Music & Mirrors

Cursed Hearts Duology

BOOK TWO

Candace Robinson

Edited by Brandy Woods Snow & Luna Imprints

Cover Design by JRC Designs / Jena R. Collins

Interior Formatting by Book Savvy Services

Music
MIRRORS
CURSED HEARTS DUOLOGY
BOOK TWO
CANDACE ROBINSON

CONTENTS

For Vic,

Who adored David Bowie in Labyrinth as

much as me

SIDE A:
Mirror
Dimension

CHAPTER 1

A melody combined with brutal anger and beauty filled the air, shouting at Ridley. It was sinister—it was lovely. The balance of the melody was uncontainable, yet he yearned for it with every fiber in his being. The music reached deep inside him, farther than anything could ever penetrate, seeping and sewing its way through his blood.

Ridley—The Mirror Keeper—picked up his pace as the music, her music, pulled him closer—to *her*. His thoughts were jumbled, as they had been during the curse. Worse now, and all because of that delicate instrument in the Piper's hands–Leni's.

As the harmonious notes flowed through every part of him, Ridley's heart rate increased, pumping furiously to each hypnotic sound. The song was achingly familiar, but he'd lost hold of its name and what it had once meant.

His gloved fingers tightened around the crushed velvet of his object, not remembering why he was holding it. He faded out from the grassy area where he was, before appearing at a spot near glass windows, a place he remembered, but couldn't recall the name of. A door opened and the clunk-clunk-clunk of washing machines reverberated in the background—the laundromat.

Ridley remembered. "Space Oddity" was still calling to him, but this was the spot where he was farthest from the Mirror Dimension. Lark and Auden were safe inside the oddity store–the curse hadn't taken them. His recollections of their circumstances cleared.

Then dark shadows surrounded him, flocking like birds in the sky, swirling and pulling him in all directions. They caressed his covered face, drawing him back to the other side, his memory slipping once more. He tried to stay in this dimension, as he had the other times, but his body blinked out, a silvery light erupting from him. Ridley's feet no longer touched cement—that world was gone.

Before him, the new place became clearer and clearer, but his thoughts still wouldn't rip free. His legs moved of their own accord across crisp, long grass, surrounded by trees leaning toward one another. Obsidian shadows lured him forward to where colorful buildings peeked out from the slits in the trees.

The melody grew louder, closer, while his eyes fluttered under the black mask, trying to find something—anything—to ground himself. In the distance, his gaze latched on to a dark cloaked figure, her charcoal hair peeping out from the hood and swaying with the wind. She stood in front of a house the color of sapphires beneath an overcast sky. The shadows pooled around her, entwining with her in their own rhythm.

Thunder clapped from above—he couldn't bring himself to be affected. If anything, the roaring beat only added elegance to the music escaping the girl's flute. Her nimble gloved fingers, so familiar, pressed and played until, finally, Ridley stopped in front of her.

The Piper yanked back the hood, her features a vacant

mask with green eyes dancing against olive skin, a button nose, and lips pursed in a tight line around the silver instrument. Her gaze flickered as it fell upon him. Dark trousers hugged her hips, boots rose to her shins, an onyx butterfly pendant sat attached to the top of her cloak … and he was hers and she was… *his*.

No, that isn't right.

Slowly, she lowered the flute from her mouth, and the shadows vanished within the instrument. She tucked it into a pocket inside her cloak, her eyes never leaving his masked face.

Something hit him then, as it had briefly when he'd been in front of the laundromat. He was standing in front of *his* home behind the citadel and Leni—the real Leni. And she wasn't his. Not anymore. That had been made clear several months ago.

"You failed, Ridley." There was bitterness in her voice, and something else, possibly disappointment, sadness.

He was Ridley—not the pre-filler who'd pretended to be Auden. If the curse had succeeded, the real filler would've been taken from liquid glass to live inside Lark and Auden's bodies—people who had not yet been created on Mira. During the curse, there was a pre-filler who would enter the body of the victim and would have aspects of the filler, the victim, and new false memories created from the mirror glass. Except this time, it had been different—Leni had done something else to make it so. This time, somehow, she'd used part of Ridley and herself to make the pre-fillers.

As the fog inside his head completely cleared, as his movements and thoughts now became his once more, everything came to him in a flash. He was *home*… in Mira. But even though he was back there, it was different in a lot of ways from the Earth Dimension, yet it wasn't. The music he listened to was the same as there.

Leni stood in front of him, watching him, a girl who was no longer his. She was someone who'd broken him, and still he couldn't help his heart from kicking into overdrive as he looked at her. She wasn't the Pied Piper, like in stories, but that was what it felt like when she'd lured him back to her snare. When she played the flute's music, it compelled him to do what she willed. He'd accepted to be her Mirror Keeper, but he hadn't known it would be like this.

Hastily, Ridley averted his eyes from her heart-shaped face and the narrow gap between her teeth before any more memories could swim to the surface. Instead, he peered at the tall pine trees scraping the darkening sky and the mirror-glass citadel in the distance. One he hadn't wanted to return to.

The citadel's shape resembled that of a Rubik's Cube except for being made entirely from glass. The façade sparkled of blue glass with splashes of yellow and green on its sides, and four cubed turrets jutted up from the top.

As Leni had mentioned, he'd failed the curse. And, mostly, Ridley was fine with that. His mission had been to pick two people from the Earth Dimension, then initiate the curse. Two fillers would've entered their bodies, then Lark and Auden would've been locked away in transparent cages—mirrors—and forever bound. The twin kings and queens in Mira used the souls to keep the Mirror Dimension's heartbeat alive, because if it died, Earth, in turn, would also die. It had been so since the beginning of time. When humans from Earth were in the womb, a mirror was created for them, giving them a soul. But people in Mira didn't have a soul, therefore, ones had to be stolen every so often. In the end, Ridley had chosen to help Lark and Auden, even if it could destroy both their worlds, because he'd once believed in love, too.

Ridley lowered the mirror to the grass, resting it against him, his worried expression concealed behind the mask.

"You may think you're hiding under your mask, the hat, the jacket," Leni started, "but your shoulders are slumping."

He straightened, clenching the mirror, preventing it from falling. Not that it would shatter, anyway. Not here. Not there. It was only possible if someone was inside the mirror, using an object from Ridley's dimension. And still, it had pieced itself back together again when the curse was broken. Without the jeweled box, with the words *For Butterfly* etched on the bottom, or the glass butterfly Leni had given to him, the mirror would've still been intact if Lark and Auden hadn't broken it.

His fingers twitched, wanting to slide into the pocket of his pants where the glass butterfly now rested, but he didn't allow them to.

"Why?" he finally whispered.

"Why what?" she asked, not meeting his gaze, her brow furrowed.

"Why did you do it differently than we were supposed to?" he rasped. "Why did you use part of *us* instead of the fillers? *How* did you do it?" This had been their first time to cast a curse—they hadn't been the ones to do them previously.

Leni reached forward and grasped Ridley's collar, her hand shaking. Despite her smaller frame, she had enough force to jolt him forward. "Drop it," she spat in a hushed tone.

"Because—because of you," Ridley said, low and angry,

then stopped. He tried to draw his words together without a notebook. "Darrin died."

"I said, *drop* it." Her eyes were wide, wild, almost frantic.

Before the curse was broken, Lark and Auden's bodies had been possessed by parts of them in conjunction with aspects of Leni and Ridley. Even if it had been the mirror pre-fillers he and Leni were supposed to use, it would've still been a dangerous and unpredictable stage until the curse was completed.

A pitch in her tone made him not question her further. He'd do it later after speaking to the royals. "Let me bring the mirror inside, then we can go to the citadel." He'd be the one to face punishment for what he'd done. And he'd keep secret what she'd done.

Ridley brushed past Leni and opened the door to his small house, then placed the mirror in the corner of the living room. His Tears for Fears album had fallen off the coffee table and onto the floor. He'd never felt closer to the song "Shout" as he did right then. But he didn't shout—he swallowed it and met Leni back outside where more clouds had gathered, and sunlight was dipping low on the horizon.

Leni strode in the direction of the citadel then whirled around, holding up her index finger in his face. "Why did you have to interfere? For once, why couldn't you just let things be? It was so simple!" Her voice caught on the last word.

She turned away from him and walked faster down the pebbled path leading to the front of the citadel. Her back straightened as she became the perfect soldier.

Quietly, he trailed her, already relieved he'd left the mirror behind. To him, the object was light as a feather—to everyone else, it could feel like lugging bricks.

Fat rain droplets pelted them as they drew closer to the glass citadel. A glistening sheen covered the colorful outer layers, with the four towers seeming to cast their hues to the next dimension. One tower for each ruler—the two queens and the two kings, just like on a chessboard.

As they neared the crimson glass drawbridge, Ridley took clunky steps across the swaying surface as it creaked and groaned. Thickly braided rope—in need of mending—held the sides together above murky water. A pair of turtles, reminiscent of the Earth Dimension's reptile species, poked their heads from the liquid.

Mira. Home. This place was his home, but it was the furthest thing from it since Leni had broken his heart.

Two guards—wearing neon-yellow, one-piece cloth uniforms and obsidian metal helmets in the shape of horses' heads—protected the tall diamond-shaped door. A zigzagging line down the center separated the glass entrance into two.

The guards bowed their heads at Leni. Her fingers fidgeted as she and Ridley bowed back, patted their chests and gestured the secret access code.

Something was bothering her. She never twitched like that.

"The kings and queens are already seated and waiting for you both in the throne room," the female voice of the guard to Ridley's left said. "They hate wasting time, as you know." She straightened to an upright position and pulled open one side of the door by its crowned handle.

Ridley followed Leni inside the spacious square sitting room. As he padded across the neon pink and green rug leading to the throne room, clumps of mud lingered behind from his boots. Mirrors lined the walls in various shapes and sizes—oval, circle, square, rectangle—like those in the Realm of Mirrors. Within them was a family eating at a table, an older man watching TV, a young guy doing karate in his room, a girl reading a book, a couple kissing. His image reflected in none of them since he didn't have a soul—like Leni. Like everyone else there. Some of the mirrors were taller and narrower, others small and short, but they all held images that led to places in the Earth Dimension. Some in rooms, others in stores, anywhere really.

At one time, he and Leni had both been a part of making the mirrors from liquid glass. Ridley had once been glass, too, and he wondered if having a soul made one different, better. He shook the thought away.

Bright lightbulbs filled the room, casting shadows across yellow walls. The slam of the door mixed with the pitter-patter of the rain as it began to pour. Two guards stood at the entrance to the throne room, both drawing open the doors without a word.

Ridley wondered what his punishment would be, slowing his pace when he thought about the weapons the royals kept in the throne room. Leni waved him on, and he rotated his shoulders as he continued. What he wanted more than anything right then and there were his headphones, his records, and his pen and paper. Lark and Auden had shared that interest with him, and it had tugged at his heartstrings. He'd mucked up the job, but he hadn't cared about it to begin with—he'd only done it because of Leni.

As he shuffled past Leni, she drew him back by his arm. "You don't have to wear that anymore." She took the items from his head and tossed the mask onto the mirror-glass chair. "Everyone can see your face now." Reaching a hand forward, she combed it through his curly hair and placed the hat back on his head.

Ridley inhaled and only blinked at her before finally speaking softly, "I know."

He remembered how Lark and Auden had been able to see his face once the curse had been broken, but he hadn't questioned it. And it shouldn't have been possible, yet somehow it was. Taking a deep swallow, he turned and crossed into the throne room.

Against one of the far walls stood a row of arcade games, and along the other was a variety of whips hung neatly. But in front of him, a trail of glistening orange carpet, spread over a red floor, led up a slight ramp to the stage where the twin kings and queens sat comfortably and regally in their mirror thrones. No reflections could be seen, not even the twinkle from the fluorescent bulbs hanging above.

"Take a seat," Portia said in an even tone, not rising from her throne, her silver gaze locked on the two of them. She wore a lavender jacket with high shoulder pads, tight jeans, and purple shoes. Portia's auburn hair fell in springy curls down her back. Her sister, Calliope, matched perfectly, except for her green blazer and heels.

Ridley stared at the shiny scarlet floor, knowing there was nowhere else to sit. Then he wondered what the royals were like when they'd once been joined—when it had only been one queen and one king. At least that was how the story went. The Earth Dimension was created to keep the balance of Mira, and the royals were split into two to keep the balance of it all.

As if hearing his thoughts, one of the kings spoke up. "Yes, please do." Brand's voice boomed from the other side.

The King and his twin—Anson—were both dressed similarly in shoulder-padded suits. Brand in white and Anson in baby blue, their dark skin complimenting the colors. Like Calliope, Anson never spoke. Both their hair was curly on top and longer in the back against their necks.

Leni and Ridley sank to the floor. Ridley wanted to ask what position he should sit in, but he kept his snide comment to himself.

"I was speaking only to the Mirror Keeper," Portia said harshly.

Leni stopped mid-movement, straightened, and took a step forward. A squeak of wheels entered the throne room. Ridley's gaze jerked to a large bar, with two cuffs hanging down. It was being pushed by two guards, their dark horse helmets tilting upward. When the bar stopped in front of Leni, Ridley's lips parted.

"Mirror Keeper, you did your duty, but Leni didn't finish hers. We didn't retrieve the two souls, so she will have her punishment."

No. No. *No.* This was his fault—he'd helped Lark and Auden when he wasn't supposed to. "Leni didn't do anything wrong. It wasn't her fault!" Ridley shouted and stood from the floor, taking a step forward.

Leni frantically shook her head and leaned toward him, whispering so only he could hear, "You keep your mouth shut."

"I will not," he said, frowning.

"You will!"

"Remove your cloak and shirt," Portia demanded, not paying attention to anything they'd said.

Leni studied Ridley, pleading, and in that moment, it was the old Leni. Words couldn't formulate in his head fast enough as she moved away from him. Two hands grabbed at him as he shot forward, and he almost slipped out of the guard's grasp before another latched on.

"It wasn't her fault, it was—"

Something hard slammed around his mouth, preventing him from saying another word. *It was me!* He wouldn't rat her out, but he wanted to say what he'd done. Why they hadn't succeeded.

With no sign of emotion, Leni glanced back at Ridley, and all he could do was blink at her, the way he had when he'd first met her.

Desperate grunts escaped his throat as she turned her head forward.

His heart thudded against his ribcage while Leni removed her cloak before dropping it to the floor. She then lifted her shirt over her head and tossed it beside the cloak, revealing a lacy purple bra. Without any defiance, she placed one hand through a shackle and a guard tightened it, followed by repeating her movements with the other.

At a leisurely pace, one of the broad-shouldered guards walked to the far-right wall and ran the tip of his finger across the different forms of whips. *Not the spiked one*, Ridley pleaded. As if listening to his prayers, the guard took a smooth black leather whip. Leni didn't lower her head, didn't slump her shoulders, only stared straight ahead at the royals.

Ridley desperately wanted to swap places with her. He could handle the pain, and no matter what she'd done, no one deserved this. Especially not her.

The guard fingered the whip as if it was his prized possession and sauntered toward Leni.

A deadly silence reigned in the room—cut only by

Ridley's muffled words. Then the whip came down, hissing through the air and striking Leni's flesh. She jolted forward but didn't scream, didn't cry—not a whimper escaped. Even without seeing her face, Ridley knew her teeth were clenched.

Tears pricked Ridley's eyes as the whip sliced downward again. He wanted to close his eyes and pretend the two of them were back in the shop making things from the liquid mirror glass, listening to records on repeat as they worked. He would admire her blowing glass and molding objects into shapes while he tried to create his own.

But they weren't back there.

They were here. And he had to watch helplessly, unable to do a single thing. When the guard finished, sweat drenched Leni's exposed skin and open wounds marked her back, leaking silver blood.

"Ridley, now you know what happens when you don't obey. This may be you one day," Portia said with a bright smile.

"Leni, you should've completed the curse." Brand shook his head. "Time is limited."

The guard released Leni from the shackles and her arms flopped to her sides as she turned toward Ridley. If he hadn't known her, he would've believed she wasn't in any pain by her stoic facial expression. The beads of sweat pebbling her forehead and the slight twitching of her lips were the only tell-tale signs.

Finally, the guards let go of Ridley and took the clasp from around his mouth. He was about to speak up when Leni stopped in front of him and murmured, "If you ever cared for me at all, then do as I said earlier—keep your mouth shut."

Ridley blinked rapidly, holding back what he wanted to

say to her, to everyone in the room. Her words caused him to swallow his own for as long as she wished.

"Thank you." Leni smiled for a brief moment. And there was that girl again—the one he'd loved—the one he would hum "Space Oddity" with while she whistled—the one who hadn't hurt him.

Leni's smile dropped from her reddened lips as her body slumped. He caught her, but in an effort to avoid her crashing to the floor, he wasn't able to avoid his hands colliding with her torn back.

CHAPTER 2

Music from "Baba O'riley" – The Who

Leni tried not to fall. She didn't want to fall. She wanted to go to him, one last time. But the pain bit at her back, causing the world to turn a purplish black.

Leni placed a record onto the player and let the rhythmic sounds of David Bowie wrap his vocal claws around her. His voice generally soothed her when she worked, but today she couldn't help feeling somber. Her brother, Romy, had been put to death months before, turned back into liquid mirror glass.

He'd fallen in love and gotten a girl pregnant. Babies weren't born here often, but when they were, they were not allowed—it could make the dimension off balance. So Romy and his girlfriend had tried to run away, gotten caught, and because they hadn't given the child up to the royals first, Romy, his girlfriend, and the baby were no more.

Leni hated Romy, hated him for dying. It shouldn't have been a difficult decision—he could've made an older child from the mirror glass when he was ready. He should've used protection when he'd been with his girlfriend. Maybe Leni was angrier because he hadn't asked for her help, hadn't even told her that a child had been born. He could've trusted her, as she would've trusted him.

Brushing a lock of dark hair behind her ear, she flipped

through each of her records and settled on playing "Baba O'riley." Her collection had grown tremendously just from slipping through a mirror and collecting what she needed from the Earth Dimension. There was always a duplicate left behind anyway. Everything made there had a duplicate, with the exception of living things.

When Leni was first created, she'd studied another girl through one of the mirrors in the home of her caretaker— Millie. Leni hadn't had a voice yet, but she could see and think clear as day as she'd watched how the Earth girl danced to music from a record player.

Day after day, Leni stared at Millie's record player until she decided to venture inside the girl's room and pluck one for herself, along with a set of records. The sounds breathed new life into Leni, and as she began helping at the mirror glass shop, the workplace was never quiet because of the music she'd brought.

A sizzle came from Leni's left, and she quickly finished pulling her hair into a side ponytail. She moved to the enclosed pool of liquid mirror glass. Bright orange flames flickered beneath, licking the sides of the boiler. Grasping the ladle's handle, she dipped it into the melted silver and poured the liquid into one of the wooden frames. Then she did another, and another, all while letting the music sweep her away.

Millie had been in charge of creating mirrors before Leni and Romy, as were her caretakers before her and the ones before that. Their line had been assigned by the royals, so one day, Leni would have to choose someone to replace her. She didn't want to have to do that because she hadn't gotten the option for herself.

Tucking thoughts of Romy into her secret place, Leni went as fast as she could to finish her mirrors for the day, so she'd be able to blow glass and shape it into things. Most of the time it was insects or spiders or any other bug she could think of. At sixteen, she was mostly alone, except for Elliot—her friend and ex-boyfriend—but she'd broken up with him months ago, after Romy died. They were better off as friends anyway.

The fire underneath the boiler crackled and cast shadows that crawled up the walls. Leni glanced up at the mirrors surrounding her in the room—no reflection. She'd never had one, none of them did. The objects only reflected places in the other world, where she was able to slip into briefly to scavenge things. When she peered down at her arm, the flesh was similar to the people in the Earth Dimension—except she and everyone else in Mira were without a soul. The only other difference was a glittery, silver sheen pumped through her veins instead of crimson.

From Leni's left, something twitched and a buzzing sound arose, startling her. She whirled to the side—nothing, only her shadow. But she knew it wasn't nothing. The shadows had been following Leni her entire life—they were part of the flute that the royals' Piper carried. Romy had been the only one who'd known about her shadows. Not even Millie knew. She thought that if she kept silent about having them, she could never be chosen to be the Piper if it came down to it.

Sometimes the shadows were worse than others—sometimes they stayed away for months, sometimes days. Over the past few weeks, they had gotten worse again. And this time, Romy wasn't there to help her through it. But she knew everything would eventually return to normal.

Pushing away her fear, Leni dipped the ladle into the glass and poured the last bit into a circular frame. These would all be taken to the citadel when Elliot came to retrieve them. She hung the tool back on the rack above the boiler and let out a breath. Throwing her hands up in the air, Leni skipped in place, because she could, because she was alone with the shadows gone again at the moment, because now, now, she could work on making a glass millipede.

Leni swiped her gloved hands together over a plastic bucket, removing as much dried mirror excess as she could. She peeled off the rubber gloves and set them on the far table, brushing her palms down her middle.

Plucking up her pack of tools, she stuck them in the pocket of her apron. Leni then took the metal bar from the corner of the room and dipped it into the glass, rotating it around and around, letting the liquid gather and harden into a small oval shape at the end. While whistling to the music, she pulled the rod back and sat on the stool, propping the metal bar right above her knee, looking as though she might be prepared to go fishing. From her pocket, she drew out a tweezer and began sketching, digging, scooping, and forming the teeniest little legs into the glass.

As she worked, Leni brought up her lighter and flicked it on to soften a few of the spots that needed it. With forceps, she snipped off parts of the legs that were too long, then molded them to size.

Behind her, a loud clatter erupted, causing her body to jerk, interrupting her pristine movements. She slowly turned around, her gaze landing on a box of records that had fallen from the table. They'd been firmly planted in the middle of her desk or ... maybe they hadn't been?

Leni frowned and scooped them up while scanning the room. From her periphery, a dark shadow moved, folding and twisting around her with indecipherable whispering. She closed her eyes. One. Two. Three. When she opened them, the shadow had vanished. It was only her.

"This is normal for me, and it will go away like it did before," she said in a low voice. A shiver ran down her spine despite her own assurances.

The door swung open and Leni jumped back, prepared to wield her metal bar, but it was only Millie who walked through the open space. Leni sighed in relief. Her caretaker wore bright pink leggings, a lime green blouse, and a leather bandana that pulled back her salt and peppered dreadlocks from her face.

In the Earth Dimension, Millie might've resembled a grandmother by the gray in her hair and the wrinkles on her skin. She'd had Leni created from liquid glass, just as she had Romy, at an older age when she could no longer keep up with the pace of making mirrors. Everyone was created from ten-year-old mirror glass. It was the age where the royals said they were old enough to start working and understand things without needing to be pampered.

When people were created in Mira, it was said they were a combination of the stars, the night sky, the earth, and wrapped in a liquid mirror sheen that seeped into their veins. When they died, there was nothing, and they became nothing, because they were without souls.

A soft shuffle came from around Millie, catching Leni's attention. She craned her neck to see who it was, expecting to find Elliot's dark head of hair. But it wasn't Elliot. Behind Millie stood a boy, both tall and broad, about the same age as

Leni. His wandering gaze and parted lips made him appear younger.

"We finally found someone to fill in for Romy," Millie said, tugging the boy through the doorway. "His name is Ridley Kol."

As he slid into full view, Leni's heart accelerated. A mop of curly chestnut-colored hair dangled from his head, right past his chin. A cluster of freckles ran across his cheeks and nose, against pale skin. He remained there, quiet as a mouse, and Leni couldn't help staring at him. But then she fully took in Millie's words, about him replacing her brother—the reason he was there was because Romy was dead.

Leni removed the arm of the player from the record so the music would stop. Her chest grew heavy at the raw emotion that wanted to form. She didn't want anyone to fill in for Romy —she wanted her brother to ask her riddles she had no answer to, sharpen the tools so she could sculpt the mirror glass, show her how to juggle plums, tell her everything would be all right when she would see the shadows. She wanted her brother to come back from the dead. But he wouldn't—couldn't.

"I told you I'm fine with working alone." Leni removed her eyes from Millie and peered down at her hands so she wouldn't cry.

"Look"—Millie took a few steps forward, lifting Leni's chin—"Sonya had created him, but wanted a girl instead. She hid him all these years, and the guards took her in after I discovered him in a closet."

Leni gasped, wondering why someone would do something so heartless. Sonya had been in charge of one of the pastry shops just up the road. "She hid him because he wasn't a girl?" Her chest sank as she said the words aloud. It still didn't lessen the fact that she didn't want him to replace her brother.

"I suppose if you don't want him, then you'll have to send him back to his tiny closet." Millie had a way of making things sound horrific, and Leni would never do such a terrible thing as that.

"No, it's fine." She glanced at Ridley, standing there quietly.

It would be weird having to share a room again. The house was small, with only two bedrooms. She and Romy had always shared a room, and it wasn't horrible, not, at least, until he got a girlfriend and started bringing her over. Then Leni wasn't allowed in the room when they were there together. She imagined this new boy bringing a girl into her bedroom, and she quickly shut out that unpleasant thought.

Biting the inside of her cheek, she decided to be friendly. "Hi."

He blinked at her.

Millie placed a hand on his shoulder. "He doesn't talk a lot—or at all—but he can write. Sonya didn't do much of anything besides give him paper, books, food ... and a bucket."

"Oh..." Leni's eyes widened, her stomach sinking. She couldn't formulate anything else. The word sorry didn't seem like enough.

Millie softly patted Leni's cheek. "I know this is hard for you, but treat him nice. And I promise, you'll find the work less taxing now." She nudged Ridley toward Leni. "Show him the process, and I'll see you two at home later this evening."

Millie handed Ridley a Post-it pad and a pen before leav-

ing. Ridley didn't move, only stood there, flicking his gaze up to the ceiling.

More than anything, he looked curious with parted lips as he took in the surroundings. Ridley's head swiveled in the direction of the table, his stare falling on her record player.

Leni guessed what he wanted—the music back on. But all she could think about was her and Romy listening to the records here together. Come on, Leni, you can share your music.

She moved toward the box of vinyl. Quickly, she flipped through her stack of records and fished out the one he would need to listen to first. Clutching the record sleeve in between both hands, she held up the cover art for David Bowie in front of Ridley. She tapped the front as Ridley studied the singer, the red and blue lightning bolt down his face, how eccentric and cool it was.

"You see him?" Leni remembered when she listened to Bowie for the first time in her room six years ago. "He's the true king of music."

Carefully, she took the record out of the sleeve and turned it on. "Space Oddity" came alive. As the sizzling sounds of the record mixed with the glorious tones of the soothing voice and the soft beats of the music, Ridley's fingers tapped lightly against his thighs.

One of her brows shot up. "You like it?"

His eyes locked onto hers and he blinked. He said nothing. She said nothing. But she smiled. And she noticed for the first time that his irises were two different colors—one brown, the other gray. Bowie had different colored eyes—not the same shade, but it couldn't be a coincidence. She loved oddities and those two little strange features made her heart flutter, and she couldn't help but like his eyes, and his freckles, and his mop of unruly hair.

She needed to work... Not think about features on a new boy.

"Let me show you how everything is done here." Leni waved for him to follow her, and he listened. As she whistled along to the music, he continued to tap his fingers to the melody.

"You see the mirrors here on the walls?" She didn't wait for him to blink. "You have a few moments where you can slip in and grab anything you want from the Earth Dimension before springing back here. But don't snatch anything twice, or it will go missing and whoever the things belong to will notice. The royals in charge of Mira have rules about it being forbidden, and you could get turned back into mirror glass for doing it." However, the owners would most likely never catch on to it—they would probably chalk it up to misplacing the item or something along those lines.

She walked to the boiler, then turned around to a flash of yellow glaring her in the face.

Ridley held up the Post-it pad with words written across in blue ink, Hi, Butterfly.

"Butterfly?" She gazed down at the printed purple and black insect on her shirt. "Yeah, I like them. You can call me that if you want, but Leni works, too."

His lips tilted up.

"Now back to business." Leni pointed at the silvery liquid churning in the large boiler. "You see this? The ingredients are already in there from this morning to get the liquid just right, so next, you pour it into frames. Elliot, who you haven't met yet, brings them to us each morning. It doesn't matter *which shapes you choose to use from the stack. I prefer the ovals because they look prettier, don't you think?" There was just something about the shape not being quite a circle that caught her eye.*

Ridley observed the stacks of frames, blinking, then reached for a rectangular one.

Leni placed a hand against the side of her face, then let out a giggle. "I have a feeling you're being stubborn."

With a smile, she took the frame from his hand and set it on top of wax paper on the floor. Using the ladle, she poured the liquid glass into the frame, watching it spread and harden. Satisfied, she picked the new mirror up and propped it against the wall—no image formed. This one would go into the Realm of Mirrors where a soul would appear once it connected to the wall.

The next mirror showed a reflection of an Earthling's bedroom. Before becoming too tempted to go in and snatch things, she pried her fingers away. This one would be going into someone's home, shop, or maybe even the citadel.

Leni wasn't the only one in the dimension who created mirrors—she'd never be that fast to keep up with all the babies being born. When humans from Earth died, their mirrors vanished from the in-between as if they'd never been there—so nothing was salvageable or reusable.

For a moment, Leni wondered what it would be like to see a true reflection of herself. She wondered what she looked like. She only knew what Millie had told her—beady green eyes, a gap between her teeth, thin lips, small nose—none of it sounded appealing. However, she liked the color of her black hair and her olive skin. On the other hand, having a reflection that basically followed a person everywhere, and could appear in almost all surfaces, was a terrifying thought at times. But it couldn't be any worse than having shadows following her.

Leni found Ridley tapping his foot against the floor to the music, creating a perfect rhythm.

"That's it for the day since I already finished up what was needed. I'm going to work on glassblowing," Leni said, picking up the metal rod in the corner. "You can mirror shop in the Earth Dimension if you want or sit and listen to music."

He wrote something on his notepad and held it up: With you.

"Really?" Even Romy had never wanted to do that with her, only give her the tools. The idea intrigued her a bit. "Come on, then."

He followed her back to the boiler where she planned to start working on a spider figurine. Leni turned to the side and scooped up the formed glass over the rod. Ridley stood to the side, silently watching, tapping his foot. Maybe this wouldn't be so bad after all.

A strange tickling sensation ran up the back of her neck. She glanced up at Ridley, standing across from her at a distance. Not him. She tried to imagine it hadn't happened, until the sensation came again, this time wrapping around her throat and squeezing tightly. A choked, coughing noise escape her lips. She tried to scream, kick off whatever was doing this to her, but she couldn't.

Ridley's head jerked up. A low hiss sounded beside her, akin to the sound of snakes flicking their forked tongues. As each second passed, her air supply lessened. The shadowy forms floated in front of her, then up toward the ceiling.

Two hands grasped her wrists and the darkness vanished,

leaving only Ridley holding her in place. His chest was heaving, and he blinked rapidly as he looked at her.

"A-Are you all r-right?" Ridley's voice came out in a deep rasp, as though he'd never used it before. He probably hadn't.

Leni's heart hammered, and she knew she should keep silent about the shadows, but she couldn't anymore. It was a secret she wanted to share with someone.

"You didn't see the shadows, did you?"

He shook his head and blinked.

"I'm fine, but you can't tell anyone about this."

"Promise, Butterfly." Ridley's palms were still lightly grasping hers, and his scent, like toasted marshmallows and cinnamon, caressed her nostrils. And somehow the smell calmed her, made her less afraid.

 Chapter 3

Music from "Let's Dance" – David Bowie

Ridley scooped up Leni's collapsed body, careful not to dig into her torn back as he brought her close to his chest. Her face appeared almost serene, eyes shut, lips parted, not a single twitch of pain as his gloved hands cradled her. He knew that if she wasn't passed out, she would've fought him to let her walk, so different from the old Leni who would've wrapped her arms around his neck and rested her head against his chest, listening to the thump-thump of how wildly his heart was beating from everything that had just happened.

In the quiet of his mind, the thrumming grew louder as he strung together the words he wanted to hurl at the royals. But he held them back, piled up on his tongue behind firmly set teeth and tight lips, and only stared at the twin kings and queens.

When he'd first come to the citadel several months ago, he chose to remain silent most of the time. At eighteen, Ridley had only been alive on Mira for eight years. Before that, he didn't know where he'd been—he supposed somewhere within the liquid glass, waiting for the stars to align just right. But what he did remember was being alone in Sonya's closet until he was sixteen. He remembered her false smile when he'd come out of the glass, the one she'd held onto until she walked with Ridley into her house and shoved him into a tiny closet. He remembered his only company were the voices from her TV outside his door. He remembered teaching himself how to read and write. The books she'd tossed at his feet, he'd studied every inch of them—the pictures, the words. Then Ridley would copy each paragraph in his raggedy journals. The words were his comfort, his lifeline, his only friends —until Leni.

He focused on the royals' stern faces. It was obvious this dimension was a mess and had been for a long time. Yet he didn't know how to make it any better, not when everyone could be destroyed on a whim. Not when worlds could be dissolved into nothingness with ease. Not when kings and queens were worse here than in any of the storybooks he'd read when he was younger. Not when these leaders made masked guards whip people who didn't deserve it, especially the girl who had been so dear to him. He lowered his eyes to her—she still was. No matter that she didn't want him anymore, even as a friend.

"You could have chosen to leave if you'd brought back the souls," Brand said with a shrug. "It's not a difficult task. But you have Leni Rose to blame for that."

"You can't blame her," Ridley replied, trying hard not to let the fire coursing through his veins surface. He adjusted Leni while trying to gather the words in his head, needing desperately to write them down.

"She's the one in charge," Portia interjected. "So, yes, Ridley, it is her fault. Even if a certain Mirror Keeper may have had a change of heart."

They did know what Ridley had done then… How could they not? They could tap into mirrors at any time. "Then why aren't I the one being punished?"

"Perhaps you are." Brand cocked his head, his dark gaze lingering on the wounded girl in Ridley's arms.

Calliope and Anson both sat tall on their thrones, quietly grinning.

Ridley's chest tightened and he gave a curt nod, because there was nothing he could say that wouldn't make matters worse. He needed to get Leni away from these people who would only do her more harm, especially if they discovered what she'd tried to do in the Earth Dimension.

"Good day, Your Majesties." Without another word, Ridley turned to collect Leni's cloak and shirt.

Portia spoke up, "Since we didn't receive the souls, the next mission will have to be sooner—a month's time. But before that, in seventeen days, there will be a masquerade party here at the citadel."

He froze. A party? The royals only held masquerades when a new Piper was to be announced. He'd only been to one of those parties before. This wasn't possible. No Piper was ever released—they worked until they were dead. The only worker out of the Piper and the Mirror Keeper who ever went free was the Mirror Keeper, but only if a curse had succeeded. And it hadn't.

"There," Portia continued, "you will meet the new Piper."

Ridley's shoulders remained stiff as he took a hard swallow. "Leni won't be the Piper anymore?"

Brand rubbed at his chin and a knowing smirk appeared. "No, she won't be the Piper anymore. Her home will remain vacant until then, so you can dispose of her wherever you wish."

Ridley's stomach twisted, turning into knots. He had planned to take her to her house, beside his, in the back of the citadel. She would've wanted to recover there, but now that wasn't an option.

"I'll bring her to my place then."

Portia leaned forward, her smile growing wider and wider. "Before you two leave, we need the flute returned."

There was a secret in that smile, something she wasn't telling him. The silver pumping through his veins stilled as his heart tried to reignite.

No one moved for the cloak. Portia wanted him to do it, even though she knew his hands were full. While trying not to disturb Leni, Ridley lowered himself and lifted the dark garment. He dipped his hand inside the inner pocket on the side of the cloak and retrieved the silver flute.

As soon as his fingers brushed the object, a light crackling sounded. He could've sworn a dark shadow floated in his periphery, ones like he'd been seeing while the curse had been going on. Leni's shadows. But then there was nothing as he tossed Leni's clothes over his shoulder.

A guard stepped forward and held out a hand. Ridley pressed the flute into his palm.

"See you back at the masquerade party," Brand called as Ridley turned on his heel and headed for the door.

Ridley didn't say anything in return.

Quietly—too quietly—he exited the room. Leni's breaths came out soft compared to his own.

He didn't know how she would feel about him taking her back to his place, but that was where she was going. Their old home had sat empty ever since they'd gone to the citadel after Millie hadn't come back. She'd decided to take a journey of her own across Mira and hadn't told anyone. Ridley still couldn't understand why she would do something like that. When Leni woke, if she wanted to go to Elliot's or somewhere else, he would take her there.

At the back of the citadel, his bright blue home slid into view, surrounded by lemon bushes and banana trees. Leni's home, now vacant, rested on the opposite side.

He drew closer and stepped over the threshold to his home. Leni let out a wounded mewl from the sudden shift, her green eyes flicking open for a moment, catching his, before shutting again.

She didn't make another sound.

Ridley angled his head to make sure he could hear her breathing—slow and even. As he entered the living room, he couldn't stop himself from humming the chorus from "Let's Dance" to try and soothe her. It always had in the past. But that was the past—this was now.

The room he and Leni had once shared at his old house had been piled with records, cassettes, and books. Back then, he'd taken anything he could from rooms in the Earth Dimension, trying to fill his space with both memories of past eras and recent things.

Now, his home was missing most of his belongings because he'd left them at their old house—they were reminders. The living room didn't have much, only an old cloth couch, a wooden coffee table, then a small kitchen to the right. He pushed open the door leading to his bedroom and bathroom. Gently, Ridley lowered Leni to her stomach on top of the mattress, as if she was a bundle of straw that could easily break apart. Then he placed her things on one of the nightstands.

His house was small, even more so than their old home. But Leni could have this room if she needed it—she could always have anything of his. And he wanted so badly to change his mind on that, but he couldn't.

As he swept a lock of sweaty hair from her face, she coughed. Her eyes opened, trying to focus, then widened for a moment when he knelt by the bedside.

"No," Leni whispered. "I've gotta go to the Earth Dimension."

He pressed his head against the mattress, his face close to hers, so she didn't have to lift her head. "No, Leni, we're here, back in Mira, remember?"

Her eyes closed, clenched tight, and she let out an anguished cry while reaching for her back. "Just go…"

"Stop," he said softly, sharpening his gaze on hers.

And to his surprise, she did, sinking into the bed and relaxing her eyelids. She wouldn't like what needed to come next, but he had to get her wounds cleaned up. He wished Millie was there to help him, because she could calm any situation. But she wasn't—it was only him.

Lifting his head from the mattress, he stood, removed his gloves, and went to the kitchen where he filled a bowl with warm water. From inside the cabinet, he grabbed a bottle of alcohol and a couple of rags before going back. He rested the things on the bed and chewed his lip while analyzing the torn, silvery stripes.

To calm them both, Ridley placed the player arm on the record. The scratchiness of the vinyl played, leading into the slow-paced song. Leni sighed, not quite as asleep as she pretended to be.

"Leni," Ridley said gently, "I need to take off your bra. Is that all right?"

She stayed hushed, and he thought she wasn't going to answer him. But then she did. "No. I'll do it."

With achingly slow precision, Leni reached behind her back, wincing. He watched her struggle until he couldn't anymore. He stretched forward to undo the clasp. A moan escaped her throat, and he helped her wriggle out from the undergarment.

Neither one spoke as he dipped the rag into the warm water and cleaned away the dried and wet silvery blood as best he could. Throughout the whole process, Leni held her breath, not making a sound.

"You ready?" he asked, dabbing the dry rag with alcohol.

"I thought we were finished." She paused and peered up at the rag, her expression full of apprehension. "Go ahead."

Ridley nodded and bit his lip as he pressed the alcohol to her wounds. She wasn't silent any longer—she inhaled a sharp breath and let out curse after curse.

"I'm sorry." He blinked, guilt coating his voice.

"Stop being so nice to me," she said through gritted teeth as tears collected in her dark lashes. "Just stop."

"What do you want?" He set the rag on the bed and leaned forward. In that moment, whatever she wanted, he would do.

"For you to leave," she murmured. "You ruined every-thing… You took away my chance."

Chance at what? Her stealing a life that didn't belong to her? She was wrong.

"It was the right choice, Leni."

Instead of shouting like he wanted to do, as he'd never

done, Ridley turned up the music and walked out of the room. But then he sighed and thought about Leni's back, knowing she hadn't had anything to drink. He filled up a cup of water and set it beside her on the nightstand, then shut the door behind him.

Despite everything, Ridley stared down at his hands, not knowing how to feel. He'd taken off the gloves, though he still wore the black attire. He wanted it off. All of it. Stripping all the clothing away, he balled it up, threw it in the corner of the room next to the mirror, and wished he didn't have to put the things on ever again.

He thought about all he'd done and hadn't done. He thought about Lark and Auden, remembering how they exchanged lyrical notes through the cursed mirror from his side. But he hadn't *known* Earth humans, not until he'd entered their dimension for longer than a few seconds as the Mirror Keeper.

"Leni's chosen you for the Mirror Keeper position," Brand had said.

"That's correct." Ridley had blinked and blinked and had accepted Leni's offer, even after she'd broken his heart, even when he hadn't known what all this would entail. But he'd taken it on because she'd begged him, and she'd given him the choice. Yet, as the Piper, she could've just picked him and made him do it anyway.

"Good." The king smiled. "You might want to try shutting off that heart of yours."

"I already have." Ridley thought he had, yet *she* had still been in it. Always.

"She can never quit, you know."

"Then I will never quit."

When he'd spoken to Brand, Ridley had meant it. He'd never thought of humans on the other side as being real, not until he truly saw them during the curse—alive, moving, vulnerable, loving. Yet there was one he hadn't really known but had considered a friend. Even then, Lark hadn't felt real, only her objects had. When he realized that wasn't the case, it had been too late for him to turn back. He'd *tried*.

Grabbing his headphones from the couch, he brought them over his ears to shut out everything he could. He picked up a spiral notebook off the coffee table and jotted down the words that needed to pour out. *Sorry. Sorry. Sorry.* Over and over again until his eyes couldn't stay open, as David Bowie continued to sing lullabies into his ears. The words had been for Lark, Auden, and anyone who would listen to his silent apologies. However, the main reason was for Leni, because if anyone was to be whipped and wounded, it should've been him.

Setting the notebook down and shutting off the lights, he lay back on the couch and closed his eyes. As Ridley's head hit the pillow, a tickling sensation ran up the side of his neck. His eyes flew open, but in the dark, he couldn't see anything. A soft buzzing sound filled the air. Then he could see it—the color black, a shadow, drawing closer and closer to him. It ran a hand down his forehead, his cheek. He couldn't move or find his voice as shadows covered every inch of the walls around him. The curse wasn't going on anymore and Leni didn't have the flute, so why were they here?

Jolting from the couch, Ridley barreled across the room and flicked on the light. The area was empty. Chest heaving, he opened the bedroom door, where he found Leni still fast asleep on her stomach.

Leni had always been able to see the shadows—never him, not until Phase One of the curse had begun. Ridley hoped the shadows wouldn't disturb Leni, but they'd never listened to his prayers before. He ran a hand through his hair, knowing deep down that something wasn't right.

CHAPTER 4

Leni tossed and turned, gasped, then tossed and turned some more. The wounds on her back throbbed with fury as she faded in and out of sleep.

The sun shone through her window, dancing across Leni's closed eyelids, turning the dark insides a glowing orange. She pulled back the blanket and rolled to her side. On the floor, against the side of his bed, Ridley sat with a pair of headphones over his ears. As she brought herself up, his brown and gray eyes met hers.

"What are you doing?" Leni asked, leaning forward. She'd never seen him so relaxed, like there wasn't a worry in the world.

"What?" He pulled the headphones back from his ears, freeing his curly hair to fall around his face.

"I said"—she grinned—"what are you doing?"

"Music." Ridley stood and turned around, searching for something beneath his pillow. He grabbed whatever he needed and handed it to her. "A gift." It was a cassette player with headphones.

Leni squeaked in excitement and folded her fingers around the player. As she inspected hers, inspected his, inspected hers again ... she noticed something. They matched! Throwing open the player, Leni slid out the tape, held it closer to her face, and read the artist's name. David Bowie.

Ridley scooted forward and scanned over her tape, pointing to a song, "Space Oddity." Then he clucked his tongue in a job well done. "It's good, right?"

Something was off. Leni looked at his player again, then leaned forward. She pressed stop on his player and ran her eyes over it as she removed the cassette. David Bowie. *Her eyes widened. It was the same tape with a scratch across Side A.*

"Ridley!" she whisper-shouted. "Did you take the same player and tape from a mirror?"

Guilt filled his face, and he shrugged with a knowing smile. "Sometimes, you gotta do what you gotta do."

Leni stopped fighting her smile as she grinned back. "You can't do that again, though, all right?" Then the smile slipped from her face when she thought about the royals and how this wouldn't be good for anyone. "Remember when I said there was a law about this sort of thing? Death, Ridley—it would mean death."

"No more," he promised, and she knew he was telling the truth. Because he didn't lie. He placed his hand on top of hers, and she drew in his warmth. "I think the word I finally found for you is 'friend.' I wanted to make you feel less afraid of the shadows, and with these, we can listen to music everywhere."

Her heart seemed to expand, and she squeezed his hand back. "Friend."

Leni woke drenched in sweat. It took her a moment to realize where she was, that she was in Ridley's bed. Before she could call out to him, like she wanted to, her eyes closed once more.

Leni couldn't breathe. Her lids jerked open. Above her, two dark hands circled her throat, choking her, constricting her airpipes. She tried to release a scream, claw, rip, tear, bite, anything to get that droplet of air. Then a gasp came— her eyes bulged and relaxed—she could barely move. Stumbling off the bed and across the floor, Leni's fist collided with the wall. Her entire arm and muscles were like gelatin, or what she assumed gelatin would feel like if a person was made of it. She was too tired to move any farther as her shoulders slumped and her head swayed.

The door flew open and the light flicked on—the savior had come. Or, at least, Ridley had. Millie's head peered over Ridley's shoulder. They must've still been up late watching movies together.

Leni's gaze darted around the entire room. Nothing had changed. Nothing was there. The shadows were gone. Only Millie and Ridley stood at the door, watching her. Leni wanted to cave in on herself, and she wished she hadn't struck the wall because Millie was going to ask questions. And she did...

"What's going on in here?" Millie whispered, her face growing concerned as each second ticked by, her hand continuously rubbing her cheek.

"Nothing," Leni lied. "I rolled over and accidentally hit my hand against the wall. It was just a nightmare—that's all." And it really had felt like a nightmare, one that wouldn't ever go completely away.

Millie pressed a palm against her chest and nodded. "If you need me, don't hesitate to call, okay?"

"All right," Leni murmured.

Ridley didn't leave. Instead, he entered the room and closed the door gently behind him. Almost swiftly, he edged forward and knelt before her like some kind of knight. Her knight. She shook off the strange thought.

"You keep lying to her," he whispered.

She peered down at her hands. "People lie." Whether they liked to or not, sometimes it was necessary.

"But you love her."

"People lie the most to the ones they love."

Leni didn't want to have to talk to Millie about the possibility that she could one day become the Piper because her caretaker would worry too much. Besides, if no one else knew, then if the time came, maybe she wouldn't be chosen. Maybe it would be someone else who could see the shadows—it wasn't only her in Mira who could.

She thought about Romy's murder for protecting his baby, how she never had a chance to even say goodbye. Being that close to the royals, who had picked death for Romy, would be worse than her nightmares.

Ridley turned around and sat on his bed. He scribbled on a Post-it note and held it up. You can always talk to me.

"Thank you."

Remaining quiet, he opened an old picture book and copied down the words on a sheet of paper in his lap. The way his hand moved was so quick, faster than the words could ever spill up his throat and out from his lips. She wanted to read them, see everything he wrote and understand how he felt. But they were his words.

To prevent her fingers from stealing his sheet of paper for her curiosity, she instead reached toward the record player and started Blondie. The singer's voice sang to them, calming her.

Leni whistled softly to the music, trying not to go back to sleep. She wished that it had only been a bad dream, but at least it had been weeks since the shadows last visited her.

"Leni?" Ridley interrupted her thoughts.

"Yeah?" She rolled over to face him.

He was chewing on the edge of his lip. "What does a kiss feel like?"

The question wasn't one she was expecting. Her eyes danced with surprise and they lowered of their own accord to his mouth, before looking back up. "It's hard to explain. Depends on the kiss, I suppose. But it can be as light as the brush of the wind or it can be as rough as a finger being pricked with a needle."

"That doesn't sound good."

She laughed and sat up on the edge of the bed while "Heart Of Glass" played around them. Her gaze fell to the book in his hand. "What are you reading?"

"A couple things, actually." He smiled. "Sleeping Beauty and Romeo & Juliet.*"*

Over the past months, Ridley had been speaking more and more, but he'd never missed a day where he wasn't writing in a notebook or on a Post-it note.

"Ah, the sleeping beauty being kissed awake. Well, princesses don't really get cursed and have to be awoken by a kiss. That would be too easy." Leni got up from her bed, sank down beside him, and picked up Romeo & Juliet. *"Do you think their love was really worth it?"*

"Love is always worth it."

"You were created a hopeless romantic, it seems." She didn't know if love really was worth it because in the end, Romeo and Juliet had both died.

Leni lay back on her pillow and patted it. He pressed his

head beside her, his marshmallow and cinnamon scent enveloping her senses.

Her hand was brushing his, and she interlaced their fingers, thinking about love. What was love exactly? She hadn't been in love with Elliot when she was with him, but she'd really liked him. And can love truly beat all obstacles?

"I have something for you since tomorrow we're celebrating your one-year anniversary here." She unlaced her hand from his and opened the drawer by her bedside. With fumbling fingers, she grabbed the glass object. "When I asked you what your favorite insect was you told me a butterfly, so I made you this after you created the glass grasshopper for me." Not meeting Ridley's gaze, she placed the silver mirror butterfly into his palm.

His index finger ran over the curve of the wing. "It's perfect, but you didn't owe me one."

"I wanted to give it to you because you're my friend, and once you have me as a friend, that means you have to put up with me forever." She smiled. "And I have one more thing, but only if you say it's all right."

"What is it?" His mismatched eyes met hers and she held them with hers as the dreaded thing in her chest pounded. Ridley didn't look away. And she knew without a doubt that her feelings for him had been growing.

"Can I kiss you?" Leni's heart beat faster, quicker. Her gaze couldn't help but fall to his lips. They looked soft, smooth. And she'd been wanting to kiss him for so long. "It's all right to say no."

Ridley leaned forward, away from her, and wrote something on his notepad. He held the words up with a smile. It's about time you asked.

Leni smiled back and cradled Ridley's face, his stubble brushing her palms as she pressed her mouth to his. It was gentle, it was sweet, but then her lips moved, and his lips caressed. The kiss went deeper and deeper until it could go no further and they both pulled back for air.

"That was like being caught in a fire, but we were the flames," Ridley said, his lips red and swollen. He shifted toward her and placed his lips to hers once more in a feath-erlight kiss. "And now it's the wind cooling down the flames."

She smiled again, feeling things she'd never felt before, and tucked her head into his chest while he returned to writing.

Leni woke again, tears trailing down her cheeks while she whispered Ridley's name—her voice still too weak—then drifted off into her hell.

A sizzling echoed as though a serpent was weaving in and out of Leni's ears. She slapped the side of her head, only to come into contact with her ear instead of a snake. Her body shook, then it levitated from the bed. She couldn't scream. She wanted to scream. Her spine arched backward, body shaking. Ridley was in the bed beside hers asleep, and she desperately wanted him to wake. The shadows swarmed around her, brushing her skin in a slow taunting caress.

Digging. Digging. Digging. She finally dug out her voice and screamed, screamed the loudest she ever had. Leni fell to the bed with a loud and heavy thump. As she caught her breath, the lights flew on, illuminating the room.

Her eyes were adjusting to the brightness as Ridley came to her.

"Ridley, you're here." Leni latched onto him, pulled him toward her, and crashed her lips against his. "Every time."

She didn't want to go back to sleep. She needed his kiss, his touch.

"Are you all right?" he asked, shifting back, scanning her face.

"I'm fine. Now just kiss me." She tugged him forward and he settled in between her legs. He let out a groan, and Leni's body shivered at how close they were. Over the past few months, they'd been in this position a lot, growing closer, growing bolder. Piece by piece, their clothing was discarded. Her lips explored his, and his explored her skin.

They'd done everything but this one thing.

"You know I love you, right?" Leni murmured. She didn't want him to think she was doing this to not sleep. She was doing it because she wanted to, wanted to be with him. But she'd never spoken the words aloud.

"I love you too." He paused and pressed a soft kiss at the crook of her neck. "Do you care that I haven't done this before?"

"No." She smiled, moving a lock of hair behind his ear. "Do you care that I have?"

"Never."

She gripped his hips and urged him on, and in that moment, she believed that Romeo and Juliet had made the right decision. Love was always worth it.

This time when Leni woke, she couldn't contain it. She screamed and shouted Ridley's name so loud she feared it would tear down the walls. Her throat was dry, and her lips chapped. She couldn't even describe the pain throbbing at her back or the one growing inside her chest.

The door swung open. Ridley flicked on the light and

stumbled in, his gaze searching the room. "What's wrong? Is it your back, or is it the shadows?"

It was the dreams—more than anything, it was the dreams. But she didn't want to confess the truth to him. "It's my back. It hurts." She thought about the shadows, and they hadn't come to her yet. But with everything in her, she knew they would return.

"Let me reapply the ointment." He looked exhausted with dark circles beneath his eyes, and she shouldn't have called for him, but she didn't want to be alone in here anymore.

Leni pressed her arms by her sides as Ridley lifted the bandages. Her eyes fluttered at the slight sting, but as soon as he put on the cool ointment, numbness consumed her flesh.

"Do you need anything else?" he asked.

"Water." Leni winced when she sat up to take the glass from him. The fluid was warm as it ran down her throat, but it still soothed it. She handed the empty glass to him and lay back down.

"Goodnight," Ridley said while shutting off the light and placing her back into darkness.

It was dark, too dark, like the shadows. "Wait!" she called, desperate for him not to leave.

"Yeah?" He flicked the light back on.

"Can you... Can you..." She couldn't coax the words out. Perhaps because she knew she shouldn't be asking this of him right now.

"Can I what?" His eyebrows drew together like he was trying to find the answer somewhere in his mind for the question yet to be asked. It wouldn't be there.

"Can you please stay for the night?" Leni murmured, not

taking her gaze off his. She waited for the word *no* to slip out from between his lips.

Ridley paused, his face softening, then nodded. "Of course." He turned off the light, and the mattress carefully dipped as he lay on his back beside her.

In the darkness, he didn't say anything else and neither did she. With him there beside her, maybe the memories would stay away. If not permanently, then at least for the night.

CHAPTER 5

Music from "Train In Vain" – The Clash

A light buzzing sounded near Ridley's ear, and his eyes shot open. Above him, a dark shadow swirled, coming closer, pushing back, coming closer again. A lithe hand wrapped around his throat, squeezing gently as if taunting him.

"Ridley," it whispered, ballooning toward the ceiling, then drifting back in his direction. "Soon."

The new curse. It was coming.

He clamped his eyes shut, like he did during the curse when he would blink out from the Earth Dimension and re-enter his, only he would be in a place where he didn't know who he was, just waiting to find a way back to help Lark and Auden. How his voice had been silenced for the duration. How the shadows that swarmed around Leni wouldn't let him confess the truth—how they had spoken to him then, too.

Go away. Stay away. Ridley's lids flicked back open, and the shadow was gone. The morning light spilled in through his window, coloring everything in the room a soft orange.

Leni was still sleeping beside him, and he couldn't help studying her serene face for an extra moment. The shadows were still there because of her. He hoped they would leave her in peace while she healed.

Careful not to disturb her, he slipped from the bed and

headed into the living room. He placed his headphones over his ears, grabbed his pen and notebook from the coffee table, then flipped it open. *What is happening? Why hasn't it stopped? Does it just never stop? I hope Leni will be all right. I hope Lark and Auden will be okay after what they went through.* His gaze focused in the direction of the covered mirror in the corner. There was a way to see if they—Lark and Auden—were all right.

Quietly, Ridley set down the notebook and pen, left "Train In Vain" pumping through his ears, and shuffled toward his mirror. Pulling the crushed velvet drape from the object, he dropped it to the floor. Inhaling and exhaling, he stared at the glass, the wood around the upper portion. Nothing reflected here in Mira. Nothing at all.

He pressed his hand to the mirror, and it passed through, the surface rippling against his flesh, glowing a light silver.

Closing his eyes, he spoke, "Show me Lark Espinoza." No one could do this but the Mirror Keeper. And even with the next curse, he decided he would do the same thing as before and help break the spell. Therefore, he would never be rid of the mirror…

An icy chill trickled up his palm followed by a licking burn—he withdrew his arm. Across the glass, an image appeared, unfocused at first. The day was early in the Earth Dimension, but outside a sun colored the sky pink, orange, and yellow. The bay's waters shoved back and forth, and in front of it lay two forms. Lark's head rested against Auden's chest, her eyes closed, but he was awake. Light gray smoke rose from a trashcan beside them as if they'd just burned something.

"This is good. They're fine." Ridley sighed. The image

slowly faded until it was gone—the mirror back to being just that, a mirror.

One of the mirrors at the shop had connected to Lark's room, and that was how Ridley had gotten to know her—through her objects. He would take her records, her cassettes, and sometimes her candy bars. But she had never known since he made sure to only take one of each item. He'd liked Lark. Not in the way he'd liked Leni, but as a friend—one he'd grown to know through her objects even though she hadn't known he existed.

But then he'd been chosen for the Mirror Keeper position. And he'd selected Lark. Ridley had been able to see into the past and watch her and Auden exchange notes in class through the cursed mirror. There needed to be another, and he'd chosen Auden because he liked his and Lark's interactions, not because he wanted them to die.

Then it was too late.

He draped the mirror with the cloth and glanced toward his bedroom. Leni still hadn't stirred. Taking the headphones off, Ridley filled another cup with water and grabbed a candy bar along with a bag of Cheetos. Keeping his steps quiet, he opened the door and found Leni on her stomach, still sleeping.

The previous night, Leni had called to him, appearing more vulnerable than ever. He wished she would write down her thoughts so he could read them, but she would prefer to keep those locked away. As he studied her back, the silver coating the gauze, he knew it needed to be treated again.

Ridley shuffled inside his bedroom and set the things he'd brought her on the table beside the empty glass. Slowly, he lowered himself on the bed, trying not to rattle her too much.

"Leni," Ridley whispered as he reached for the ointment.

She didn't answer.

"Leni?" He pressed a hand to the skin of her neck. Heat spread to his palm—she was burning up—like a tiny fire nipping at her flesh. "Leni!"

"Mmm," she replied, not lifting her head, her teeth chattering. Had he done something wrong when mending her back? He'd made sure her wounds were clean. "You're running a fever. Let me get a few more things."

Ridley rushed out of the room to the kitchen and filled the bowl with cool water. He started placing wet rags on her hot forehead and arms before changing out the gauze to reapply the ointment. She didn't say anything as he worked, and he didn't like her silence. As a cluster of words formed in his head, he wanted to transfer them to paper to figure out what they articulated, to explain how he was feeling, but there wasn't time for that. He would remain by her side until she got better and the fever broke.

Almost two weeks went by with Leni in and out, and the fever hadn't gone away. Every time there was a glimmer of hope, it recurred as hot as before. Her back was healing, but her skin still burned like it was its own wildfire.

The healer at the citadel had come and checked on her but said Leni was fine except for the fever. She wasn't *fine*. If her back was healing, then there shouldn't be a fever … unless there was another reason. There was someone who needed to know anyway, but Leni hadn't asked for him.

Ridley pressed his hand in his pocket and brushed his

fingers against the glass butterfly Leni had made for him. "I'll be back." He ran a thumb across her damp forehead.

"Where are you going?" she whispered, cracking her eyes open.

"I'm going to bring someone to help, and then I'm going to fix this." He placed his headphones around his neck.

"You can't fix everything with music." She smiled.

"If I could fix everything with music, the dimensions would be a much different place. Try and get a little more rest."

As he shifted the blanket, he noticed she'd already passed out again. She looked so small, so tired, so un-Leni. But at least she'd listened this once.

Ridley put the headphones over his ears then his pork pie hat on his head. He didn't want to leave her alone in case something happened, but he wouldn't stay gone that long.

Gently, he shut the front door behind him, despite a part of him wanting nothing more than to slam it. But that wasn't him.

For Ridley, the world ticked a certain way, and he liked the quietness, the stillness, that allowed his thoughts to flow properly. But they weren't flowing anymore. Whatever was going on with Leni had him on edge, and as he had with Lark and Auden, Ridley would come up with a solution.

Clutching the handlebars of his bicycle, Ridley took off down the pebbled path, out from the citadel to the cobblestone street. He'd always believed that this world was how things were supposed to be, but once he'd landed in the Earth Dimension, he couldn't help seeing how everything there felt more real than it had in Mira. And his time in the Earth

Dimension those weeks during the curse was when he'd truly learned right from wrong.

Ridley skirted past tall colorful buildings and weaved in between several hot pink glass shops, until he stumbled upon his destination. He lowered his kickstand and approached the door with black and white checkered curtains cloaking the glass. Not bothering to knock, Ridley pushed through and stepped inside. The earthy scent of recently cut wood permeated the air. All kinds of frames—wooden, metal, iron, glass—filled the room. They were all organized neatly and hanging on neon green hooks.

"There he is," a voice called from the other side of the room and inched closer. "After all this time, stepping into my abode. You didn't bring Leni to this party?"

Ridley blinked, the silver glass pumping hard through his veins. He didn't want to be here.

"I can always get a rise out of you." Elliot grinned, his dark brown eyes smiling in sync. "Even though you're trying to hide how you feel, I can easily see that little vein thumping on the side of your neck." Setting down a square frame, he stepped back to lean against the wall, arms crossed over his chest, head cocked. He wore a purple collared shirt paired with jeans. His corkscrew black curls had gotten a little longer, hovering right at his brow.

No one else worked at this shop besides Elliot, and the other frame makers each had their own places.

"Listen, I need your help," Ridley rushed the words out in desperation. Elliot wasn't a friend—he didn't know what Elliot was to him exactly. An acquaintance? Maybe a side character in one of the stories he'd read that stood in the same room, but they never really conversed. He hadn't wanted to see Elliot, though, because Leni was … in love with him. And he didn't know if Leni had ever ended up telling Elliot how she felt or not. He didn't care to know either, not after she'd broken Ridley's heart when she'd chosen Elliot.

"Doesn't someone always want something from me?" Elliot didn't appear as if this was a burden to him—he appeared pleased as he walked toward Ridley and twisted his hat a bit. "It wasn't on right."

Ridley didn't care if his hat was lopsided, not as long as it was on his head. "Listen, something's wrong with Leni."

The smirk fell from Elliot's face. "What do you mean?"

"We didn't complete the curse, and she was punished for it." Ridley's voice trembled as he remembered the snap of the whip coming down and tearing Leni's flesh. How she'd held her tongue while it had happened.

Elliot's friendliness disappeared. His eyes narrowed and his spine straightened when he took a step back from Ridley. "The curse… I don't know when you two started, but I should've realized too much time had already passed. It wasn't completed? Why?"

"Who cares about the curse?" Ridley slapped his leg. "Something's wrong with Leni."

"Hold on." Elliot put a hand to his forehead and shut his eyes. "I'm confused."

Ridley rubbed his own burning cheek, anxious to write everything his thoughts were saying and shove it into the idiot's face. "We failed because of me, but the royals punished Leni, stripped her of her title. She's healing just fine, but she's still weak, running a fever, and mostly sleeping."

"Oh shit." Elliot's hand flew up and covered his mouth. "Oh shit. This isn't good, not fucking good at all."

"What are you talking about?" Ridley asked, his brow furrowing.

"You don't know, do you?" Elliot's eyes were the widest Ridley had ever seen them.

"Know what?"

"If you become a Piper, you work until the day you die—"

"I know that already," Ridley interjected, not needing a history lesson on how after you became a Piper you worked forever unless the royals released you from your duties like they had Leni.

"But not the rest?" Elliot clenched his teeth as he spoke.

Ridley blinked and took a deep swallow, his Adam's apple bobbing. He felt as though the news coming was something he should've already known and that it wasn't going to be good.

"If a Piper is stripped of their title, they will die at the next masquerade party when the new Piper is announced. Didn't Leni tell you this?"

Ridley stiffened, unable to swallow. Die? Die? *Die…* It couldn't be. He thought about his time with Leni while she was the Piper and he was the Mirror Keeper. She'd never told him this, and since she'd been with him, he hadn't even thought about her being released from the position. The shadows hadn't appeared since that first night and the following morning they'd come to his house.

"No, she doesn't know," Ridley murmured, meeting Elliot's dark eyes. "She's been too sick, and I didn't think about telling her with everything going on. In fact, I was glad she didn't have to work for those people anymore."

"But you still do…"

"It is what it is." Ridley shrugged a shoulder. "But you're wrong … she isn't dying."

Elliot gripped his hair tightly in his fists. "We're going to talk to Leni right now."

"Talk? We need something to fix her."

"I don't know if there's going to be any fixing this, Ridley. I knew she was going to fuck this up somehow. I knew she was making awful decisions, and now here we are."

"What are you talking about?"

"You're not one to use a curse word, but believe me, once you hear all this, you will be. As for the fever, I might have a temporary fix." Elliot left the room and came back with a pale blue bottle of pills. "I took a few bottles of these from the healer's cabinet at the citadel when I was really sick."

"What?" Ridley seethed. "The healer didn't give Leni anything when she came by."

Palming the bottle of medicine, Ridley followed Elliot out of the shop. He got on his bike and led Elliot down the path back to his place. Ridley had never seen Elliot quiet like this. He was normally laid back, teasing, and flirting with everyone —him, Leni, anything that walked. But maybe he did care about Leni, the way she did about Elliot, and maybe Ridley should be okay with that.

An icy chill washed over him as he pedaled down a dipping hill, like he was back in Sonya's closet again, accepting that this was how his life was supposed to be. What it always would be. Where the words would be his mother, his father, his friends. They comforted him when he was sad and alone, when all he could do was blink, not truly cry.

The wind slapped his face, pulling him out of his own head when they approached his bright blue house. He stepped off his bike and pressed the kickstand down, hoping the medicine would work. His breathing came out uneven, lungs not working properly, because he was desperate to get to Leni so she could tell him that Elliot was wrong.

As he took a step forward, the trees and the world around him grew brighter and brighter. He tried to refocus his eyes, but a darker image expanded from behind him, encircling him. His head started to pound.

"Ridley, what are you doing?" Elliot asked, wrinkling his nose.

The throb on the side of his head beat harder, and the sizzling sounds the shadows whispered in his ear were things he couldn't decipher. Dark fragile fingertips, with sharp talons, caressed the side of his face. Two hands shook him, and he couldn't tell if they were Elliot's or the shadow's. Something or someone rattled him again.

Ridley's eyes finally cleared, but his body couldn't hold itself up any longer. His knees buckled and he collapsed to the ground. The shadows faded out while his head continued to throb harder, fiercer, to the point where he thought it would explode. And he shouted then for the pain to stop, but it wouldn't.

Elliot hovered over Ridley, looking as if he'd just seen a ghost. "You're seeing the shadows, aren't you? Even though the curse is over."

Ridley blinked, telling him yes in that movement, because that was all he could do.

"I don't want to have to tell you this." Elliot paused, his lips pursed. "But I think you're the next Piper."

CHAPTER 6

Ridley, I need you to be the Mirror Keeper," Leni pleaded, demanded. "I'm supposed to choose one, but I'm asking you." But even if Ridley said no, she would have to choose him anyway. She wanted to give him the opportunity to say yes, not take him by force.

"Why should I?" His eyes were swollen like he'd just been crying. He had. Because of her.

"Because I trust you." Even though she knew he couldn't trust her because of what had happened.

"What about Elliot? Why don't you choose him?"

He was making things harder already, but she couldn't tell him the truth. Not yet. "He's the best frame maker, the royals need him here," Leni lied.

"Always second choice," he whispered. "But it doesn't matter. I'll do it, because I want you to be safe."

Tears pricked her eyes and she didn't want him to see, so she spun around on the heels of her boots to leave. "Good, that matter is settled."

Leni's eyes flew open and her head lolled to the side as she peered around the room. Her body felt like it was made of lead, but her teeth were no longer chattering. The coldness had left her. Had the fever calmed down a bit? The days had all melted into one long, endless daze.

"Ridley?" she called in a rasp, pushing herself up to a sitting position against the headboard.

He didn't answer.

She ran a hand across her forehead, recalling that he was going to get help or something. How much time had passed? She'd been in and out, in and out. Her back no longer ached like the dickens, and the scabs had mended her skin. Raised scars still lingered behind.

Leaning forward, she grabbed the full glass of water at her bed side and drank it. In that moment, she wanted to drink an entire ocean, but without the salt … and the fish.

Leni dropped her feet to the floor and shakily stood from the bed—Ridley's *Blade Runner* T-shirt that she was wearing fell above her knees. She thought about the first time they'd watched it together, when he kept holding up notes during the film, the way he still blinked more than talked back then.

Suddenly, the room seemed to spin around her, and she waited for the shadows to come, to pour out from her, surround her, play with her. But they didn't come. She was truly alone. For the first time in a long while, it was only her standing there.

It's the fever playing with my emotions, she thought as she hobbled to the bathroom.

Everything inside the cozy space was black and white—checkered tiles, checkered walls, checkered counter. Was the damn bathroom trying to tell her to play a game of checkers with Ridley?

Slipping out of the baggy shirt, she stepped into the shower and let the water cool her down. She didn't think about anything, only hummed a melody inside her head to make it remain that way.

The thoughts didn't stay gone for long. Too many days had been wasted, and as soon as she got dressed, she would go to the royals and find out when the next mission would start. There wasn't time to lay in bed and be sick. Besides, she was starting to feel a bit better.

She wouldn't cry. She wouldn't cry. And still … she cried. The tears came in waves, a choked, ugly mess, blending in with the water. Wounded and guttural noises escaped her throat, and she was relieved that she was the only one in the house to witness it.

When no more tears came, Leni took a deep breath, shut off the shower, and stepped out onto the cold tile. She snatched a fluffy blue towel from the rack, still slightly damp. As she brought the towel up to her nose, Leni caught a whiff of Ridley—marshmallows and cinnamon.

Wrapping the towel around her body, she headed into Ridley's room and grabbed another movie shirt from his drawers. This one was of *The Dark Crystal* with the two puppets on the front. The shirt was just as long as the other one, so she took a belt and buckled it in the center to make the cloth into a dress. There wasn't a single mirror on the walls that she could slip into to search for something else to wear. She wondered why he chose it this way. Her chest clammed up because she knew this was another side effect of her stupidity.

If Ridley returned home before she got back, he would probably wonder where she was, but she wouldn't take long. What he didn't know then, as well as now, was that she was the one trying to keep *him* safe.

Ridley had left her favorite snack beside the bed. Cheetos. It wasn't coincidental. She banged her hand against the table. "Dammit, Ridley."

Because of that one bag of Cheetos, she couldn't help thinking about what they'd had, all they'd shared, and how much she'd missed him. Even when she'd worn that stupid cloak, she still had a black butterfly pin on it—so she would remember why everything she did during the curse was worth it.

Leni opened the bag and forced down the chips, just to get her strength up, before heading out the front door.

The cool breeze nipped at her skin, smelling of bananas and lemons from the surrounding trees and bushes. Still no sign of Ridley. Before she could think about what she hadn't accomplished, missed people who weren't there, Leni strode toward the citadel. Her body swayed as she walked the glittering orange mirrored path toward the front of the building. Glass molded flowers were planted beside the path. The flowers reminded her of her glassblowing days, and she had to shut that thought out, too. Happiness wasn't possible right then—but it would be. Once the next mission started.

The glass bridge loomed ahead, and she continued forward with her spine straight, trying to appear unfazed—as if she hadn't been whipped, like she hadn't failed—even though her body wanted to topple over right there.

Leni had never wanted to be the Piper, but at the back of her mind, she'd always known she could one day be. When she found out what the shadows were, because Romy had told her why they were leeching onto her, she was shattered. She and her brother knew they needed to keep quiet about it. But then came the masquerade where she was indeed chosen. And shortly after that was when she'd hurt Ridley. Then there had been a possible solution once she discovered what the Piper actually did and the truth about the fillers—that she could use her and Ridley to escape this dimension.

For a moment, Leni's hand brushed her stomach before she lifted her chin and padded across the glass bridge, the wind making it sway and groan more than usual. Two guards stood outside the front of the citadel in their yellow jumpsuits and wearing their expressionless black horse helmets.

Leni didn't drop her gaze, didn't look at the blue sky nor the cloudy water below, but only at the two guards who were watching her in return. She came to a stop in front of them, holding her shoulders back, and used the secret hand signal to get inside. "I need to speak with the royals. It's important."

"I believe they've been waiting for you to come. Let me see if they're busy," the shorter guard said and left Leni standing in silence with the other.

After what seemed like hours had passed, when in fact it had only been a few minutes, the guard returned and held the door open. He motioned her inside. "They will allow you this one request."

One request? Has something happened?

Leni entered the sitting room filled with the assortment of mirrors hanging on the wall. Within them, families were chatting to one another, others played video games, rooms empty. The emptiness of the rooms reminded her of her heart and how hollow it had become, so easy to crack.

She followed the bright pink and green ornate carpet to two more guards holding open the doors to the throne room. Gathering her inner courage, Leni walked across the shimmering floor, while trying not to think about the last time she'd been there.

Leni met the dark irises of the royals. Brand and Anson were dressed in similar styles—canary yellow and baby blue jackets with faded jeans. Portia and Calliope wore slim suits of different colors—hot pink and orange. Their curly auburn hair cascaded down their backs, against their pale skin.

"You've returned," Portia cooed, picking at invisible lint on her jacket.

Leni took a step in the queen's direction, nervousness slinking inside her. "I wanted to ask when the next mission would begin."

Brand pursed his lips and pressed his index finger beneath his chin. "That was your only shot. The shadows have already left you and flocked to someone else. The flute is back with us."

Her heart dropped, literally feeling as if it had broken free from her chest and plopped on the floor. There was no way she'd heard him right. "What do you mean?" She crept closer, prepared to drop on her knees, bow, and kiss the floor before these jackasses.

"The Mirror Keeper may be allowed to lose a curse, but the Piper isn't," Portia said in a bored tone. "Did we forget to mention that? You may be required to work until you die, but only if the curse wins. Every. Single. Time. Besides, even if it was possible, we wouldn't let you try again. No time for failure."

Leni had to keep from screaming, from trying to rip them to pieces. "But you have to let me work," she practically pleaded.

"And why is that?" Brand asked, leaning forward, dark

eyebrow arched. "I vaguely remember you begging and crying to not have the job when you were chosen, for us to take the shadows away. Well, now your prayers have been answered—they're gone."

He was right—she wished she could take that day back.

"No, please. I don't want to do this. I don't want to take people's souls."

"You can't tell the shadows no when you've been selected. It's this or be killed," Brand said.

Leni had thought about choosing death, but she hadn't wanted to die. That wouldn't have solved anything because the shadows would've just gone to someone else.

"You were late cleaning out your place, so we've burned everything already." Portia shrugged.

Her body felt as though it would collapse right there on the floor. She'd left most of her things at her old house where she'd lived with Millie and Ridley, but not her cassettes. So many of her tapes had been there, along with the player and headphones Ridley had given her. To others, they may have just been material things, but to her they were *everything*. They spoke to her—they helped her get through the days. But there was nothing she could do about them now.

Leni remembered something. It should've hit her as soon as she was told she wasn't the Piper. "If I'm not the Piper then that means… That means—"

"That means you'll be dead when the next masquerade comes and the new Piper is crowned, which will happen in a little over a week." Portia's downturned lips turned into a wicked grin. "And I think you may like this new Piper, except he does blink a lot."

Leni's eyes widened. She couldn't breathe, couldn't find

any oxygen at all. *No, no, no.* The shadows hadn't been with him from his creation. And just because a person had shadows didn't mean that they would necessarily become the Piper. The Mirror Keeper only saw shadows because of the Piper… Was it possible to inherit something like that? What had she done?

"You may go now," Portia continued. "See if maybe your fortune is wrong."

Leni turned on her heels, her nostrils flaring from her rapid breathing, but she tried not to let her mask slip. There needed to be a Plan B. But was there any way to fix this?

Once out of the throne room, then out of the sitting room, then outside, then back in Ridley's house—she slammed the door and did it then. She screamed, punched the couch, and fell to her knees against the carpet.

With tears in her eyes, she finally glanced up, resting her gaze on the covered mirror in the corner. That was why Ridley didn't need mirrors on the walls—he had a mirror with him at all times.

She'd never been inside for that long. Not really. But a part of her wanted to slip through and see them… That would be the easiest place to find them. As an emotion—possibly regret—rocketed through her veins, she stopped. *You did what was right, Leni. It was the best you could've done with what was handed to you.*

Crawling forward, Leni ran her fingers against the crushed velvet and ripped it free. The mirror stared at her, and she peered at it. As self-centered as it was, she still wondered what she looked like. Even if she was ugly or beautiful, either would be better than seeing nothing. She inched closer and slowly pushed her form through the glass. There wasn't a silvery glow like when Ridley touched it, only a ripple and a tickling of skin as she entered.

As before, the room was triangular, purple, filled with mirrors, and a woodsy scent, but when Leni's gaze landed on the table, her heart froze in her chest. There, in the center of a circular table, rested a box—a familiar box—*her* box. It was the gift Ridley had given her. Tears pricked her eyes as she lifted the golden metal with silver jewels on top, and rotated it in her hands to its bottom. The words were still there. *For Butterfly.*

This was the object he'd chosen? This was one of the reasons Lark had asked her if she was Butterfly? In that moment with Lark, Leni had been tempted to stop, but she couldn't, the curse had already started, and the shadows were too strong, controlling her at times, just as she'd done to Ridley. Carefully, she set the box on the table and wandered to the center where the two walls formed an opening, leading to a hall. Down the hall, mirrors hung perfectly straight—rectangle, square, hexagons, triangles, ovals. Most of these she hadn't made—she hadn't been created yet. Leni read the names of the placards above the mirrors, not recognizing any until she came across the one she was searching for—Lark.

In the glass, the face of a girl with windblown curls, light brown eyes, and red lipstick looked out at her. On the opposite side of the wall, in a cluster of other mirrors, rested Auden's. His hair was swept back, his hazel eyes shining, no smile, as if he knew Leni was studying him.

"I'm sorry," she said to them both. "But I had to. Maybe if you knew why, then you would understand, yet we'll never have the opportunity to meet again."

They wouldn't have forgiven her, anyway. Not when their

lives had been at risk. Not when Auden's best friend, Darrin, had died. Not when Lark's sister, Paloma, had gotten hurt. And for that moment, Leni pretended she and Ridley had won the curse, were in their bodies, and she could finally tell him the truth.

She shook away the thoughts, but couldn't help imagining how things could've been, how *they* could've been. Free. But something about it now tasted bitter, no longer a sweet dream of what could be.

Leni stood in the room for a few more minutes before crawling back out of the mirror. As she rose from the carpet, a loud thump came from outside. She hurried and flung open the door, finding Elliot holding Ridley on the ground.

What the hell?

Ridley gripped his head and she knew then that the royals hadn't lied to her—he was seeing the shadows. And she couldn't see them. All her life she'd wanted them to stop— now she wished they wouldn't have.

His mismatched irises caught onto hers, never leaving. "Do you remember why purple is my favorite color?" Then his body slumped to the side and his eyes closed.

Leni jerked forward. A swishing and fluttering sound echoed around the room. She pressed her hands to her ears and curled up on her side. She didn't open her eyes, wouldn't open her eyes. This had become all-too familiar. A nightmare of a dance.

In her sleep, she dreamed of her fingers on a flute. In her sleep, she dreamed of herself cloaked in darkness, of her mind giving in to a song. Somehow, she knew it was a song, even though she couldn't hear the melody. It was as if she could choose the song if she wished, but she never did. She always ran.

A light movement drifted down her face, and she opened her eyes. The shadows were there once more, like they had been night after night again, when they'd been gone for months.

"Go away," she seethed in a low voice.

They crept closer, a shadow's nose almost touching hers. Leni shivered, her heart accelerating. She screamed. Loud, so very loud, not wanting to, but she couldn't take it anymore.

The lights flicked on. It took Leni a moment to adjust to the bright light, but when she did, her gaze settled on Ridley's concerned face. He came and sat beside her, entwining their fingers together.

Leni ran a hand through her hair, drenched with sweat. She wanted it gone, so she leaned forward and opened her drawer, pulling out a pair of scissors. Her focus turned back to Ridley who held up a note.

We need to fix this.

"Can you do something for me?"

"Anything."

"That's not a word you ever want to use around anyone, even me. The only person you ever need to do anything for is yourself, all right?" Yet she would do anything for him.

"You can't choose things for me." His brow furrowed. "Now what do you want me to do?"

She took his hand and pressed the scissors into his palm. "Can you cut my hair for me?" With no way to see her image in a mirror, she wouldn't be able to do it right.

He studied the scissors and bit his lip. "Are you sure? Your hair is so soft."

"It will still be soft." She laughed, then stopped when she remembered the shadows, their touches, their caresses, like they wanted to possess her.

"Just tell me how."

Leni reached over to the record player and let "Love My Way" sweep her away into a pretend place, while she explained to Ridley how to cut her hair above the shoulders with chunks shorter in areas.

Taking a long lock of hair in his thumb and index finger, Ridley rubbed it before he chopped it right below her ear. He studied her, blinking, his lip between his teeth.

"Keep going." Leni nodded. "I trust you." She liked her hair long and would miss it, but there'd been nights where her locks had been floating around her—out of her control. If it was kept short, that wouldn't happen.

Ridley continued with steady movements, leaving his bottom lip tucked in between his teeth, sailing the scissors across her hair. Chop. Chop. Chop. The locks pooled around her body, freeing her. She whistled while he hummed to the music. After the last of the hair needing to be cut cascaded downward, he placed his hand against her head, gave it a stroke, and patted it. "Still soft."

"You have the best comments. Never stop." She studied the color of his eyes. "What's your favorite color?"

He puckered his lips, seeming to ponder her question. "Purple."

Purple was a good choice. But when people asked what someone's favorite color was, they never really asked why, and she was curious. "Why is that?"

"Because," he said with a grin, "it's the perfect blend of blue and red—two of the most immaculate colors."

"So then why isn't your favorite color one of those?"

"Because then what would become of purple?" He paused, creating his own dramatic effect. "It would be dead, stripped apart by two colors that pulled away from each other."

"Wow." Leni laughed. "There's a lot spinning in that head of yours."

"It's hard to keep my mind quiet." Ridley swept a lock of hair from his face. "I have something for you."

"Oh?" She perked up and looked at his empty hands.

He left the mattress and reached beneath his bed, withdrawing a box. It was golden and covered in jewels.

"Where did you get this?" She took the box in her hands, studying the silvery jewels on the top.

"I made the jewels from blowing glass, and I got the box at an old antique shop in town. It was made here a long time ago, but I bartered with the seller for it." He smiled. "Look at the bottom."

Leni flipped it over and read For Butterfly *engraved. She opened the lid and peered inside, finding purple crushed velvet lining. A grin spread across her face because she would never be able to see the color the same way again.*

"I love it." Leni reached forward and threw her arms around Ridley. "Just so you know, purple is also my favorite color, and I think you might be my purple."

 CHAPTER 7

Music from "Only You" – Yazoo

The thrum against Ridley's head continued to fire. His thoughts wouldn't collaborate with him—he should be used to not gathering words, but this was far worse than it had ever been. He exhaled, inhaled, exhaled, inhaled. There wasn't enough air. But a familiar, vanilla scent consumed him, comforting him as he lay on the ground.

His name was being called in the background, but he couldn't tell who it was. A shadow floated down, cramming its hands against the sides of Ridley's skull as the other black silhouettes swarmed beside it.

Ridley's vision took him somewhere else, where hands were holding a silver flute. *His* hands. The instrument came to his lips, and a few notes trickled out, but he couldn't hear the song. But somehow, he felt it in every fiber of his being.

"Ridley!" a voice screamed. Female. She was calling him, and he wanted to go to her like he always had. His body fought with him not to.

He blinked, then blinked again to tell her he was trying. The shadows came toward him, like a flock of birds, and were gone—somewhere inside him.

A bright sun shone in Ridley's eyes, and it took him a second to focus. He lay slumped on the ground outside with sharp pebbles digging into his back. His head was shifted upward, in a lap, a face leaning over him. Bright green eyes connected with his, and he blinked to tell her hello. Tears were gathered in Leni's eyes, and she continued to cradle his face with his head in her lap.

"I'm so sorry, Ridley," Leni murmured. "This is all my fault. Purple, always remember that."

The words jolted him—he was confused by what she'd said. Why was she telling him this? Purple was something they'd shared, something she hadn't wanted anymore.

Another face appeared over theirs, a few of his tight curls falling forward. *Elliot.* That was who she wanted.

Ridley pushed himself to a sitting position. The ache in his head was gone, but the one in his heart lingered. Especially now that Elliot and Leni were there, together. But he couldn't think about that now. He had to think about Leni and fixing her.

"You should be inside, resting." Ridley pressed a hand to his head.

"I'm not going to rest." She scowled. "The fever broke for now."

"You're not the Piper anymore," he said. "I went to Elliot's and he thinks he knows why you're sick."

"I know... I just came from the royals and found out." She got to her knees, her fingers digging into her thighs. "I've been weak because I'm dying. And when you're announced as the Piper, I'm going to die."

She knew. She already knew. And he'd sat there and wasted two weeks when he could've been trying to figure out another solution. There wasn't much time left at all, less than a week until the party.

"There has to be a way to prevent all of this," Ridley said. "I won't be the Piper and you're not going to die. I should've understood before that you're in love with someone else." He couldn't control the shift in his eyes as they glanced at Elliot.

Elliot blew out a puff of air and focused on Leni with pursed lips. "Tell him."

"No." Leni shook her head and rose to her feet.

Ridley frowned and pushed up to stand. "Tell me what?"

"Give her the meds, Ridley," Elliot started. "And then we're all going to sit inside and have a real chat."

"What are you talking about?" Ridley asked, clearly confused, scanning both their expressions and finding nothing.

"Please, just come inside." Leni's shoulders slumped as she opened the door, her face tired. Ridley didn't say anything else as he and Elliot helped Leni to the couch when she started to stumble.

Elliot filled a glass with water and handed it to Leni while Ridley poured out two red pills into his palm. Without question, she took the pills and guzzled down the water.

"I think it's time for you to be up front with Ridley," Elliot finally broke the uncomfortable silence. "I thought you should've told him from the beginning, but I also know you did the right thing. He's not impulsive, but when it comes to love and saving people, he would've been. Honor and Chivalry should be Ridley's middle and last name."

Ridley folded his arms over his chest. "What the heck are you talking about?"

"Fuck, Ridley, just say *fuck*. Because you're going to be cursing like a sailor when you hear this story. I know you don't like to have a potty mouth, but sometimes you need to have one. You listen to dirty words, you watch dirty words, you read dirty words, you've done dirty things, just say the dirty words. *Please.*"

Ridley wrinkled his nose and parted his lips, ignoring the idiot. He instead turned his attention to Leni, who wasn't looking at him or Elliot. She was peering down at her hands, seeming lost in her own head.

"Well?" Ridley asked. "Do you have something that's going to put me on edge? Or is Elliot just being Elliot?"

"I lied," she whispered, still not looking up.

"Lied about what?" He stepped closer to her and sat on the end of the coffee table. Was it something with the shadows? But she'd already known what those were when she became the Piper.

For the first time since they'd been inside the house, her gaze latched onto his. "Remember how I once said that you lie to the ones you love?"

He nodded. It was one of the only things she'd ever told him that he didn't understand or could ever agree with. They'd argued over small things like music or movies, but nothing too terribly big.

"When I told you I was in love with Elliot, I lied to you. He's only a friend. Since he and I broke up, that's all we've been."

"And in case you're wondering, I'm not in love with her either," Elliot said. "Not that it matters if I was or not."

Ridley's heart pounded, and he couldn't speak. His fingers twitched, needing to write something down. He grabbed the Post-it pad and pen, remembering the day Leni had confessed to him.

"Ridley, I can't be with you anymore," Leni said.

"Why?"

They had been fine. There weren't fights before or after she was chosen to be the Piper. He promised to wait for her, even when she confessed to him what she would have to do in the Earth Dimension.

"I'm in love with Elliot," she said hurriedly. "It's always been Elliot. I'm going to wait to tell him, but I think he still feels the same."

"But you said you loved me." Ridley touched his chest, wanting to break through his ribcage to get to his heart and crush it. So he didn't have to feel this, whatever this new emotion was.

"Love doesn't always last forever." She opened his hand and placed the glass grasshopper he'd made for her into his palm. "And sometimes we think we're in love, when we're really not. It happened with you because I missed my brother. I know that now. After becoming the Piper, I realized that my dreams changed too."

A single tear slid down Ridley's cheek as she walked away, leaving him alone in the mirror shop. He stared at the ceiling, looking at all the glass objects dangling that they'd created together.

*Ridley slipped out the glass butterfly from his pocket that he always carried with him. Holding up the grasshopper beside the butterfly, he inspected them both. Whirling around, he scribbled down the words on his notepad—*hurt, anguish, destroyed.

He crumpled up the paper and threw it in the trash. Taking the grasshopper in his hand, he hurled it across the room, but it didn't shatter when it struck the wall. He'd yearned to hear the sound echo over and over in his ears, but it didn't. So instead, he scooped up the grasshopper and dropped it into the boiler, letting it dissolve back into liquid.

Ridley held up the butterfly, wanting to throw that in too, but he couldn't because Leni had made it for him. And while he could destroy anything of his, he could never do that to her. Even then.

And in the end, he would give her what she wanted and let her go, despite knowing for him, no matter how much time passed, it would only ever be her.

Ridley shook off his backward thoughts and held up the note, hand shaking. *I don't understand. Why?* The only thing he could think of was because she'd been chosen for the Piper position, but then she'd picked Ridley. So now nothing made sense.

"I can't tell you," she said through gritted teeth, worry lines creasing her forehead.

Ridley scribbled down the words. *Tell me.*

"If something happens to you, Leni," Elliot started. "Then maybe Ridley could still try what you were going to."

She shot him a dirty look. "That would mean getting another girl."

"I'm not trying to be insensitive here," Elliot bit back.

Leni stood up, not as weak as earlier, and sat beside Ridley. "You remember how I told you about my brother, right?"

"Yes, of course I remember." After hearing the story, it was the seed of him starting to see what was wrong with this place.

"If I tell you this, you have to promise not to do anything," she pleaded. "To not go and try to do something heroic, because it could get her killed."

"Her?"

"The baby," Elliot said in a hushed voice.

An eyebrow flew up on Ridley's forehead. *Baby?* As in a baby created in Mira? "Are you saying Romy's baby is still alive?"

Elliot was chewing on a finger while Leni gripped the back of her neck. She shook her head, pointing at Ridley, then at herself.

Ridley blinked. And blinked. And blinked. And blinked. He'd done a lot of blinking in his life, but never so much at once. Then he took a deep swallow—his network of veins shot off like fireworks as the blood rushed through them. "You and me…"

She lifted a finger to her lips and nodded. They'd created a baby together. One he hadn't known about. "Butterfly…" He couldn't control her nickname from rolling off his tongue.

Leni picked up the notepad and wrote, *"Only You."* And he closed his eyes and let the Yazoo song play in his head. He and Leni had created a baby… Together…

Ridley couldn't contemplate any of this. Was he happy? Was he furious? Was he scared? Was he hurt? All of it. He was all of those things and more.

"Where is she?" he asked, when his thoughts stopped moving in every which direction.

Leni glanced toward Elliot, and he gritted his teeth. "We don't know," she said, pressing a hand over her mouth.

"What?" How could she *not* know?

"Millie," she said softly.

It was as though he'd been kicked in the chest. Was this why Millie had left? "Took the baby with her?"

Leni wrote the word. *Safe.*

"So she didn't tell you where, just in case, right? To prevent something from happening to you?" Like it had with Romy…

"Or you. I thought since I was the Piper that it would be better since I couldn't escape with her. And I couldn't risk you getting killed if you tried."

"You didn't give me a chance to decide, though." He couldn't wrap his head around how he felt or how he should be feeling. "And then what changed that?"

"I had a solution."

The pre-fillers. The curse. Leni using her and Ridley to take over the bodies if the curse had won. "This is why you planned for us to take over Lark and Auden's bodies."

She slowly nodded.

"But how would that even work?" That wouldn't help the baby situation. That would only move Leni and him into the Earth Dimension permanently, not the baby.

"I kept a lock of her hair—Rebel's—that I joined with mine, yours, and liquid glass. During that time, the pre-fillers would've conceived. They didn't hold all our memories, just false ones that were infused from another source…"

Ridley clamped a hand around his mouth. "Holy shit."

"I knew you were going to curse," Elliot said with a small smile.

"Are you saying the pre-filler was *pregnant?*" Ridley's deep voice went up an octave, never sounding so high-pitched.

"I don't know!" Leni held up her hands. "I mean, there was a 50/50 chance. But there was also the chance that she wouldn't have been until the end of the curse."

Ridley grabbed at his cheeks and ran his hands down

them, wanting to throw up all over the carpet. "You should've told me."

"Would you have changed your mind about helping Lark and Auden if you'd known?" she bit back.

That was a tricky question. Too tricky. "No. I don't know?" He shook his head. "No."

"And that's why I didn't tell you." Tears streamed down Leni's face. "Because I could've done it. I know it's horrible, but I've held her—I've seen her face."

What if he'd seen the baby's face? Would that have changed anything? "I can understand where you're coming from, but what do we do now?" Ridley stood and paced back and forth. "You're dying, and we need to prevent it from happening."

"I think we should go see Quinna," Elliot suggested.

"Quinna?" Ridley asked.

"She works at the creation place"—Leni pushed up from the table—"but she knows things. She's the source who aided me with this, and Elliot's been working with her for a while."

"You think she can really help stop this?" Ridley had heard of Quinna, but he didn't know anything about her besides her job of creating people.

"We won't know unless we find out," Elliot said.

A spark seemed to flicker across Leni's face, something akin to determination. "Then tonight, we'll go."

CHAPTER 8

Music from "Runaway" – Bon Jovi

Leni had confessed everything to Ridley and couldn't help thinking about the song "Runaway." She wasn't a runaway any longer, even though she hadn't planned on telling him until he was safe in the Earth Dimension. But that plan had backfired, and now she was going to die. She didn't know where Millie and the baby—Rebel—were anymore.

Rebel was safe. For now. For now. For now. But for how long? As her eyes closed, she needed to make sure Ridley was safe, too … before she died.

Leni twirled the rod in the liquid glass when a cramp ripped at her stomach. She wasn't supposed to be here—she was supposed to be packing and preparing for when the royals would need her to serve them. All this time she thought she could live the rest of her life with the shadows and just not be chosen. But she was wrong. Because she had been, it meant she wouldn't have a real life. Ever. Yet she'd vowed to make it work with Ridley.

"What's wrong?" Ridley asked, forming and shaping the glass into a flower.

The convulsion came again like she'd just been kicked in the stomach. "I don't know." Leni pressed a hand to her abdomen to try and make the pain go away. "My stomach's hurting really bad."

"Go home and rest." Ridley took the rod from her hand and set it in the corner. "I can take care of the shop until Jerry comes back." For the past couple of weeks, Ridley had been put at a different mirror shop after Jerry's caretaker had passed, so the royals assigned Ridley to work there until he found someone else. Leni didn't know Jerry well, but he seemed nice from the few times she'd seen him.

She wanted to stay but the cramping continued. "All right. I'll lay down for a bit then work on packing for the citadel."

"Do you want me to walk you home?"

"No, the royals would want you to stay." Tugging him by his collar, she brought his face close to hers. "Purple." With a smile, she kissed his lips softly before leaving.

As soon as Leni stepped outside in the cool breeze and gripped her handlebars, a sharp pain struck her stomach worse than before. She took a slow breath and pedaled her bike down the cobblestone path. Perspiration beaded her upper lip and back of her neck as she skirted and weaved through blue and pink buildings. A crushing ache came again, and she had to stop. Heart thrusting forward, she placed her forehead against her arms on the handlebars.

Her stomach had never felt this bad, even when she'd had food poisoning. What the hell was wrong with her? Leni kept her feet planted on the ground, trying to think about anything else to take her mind off the pain.

"Leni?" a familiar voice called from behind her. Elliot.

"Hey," she choked out and glanced over her shoulders, meeting his dark irises.

Elliot was wearing shorts and a gray blazer, his hair covered with a vintage newsboy hat. His hands were empty. He must've just dropped off a set of frames or he was going to pick some up.

"What's wrong?" He took a step closer, his forehead creased with worry lines. "You don't look so good."

"I don't know," Leni rasped. "But if I pedal anymore, I think it will just make my stomach worse."

"Here"—he clasped the handlebars—"let me walk you home. Make sure you get there and all." She felt too sick to argue.

Elliot pushed the bike forward while she held on. Her stomach continued to ache, but she could at least breathe again, even though she didn't want to be coddled like this.

"So, you and Ridley going to make it work?" Elliot curved the bike around a sharp corner.

"Yes." There was zero doubt in her mind that it could work.

"Good, because I was going to tell you to." He smiled. "I just wish you would've told me about the shadows. You know I wouldn't have said anything to anyone."

Leni wished she would've told him and Millie, but it was too late now. "It is what it is."

"Maybe."

Before she could ask what he meant by that, another sharp pain tore across her insides. Thankfully, they weren't far from her house. Stepping from the bike, she tried to walk faster when something seemed to shift within her belly, like she might hurl up her lunch at any second.

At that moment, she thought it was the shadows that wanted to come out and play their little game with her. But they didn't rise, didn't stir, didn't whisper. Even then, this felt different—something she'd never encountered before.

Leni remembered the night at the masquerade when she'd been there with Ridley and was announced as the new Piper. Her heart had twisted, and she'd sank to her knees, wanting desperately to run. There'd been nothing she could do. Nothing at all.

As she stumbled forward, she sank down to her knees then, too, but this was more physical than emotional pain. There was no holding herself up any longer. Two strong hands scooped her up and opened the door—she wished it was Ridley.

Elliot set her on the couch and called for Millie.

"She's not home yet," Leni groaned on the last word, her spine arching when a rush of agony blasted through her lower back.

Jaw lowering, Elliot's eyes widened as he peered down at her stomach. "What the fuck is going on?"

Leni followed his gaze and lifted her shirt a few inches. She gasped and kicked her legs so she was sitting up. Her stomach was moving. The shadows. She'd been wrong outside —it was them here, making her life hell.

"What are the shadows doing? They've never done this before." She paused, desperately searching his face. "You're seeing this, right?"

"I'm seeing this, and it's fucked." Elliot ran a hand through his hair, looking as though he wanted to get out of the house. "No one's supposed to see the shadows except for the Piper and their Mirror Keeper. And I'm not your Mirror Keeper."

Leni hadn't chosen one, hadn't wanted to choose one. But she would have to at some point. The royals hadn't even told her when her first mission was supposed to take place. No matter if it killed both their dimensions or not, she wouldn't take anyone's soul.

"Well, you're not technically seeing the shadows yet and neither am I." Another harsh wave of pain came, and she released a scream.

Elliot drew closer and grasped her shoulder. "Should I get Ridley?"

Why couldn't Ridley have just been at the shop next door? "I don't—"

The door opened, and they both turned their heads as Millie walked in with a sack of groceries. Millie froze when her gaze found Leni on the couch. Her stare became questioning as it dropped to Leni's twitching stomach. The bag of groceries slipped from Millie's hands and crashed to the floor. Several things made of glass shattered and two bright red apples rolled out.

Millie didn't stop to pick up anything—she hurried and slammed the door shut. "What have you done?" she whisper-shouted, her face full of panic.

"I didn't do anything!" Leni snapped. She hadn't asked for the shadows or to be the Piper. Not a single damn thing of it.

Millie clenched her teeth, her voice coming out in a squeak. "You're going to have a baby?"

Elliot's face paled, his jaw falling down.

What was she talking about? Leni shook her head and waved her hand rapidly side to side. "No, it's not possible. Ridley and I used protection." As she glanced down at her flat stomach, the skin and muscle were shifting. It looked like tiny hands were trying to punch their way out.

There was no way. No. Earthly human births took nine months. Here, when it happened, no one knew about being with child until the baby came, like with Romy's. She couldn't help thinking about what had happened to Romy and his baby after…

"Elliot!" Millie shouted as he started to back up, "You're not going anywhere. I need your help."

"Um." He nodded, his hands trembling and his eyes like saucers. "This is already looking like some Rosemary's Baby *shit, so I just need a moment." Leni had heard of the movie but had never seen it.*

Millie shot him a glare. "Go get me a few blankets. Hurry."

Without a word, he jolted in the direction of Leni's room. "This is all my fault," Millie whispered.

Leni couldn't think of anything to say because she was in shock. Maybe even delirious. Then she thought about what would happen next. She'd have to bring the baby to the citadel to be killed. Nausea swirled inside Leni, and her hand flew to cover her mouth.

"Here!" Elliot said, handing Millie three fleece blankets.

Millie removed Leni's shoes and placed two blankets beneath her, then concealed her lower half with the other. "You're going to need to take off your pants."

With a nod and hands shaking, Leni pushed down her leggings, her emotions being pulled in too many directions as her chest frantically moved up and down.

Peeling up the blanket a notch, Millie told Leni to take deep breaths. She wanted to tell her she couldn't. Instead, her screams sounded, her cries hitched, her body feeling as though it was being mutilated by a slasher with a knife.

After what felt like forever, the baby finally came, entering the world in a liquid sheen of silver before shaping and molding itself. Exactly like when she and everyone was created in Mira within the mirror pools.

Millie lifted the infant, its silvery flesh changing and morphing until an olive coloring appeared.

The room was quiet, so very quiet, until a loud wail echoed off the walls, straight from the baby's pink lips. Leni trembled with fright.

Millie placed the infant in Leni's arms and the world grew quiet again. The new guest was a girl—a miraculous sight with soft brown curls. How could something she didn't know existed the day before, now inspire so much love? But a cold sweep of fear washed over her. Romy, his girlfriend, their baby. Dead. As Leni studied the tiny face, she understood at that moment why Romy did what he did, and she could no longer hate him for it.

"You have to turn the infant in," Millie said, tears filling her eyes.

The thought of the royals putting an end to her baby's life horrified her. "No." She knew why Romy couldn't. Why she wouldn't. "I can't."

"If you wouldn't have been picked as the Piper, you could've tried to run." Millie knelt beside her, wrapping her hand around Leni's arm. "But you can't do that now because you're connected to the flute and they would easily find you."

"Ridley?" she whispered, even though it would hurt more than anything.

Millie closed her eyes. "He wouldn't make it. If something happened to him, the way it did with Romy, I can't. And I know you wouldn't be able to handle it either."

"Then what?" Leni asked. She wasn't going to give the baby up to the royals.

"There's somewhere I can go." Millie sighed. "I won't tell you where I am, so you won't be a part of it." She left Leni for a few seconds and came back with a pair of scissors. There was the tiniest patch of curls on the baby's head and Millie cut a few locks off. "This will be to remember her."

Leni couldn't hold back a choked sob as she stared at the sleeping baby. When she'd first met Ridley, the first album they listened to together was from David Bowie. She picked a song from it. "Rebel. That's her name. Please take care of Rebel."

And that was what Leni felt like she was, too—a rebel.

Two hands shook Leni's shoulders, waking her. Somehow, she'd drifted off and now found Elliot grasping her arms. Sitting up, she looked around the living room. "Where's Ridley?"

"He's inside the mirror." Elliot motioned his head at the corner where the cursed thing rested. "Took his notebook and a pencil with him."

Leni couldn't help but think about Rebel, the day she'd been born, things she should've done differently. "You think I should've told him sooner, don't you?"

Elliot sucked in a breath of air. "That's tough because from where I'm sitting, you did the right thing in protecting him, especially after what happened to Romy. *But* if I were him, I'd be pissed."

Her stomach sank. "Is he livid?" If the roles were reversed, how would she feel? Would she be angry? Or would she be relieved Rebel was safe? Would she love the baby the same way if she hadn't seen her face? All she knew was that she loved Rebel and couldn't second-guess her decisions right now.

"It's hard to say." Elliot shrugged. "It's Ridley. But yeah, I think he's mad. However, I don't think he's going to stay that way with you for too long, especially in your condition."

"You mean because I'm dying?" Leni had never been concerned with death. Maybe it was because she always saw herself withering away at an older age. Definitely not at eighteen.

"No, because he loves you, and I do too," Elliot said, smiling sadly. "Not in the way that Ridley does, but a different way. The world would be awful without you."

"Yeah, yeah, well, I'm not dying today." She rolled her eyes. "So let's not talk like we're having a funeral right now."

"You're right. Let's hope Quinna really does know something. She's helped you before."

Because of Quinna, Leni and Elliot had learned more about possible ways of going around things, like with the pre-fillers.

"And let's hope I don't pass out and neither does Ridley." Her body was still weak, and she knew from experience that the shadows could come out at any time. That was something Ridley would have to face, and she wished with everything in her that she could deal with them instead. For him.

CHAPTER 9

Music from "When Doves Cry" – Prince

Ridley sat against the wall with his legs crossed, leaning over with his elbows to his knees and gripping the sides of his head. His eyes focused on the jeweled box in front of him, the gift he'd made for Leni. He'd chosen this to use for the curse because she'd given it back to him a little after she had the glass grasshopper. And as soon as the curse began, when he couldn't take back how he'd helped to start it, he'd figured out a way that could possibly save Lark and Auden.

The letters inside his head were still tick, ticking, mending and forming words—ones he couldn't fully develop. He'd written lyrics to "When Doves Cry," then a list of words in the notebook beside him. *Angry. Beautiful. Quiet. Relieved. Broken. Happy. Nervous. Frightened. Frustrated. Possibilities.* They went on and on and ended with *Her.*

Ridley finally stood and gathered his things. He walked away from the spiraled staircase toward the hall where Lark and Auden's mirrors still hung with the others.

They were where they were supposed to be—back to the living. When the next humans were chosen, Lark and Auden's mirrors, as well as the others, would be shifted downward for the new cursed victims' family and friends. He exhaled a sigh of relief. They'd be okay. But Ridley wasn't okay—his next mission could be playing the flute, leading to the entrapment of other innocents.

Ridley took one last glance at their mirrors, imagining that maybe Lark and Auden were at a record shop together, flipping through albums.

Dipping his hand into his pocket, Ridley brushed his fingers against the glass butterfly. The truth had been revealed, and Leni had told him her reasoning for everything. A baby. *His* baby—named Rebel.

His hands trembled at the thought because he'd only ever seen babies in movies and in the Earth Dimension. Ridley wouldn't have even known what to do with one, and Rebel didn't feel real because he'd never seen her. But he wanted to know her, see her, hold her. He was frustrated because Leni hadn't told him sooner, but he knew she'd done the right thing by hiding her.

Yet, it was still wrong what he and Leni had been doing, what the royals were continuing to do. Could he try following the path like Leni had? Take someone's life in order for them to be safe? Because even if he did, another Piper would just be chosen to replace him while the repetitive curse continued with others.

Ridley came to a stop in front of the two nameless mirrors that were used for the pre-fillers when the curse started. Something didn't feel right about it, because no pre-fillers were in use yet, so how could there be mirrors in the room at all? He had never noticed it before, not until right then.

Blinking, he took a step toward the one on his right and pressed a hand against the glass. A cool sensation rocketed through him, causing a chill to run up his spine as freezing air escaped his mouth. It was as though life was in there, when there shouldn't be.

Yanking his hand back, Ridley couldn't do anything else but blink and think about how the dimensions were connected through this realm. The people of Mira seemed to only be around to make sure the Earth Dimension didn't destruct in order for theirs to survive. He came up with no conclusions.

Enough time had passed, and he needed to face Leni, not hide away forever. After she'd told him everything, his mind felt trapped, like he was back in Sonya's closet, alone. He'd needed the temporary break.

Setting the jeweled box back on the table, Ridley pushed out from the glass, the mirror rippling around him. When he finished dragging himself out, he stood and found Elliot and Leni seated on the sofa, talking. Before, there would've been this envious green monster pulling at him, like it had been for the past few months. Now, he was bothered that Elliot had known about the baby when he hadn't.

"Are you ready?" Leni asked, not meeting his gaze. "Or do you need a few more minutes?"

Ridley studied her exhausted face. There were light purple bags beneath her eyes and her shoulders hunched forward. "Do you want to rest while me and Elliot go?"

"No," Leni said and stood, only slightly shaking. "I'm not going to lie down anymore. It won't fix anything, and the meds are helping. Just"—she exchanged a glance between them—"can one of you pedal?"

"Of course," Elliot said, winking at Ridley. "I'm sure Ridley's bike has more room."

Ridley narrowed his eyes at Elliot, and Elliot only cocked his head.

Before they all left, Ridley packed a few things in his waist pouch and handed an extra to Leni to put her medicine bottle in. Ridley got on his bike and held it steady as Leni took a seat on the handlebars, then leaned back onto his chest. Her warmth seemed to seep into him.

Leni placed Ridley's spare set of headphones over her ears, and he couldn't help wondering what she was listening to, what she was thinking. But neither of them spoke, the breeze doing all the talking, as he pedaled behind Elliot.

The night was dark, and they only passed a few other travelers on the way, who looked to be up late doing their required jobs for the royals. Quinna's place was farther than he'd remembered. He hadn't been there since he was first created, so the memories weren't very clear.

After passing rows and rows of nothing but trees covered in thick moss, they approached a part of the woods containing a cluster of about five small red houses with orangish light shining out from their windows.

Elliot rode his bike down a gravel trail and looped around to the back before coming to a halt in front of the one on the far right. Slowly, Ridley pressed the brakes on his bike, careful to not jostle Leni.

As Ridley and Leni peeled themselves off the bike, Elliot placed a finger over his lips. Ridley frowned because what was he going to do? Shout to the world they'd arrived?

Lifting his knuckles, Elliot knocked on the door. Several moments later, a girl with dark brown eyes and short red hair sticking up in all directions opened the door. He'd never seen her before, but she was maybe a few years older than him.

"Hey, Quinna," Leni said in response to the girl's surprised stare. "We need your help."

Hastily, Quinna looked left then right, before waving them inside the narrow hallway. After shutting the door, she turned to Ridley, studying him. "And you must be Ridley… The Mirror Keeper." She grinned with a knowing expression. "Leni told me about your eyes."

"Oh." Ridley glanced at Leni, whose cheeks were turning red. Was she embarrassed? She'd always told him she liked his eyes, but he'd never seen them. He only knew one was brown and the other gray.

"Anyway, this way." Quinna pivoted on her heels, her skirt swishing as she led them down a yellow hallway with bare walls.

A metal scent grew stronger as she brought them to an area the size of a small bedroom with a blue chaise and two chairs. Quinna and Elliot slumped down onto the chaise while Ridley and Leni both took a seat in the chairs across from them. Along the walls hung posters of Johnny Cash and Hitchcock films.

"I suppose your plan didn't work," Quinna interrupted Ridley's staring spell as she focused on Leni.

Covering her mouth, Leni shook her head and Quinna sighed. "No," Leni said. "I'm dying and Ridley will become the next Piper at the masquerade."

What exactly had Leni told Quinna before? And why had Quinna helped her? Was there something in it for her?

Ridley had so many questions he wanted to ask, but he decided on the most important one first. "Is there a way to prevent me from becoming the new Piper?"

Quinna placed her elbows on her knees and leaned forward. "By killing yourself or having someone do it for you, but that wouldn't save *her*, which is what you want to do, right?"

"Yes," he said in a low voice.

"I'm sorry, but that would only lead to another Piper being chosen." Quinna squinted her eyes like she was trying to think of another possible way.

"We'd like an outcome where no one ends up dead." Leni reclined against the chair.

"Tricky, tricky." Quinna paused, tapping the ends of her fingers together. "Do you know who any of the Mirror Keepers were before you?"

The royals didn't have masquerades when a new Mirror Keeper was chosen. He had never seen the other Piper in person since the last masquerade had been before he was created. All he knew was the Piper had died of old age.

"No." Ridley shook his head.

"I was one." Quinna smiled, almost bitterly.

Ridley straightened and looked over at Leni, who confirmed it with a nod.

Taking a deep swallow, Ridley remembered everything he went through when dealing with the curse. "So then that means…"

"We succeeded with a curse, and I chose to leave," Quinna said. "Then I came back here and returned to what I did before as though I hadn't gone through what I had. In case you want to know how it feels, I regret it every single day. I regret all of it. And that's why I've been digging and digging into uncovering things."

Ridley recalled his moment earlier when inside the mirror. "I noticed something recently in the Realm of Mirrors. When in between curses, why are there still two mirrors hanging in the spots where the pre-fillers go, with coldness inside them?"

Quinna nodded. "I noticed that when I first started, and I may have a theory."

"What is it?" Leni asked.

"There's a history here that we all know the basics of, but Elliot's been helping me gather things from the citadel when he drops off the frames."

"*Huh?*" Leni whisper-shouted, shooting an icy stare at Elliot. "You're risking your life even more now?"

"After seeing what you went through when you were chosen, then what Ridley had to go through, yeah." Elliot shrugged.

Ridley could only find himself able to blink, but something like respect had stirred in him for Elliot, and possibly even fear.

Quinna cleared her throat and continued on with her story. "You know the history of the four royals, I'm sure. Two sets of twins who are immortal—two kings and two queens. And at one point, they'd been joined and lived as one individual king and queen."

"Yeah, we already know this," Leni said.

"But what if that wasn't the whole story?" Quinna arched a brow. "Let's say there's a specific reason they were split apart that wasn't about saving dimensions."

Ridley thought about this, about all he'd read and all he'd studied. People weren't born here, they were created. No one looked the same—no one had a twin except for the royals. Why weren't they questioned more about this? Or maybe they had been? And he knew if they had been, then it probably didn't end well.

"Even if they were split apart, why would that make them immortal?" Quinna continued. "If I split you apart, your ass would be dead."

"So then how are they immortal?" Ridley asked.

"My family has worked here for a long time, and when I came back from the Mirror Keeper position, I dug through the glass here, along with everything Elliot brought me. None of this nonsense with pipers and mirror keepers used to occur. There were two royals who attempted to make a deal with possibly another dimension, and in turn, got split into two. How? For what reasons? I can't give you an answer for that."

"I'm not quite understanding where this is going," Ridley said. "And I don't know of any other dimensions."

"Me neither," Leni agreed.

"What I do know is neither one wanted to become the reflection after being split apart, so they chose to remain that way. And to stay that way, they have to use the mirror curse. Otherwise, one will have to become the reflection and none of them wants that. Again, how? Why? I'm not a part of their brains."

Quinna's words repeated over and over in Ridley's head, and there was only one question he could think to ask. "Is there a way to make them whole again?" And would it even matter?

"I've been sitting on that for a while, trying to figure it out. But it couldn't have worked before, not until now..." Quinna trailed off, pursing her lips, her left knee bouncing.

"Come on, Quinna," Leni pleaded, her eyes appearing heavier than before.

"Okay," Quinna blew out. "But, just know this could make everything worse, especially if the royals found out."

"We're already too deep in now anyway," Elliot said.

"Our dimension," Quinna started, "is linked to the Earth Dimension, right? You'll need to bring two humans from there to here willingly. Once you do that, we can gather what we need from the Realm of Mirrors and then the last piece from here."

"Hold on." Leni held up a hand. "That isn't possible."

Ridley had a sinking feeling he knew what and who Quinna was going to mention next.

"It wouldn't have been possible before," Quinna said. "But you already linked yourselves with two humans from there. You hadn't used actual pre-fillers, you used parts of yourself and Ridley, therefore, the connection is still there, even though the curse is over."

The last moments Ridley encountered Lark and Auden, when he'd pulled his mask from over his head. They'd *seen* him. They weren't supposed to be able to see his face, but he hadn't thought anything of it because too much had happened since then.

"We can't last there more than a couple of minutes if we don't have the flute," Leni said. "The flute is back with the royals."

"Tut, tut, that's not true." Quinna waggled a finger back and forth. "You're still linked to the flute until Ridley is chosen, and Ridley is still linked to you because he's the Mirror Keeper, even though he's 'transitioning.' And even then, he'd be linked to the flute, too."

"Why are you even trying to help?" Ridley narrowed his eyes. "And tell us why we can't do this without Lark and Auden. They aren't going to want to come here." He knew for a fact that he couldn't get Auden to come.

"Oh, yes they will," Leni shot back. "If this can cut out ever needing to have a curse in their dimension, then their asses will come."

Quinna leaned even more forward. "To your first question, there was a baby I once knew who died. Leni can relate to that—she told me about her brother. There may be a way to end babies having to die. And to your second question, if we want to unlink our dimensions, the first step is to have the two humans from there and the two of you."

That made more sense. However, something nagged at Ridley, and he wondered if the baby had been Quinna's that she'd given up. But he didn't ask her because he knew it probably was by the glint in her eyes.

"I suppose I'll have to stay here," Elliot said. "I'm not linked to the flute, but I'll make sure to keep everything undercover."

"You have only a few days to do this since the masquerade is coming soon." Quinna stood and waved them to follow her to another door.

It led to a room filled with mirrors and small pools of shimmering silver with light smoke hovering over each one. The metal odor intensified as Ridley stepped inside. Long rectangular mirrors hung all around the room.

This was one of the places where people in Mira were created. But not all—not Rebel. If they could really unlink the dimensions and not have to take souls from unwilling victims, then this was the right choice.

Quinna walked toward a large mirror, taller than Ridley. She pressed her hand to the glass, and it rippled. "Please, make it fast because I don't know what excuse I can give for having a part in this."

Ridley couldn't tap into the combination of emotions in that moment—too many to decipher. He held out a shaky hand to Leni. "Let's try this, Butterfly."

For the first time, the old Leni bubbled forth, smiling at him with determination. Together, they stepped through the glass.

SIDE B:
Earth
Dimension

CHAPTER 10

Music From "In A Big Country" – Big Country

An electric current zinged its way across every inch of Leni's flesh as she slipped through the mirror with Ridley. It was different going through a mirror to the Earth Dimension, not like the one Ridley carried where there was more of a rippling. It was as if she was buzzing with electricity, but she was used to the feeling because the same thing happened when she ventured through mirrors to collect items.

Leni should've looked where she was going because when she stepped out, the floor was below her. But darkness also covered the area. She folded forward, pushing Ridley in the back, causing him to trip and whirl to face her. He grunted in surprise, his eyes closed as she landed in a heap on top of him, knocking the breath from his lungs. They'd collided on what she guessed was a carpeted floor in the minimal light—not complete blackness as she'd thought.

"Are you all right?" he asked, sitting them both up.

"Yeah." Leni smoothed her hair. "Didn't mean to fall through like that."

"Lights inside would've helped." His arms were still around Leni. He picked her up and placed her beside him.

Scrambling to her feet, Leni peered behind her to where soft lighting filtered in through large windows. Where were they? This couldn't be a house. She'd assumed they would've come through at Lark's or Auden's. She should've asked Quinna where they were going first…

Using caution, she walked toward the glass door. In the center, a switch rested beside it—she hurried and flipped the light on. Bright fluorescent bulbs illuminated the room, and for a moment, she felt like Dracula, about to turn into ash and die. But it wasn't the sun and she wasn't a vampire.

When her eyes finally focused, scanning the area, Leni's breath caught in her throat. The space before them was familiar. Animal skulls and bright tarot cards hung from the ceiling and gently swayed. Venus flytraps and aloe vera in skull vases sat on a glass table to her left. Along a carved wooden shelf on the wall, clocks ticked, ticked, ticked. She moved farther into the center of the store, examining every single thing she could. Maces, ancient swords, stuffed horned animals, paintings of shrunken heads and skeletons. Leni breathed in the musty smell—if she survived this, she would come back here and shop through the mirror to decorate her home with all these things.

Bubble's Oddities—the place where Lark and Auden worked, where Ridley had dropped off the cursed mirror to them for the first time.

"I thought Quinna was sending us to Lark's or Auden's?" Ridley asked, interrupting her staring spell as he examined a walking stick with a skeletal hand at the top.

"Me too." Leni observed the Kit-Cat Klock on the wall, its tail clicking and clacking back and forth, as though giving Ridley and her their final countdown.

Ridley walked back to the mirror, where they'd fallen through. Ornate brass and braided trim surrounded the large rectangular glass. Objects reflected in the store, but not him, not her. She wondered if Quinna and Elliot were watching them right now or if they'd gone back to do other things.

Striding up next to him, she pressed her fingers against the cool metal texture. "We need to make sure we get Lark and Auden to come with us through this specific mirror."

"Yeah, wouldn't want to pick another mirror and end up on the other side of Mira."

That wouldn't be good. Leni glanced outside at the dimly lit parking lot, then back at one of the coffin-shaped clocks on the shelf. "I think it's better we came through this way instead of in one of their rooms, especially this late at night."

During the curse, she remembered the things the flute would make her do. The shadows made her appear, disappear, and have the pre-fillers do strange things through the night. She'd chosen to start the curse, but she hadn't been the one doing everything by choice.

"I agree," Ridley said, patting his pocket.

Leni's fingers thrummed with anxiety against her jeans. "Should we start now?" They had a handful of days until the party.

"I don't think so." Ridley blinked several times. "Not after all they've been through. Going to them in the middle of the night would only make matters worse. Besides, do you think us tapping on their windows would entice them to come?"

Leni imagined their reaction, and it probably wouldn't be good. "You're right, but I'm not sure if morning will be much better." Even as part of her wanted to get it over with, the other, larger part, clamored for rest. Exhaustion washed over her, making her knees wobble until it was hard to stand.

She peered at the non-existent furniture around the store,

not knowing where they should sleep. "Wanna stay here for the night?"

"I'm fine with it if you are. You already know I can sleep anywhere." Reaching inside his pocket, Ridley turned and walked away from her with an indifferent expression.

Her heart dropped, like a treasure chest falling to the deepest level of the sea. Leni stood in the middle of the store alone, while he observed bottles lining the wall, reading each label.

Giving him space, she spotted an old record player in a corner. Beside it was a cardboard box with about ten records inside. Leni steadily flipped through each one, absorbing the pictures and names across the front. Three were from Elvis, then there was Ella Fitzgerald, Patsy Cline, Buddy Holly, Frank Sinatra, Billie Holiday, Ray Charles ... and Big Country.

She smiled to herself. That last one felt out of place, yet perfect for her in that moment.

Pulling the record from its sleeve, Leni placed it onto the player and let the music fill her heart, her thoughts. As the band played, she whistled along and kept sneaking glances at Ridley. He was still poring over the bottles on the wall underneath a small white sign that read, *Miracle Remedies*. His fingers tapped against his thighs like they always did with music, and he hummed softly, too. Or perhaps it was her imagination.

With a sigh, unable to take the distance between them anymore, Leni padded across the carpet toward him. "Ridley?" Her voice came out snappier than she'd meant it to, but she couldn't control it.

Spinning toward her, he smiled a small smile, but it didn't reach his eyes. "Are you all right?"

There he was again, concerned with her and how she was feeling, when she was worried about him. "Do you hate me?"

"No," he drawled, his shoulders hunching forward. "I could never hate you, Leni. It's just, everything that you told me is hitting me all at once. Millie and Elliot knew, and you didn't tell me. But you've always told me everything, so I don't understand."

"I know…" she whispered, wanting to reach for his hand but not doing it.

"And then when we were here with the curse"—he gripped his hair—"you kept using me to do these things… At times, I started not knowing what was real and what wasn't."

"No, Ridley, I didn't," Leni said. "You may have thought you were being worked by a puppeteer the whole time, and maybe you were. But *I* was being told what to do by the shadows and the flute, too."

"But not always."

"No, not always," she agreed. "Not at the beginning."

He shifted closer. "I don't hate you—don't ever think that. That wouldn't ever be possible. Right now, it's just hard for me to find air, you know?"

She grabbed his hand then and intertwined her fingers with his because he'd always been her air. "I know."

Ridley's arm twitched and his back arched. *Not again.* Leni held his shoulders as he let out a pained cry.

"Fight it," Leni said in an even tone. She couldn't see the shadows, but she knew they were there, and she bet they were watching her, all while punishing her by doing this to him.

Hurriedly, Leni pressed her palms to Ridley's cheeks. His

eyes were unfocused, looking at her but not really seeing her. "Fight it," she demanded this time.

He clenched his teeth, muttering incomprehensible words. This reminded her of how she must've appeared to him when she'd been going through this same process. With each moan that escaped his chapped lips, Leni was reminded of her own pain. Her own experience. The shadows' unrelinquished hold on her. The same hold that now held Ridley captive… And she couldn't do a damn thing.

She remembered the week before the masquerade, how the shadows had gotten worse for her, so much worse. And even now, she could still feel them brushing their shadowy fingers against her skin while luring her to choose a song.

After several excruciating moments, Ridley's eyes refocused, the pain still written across his face.

Wrapping her arms tightly around him, Leni mumbled into his shirt, "You can hate me—I don't mind. Because I hate myself every day. But I promise before I die, I'm going to save you, and then you're going to save her."

Tears slipped down her cheeks, and Ridley drew his arms around her, holding her back. "No," he said. "*We're* going to save her."

Together, they sank on the carpet in between an aisle of candles and seashell art, latched onto each other. Neither said anything else, but no more words were needed.

Leni woke early, and she wasn't so lucky as to find herself in a place where time was reversed. But she did discover Ridley still curled on his side, appearing otherworldly to her when he slept. He always had, like he'd come from one of the fairytale stories he would copy words from. And maybe he did come from one. Maybe when they were created, they were pulled from another dimension entirely, and they just didn't remember. Maybe…

Leni nudged Ridley awake. "Let's go. My heart is getting all weird with impatience."

His eyes flicked open and he covered his mouth as he yawned. He glanced at the clock. "It's super early."

"We shouldn't waste time, especially if it's going to take some convincing." She smiled, needing to figure out how she could do that if she had to. Perhaps saying the curse could not happen to anyone else might be enough.

"All right. Let's just grab something to eat on the way." Ridley pushed himself up to stand.

"That's the best idea of the day." Her stomach ached with hunger, her limbs weak. It wasn't as bad as it could be—as it had been over the past few weeks.

On the way out of the oddity store, they stopped at the McDonald's in the next parking lot. She confiscated several hash browns and sausage biscuits while no one noticed, then grabbed an orange juice.

"Lark's first," Ridley said when they stepped back outside. "I still think she'll be the easiest to convince."

"I agree with you."

Lark might be a little feisty, but Auden was pricklier. If they convinced Lark, she was sure they would have Auden.

The sun beat against her face while she walked, but at least she was wearing normal clothing this time, not a cloak and gloves. Leni really took the time to observe this dimension because she'd never cared to before, not when she'd mainly gone into rooms. Earth wasn't all that different from her dimension nature-wise—the sky was the same blue shade, the sun yellow and blazing, the trees leafy and green. Besides the absence of a gleaming glass citadel or brightly-colored buildings, the main difference seemed to be the number of cars skimming by. They only used bikes in Mira.

"Do you need more of your meds?" Ridley asked when they'd made it to the front of the trailer park entrance. A faded green sign with missing letters announced their location.

Leni's chest had started heaving again and perspiration beaded her skin. "Yes." Her voice came out rough.

Pulling out the bottle from her pouch at her hip, Leni poured two pills onto her palm. She placed the bottle back inside her pouch, then popped the pills into her mouth and downed them with the remainder of her orange juice.

The effects were immediate, her strength coming back in quick waves. They continued into the trailer park, the bright sun glaring down at them. A few of the homes looked like they would collapse at any moment, their siding and roofs missing pieces. Others appeared in better condition—Lark's included. Everything was still intact and painted a light gray and white. A plastic yellow and white flower spun in front of the trailer, like the last time she'd been here. When the original curse started, they had both instantly connected to Lark and Auden.

As they approached Lark's trailer, Leni stepped through the small patches of grass and around the back to Lark's window.

Ridley stood behind her as Leni peered in through the slit in the mushroom-printed curtains, not seeing anything except for the mattress on the floor and Lark's cat sleeping on it. Her nerves were like a volcano about to erupt—she whirled to face Ridley. "She's not here!"

"She should be." He pointed at Lark's rusty bike. Leni moved to touch it, right as a familiar engine sounded from the front of the trailer. Auden's van. This was possibly a dream come true with both of them there, and *together*.

Leni hurried to where she could get a better view of the front of the trailer. She and Ridley both peeked their heads around it.

Auden was out of his van wearing jeans and a T-shirt, and he handed Lark a small notebook. Lark stood in dark jeans and a baggy shirt, her curls rumpled by the wind.

"What are they talking about?" Leni asked, studying Lark's sad eyes.

"I can't hear." Ridley leaned closer to her, and his marsh-mallow and cinnamon scent comforted her.

She stopped distracting herself, focusing on Auden getting into his van and briefly hearing something about him going away. "Wait!" she whisper-shouted. "He's leaving town?"

Leni's eyes bulged and her breathing increased as the van drove away from Lark's trailer. What if they could only get Lark and not Auden! Why hadn't she yelled something?

From the slump of Lark's shoulders, she looked as if she was about to melt into the steps right there, and Leni didn't know what the hell to do. Why didn't Lark just tell his ass to stay?

Leni jerked her head up when Auden's van came barreling back around the trailer park, like a dark horse seeking vengeance—or possibly redemption.

Auden and Lark talked for a few moments but Leni still

couldn't hear until he stepped out of the van for some kind of two-minute reunion.

"Do we say something now?" Leni asked, not wanting to be *that* person, but also needing to be.

Ridley shrugged, crinkling his nose. She knew he was tired of having to bother them with shit, but what else could they do?

An idea struck Leni then, a good one. "They haven't seen my actual face before. Let me try something and whatever you do, stay here!"

Ridley blinked at her three times, his way of telling her not to try anything stupid. Stupid felt like her middle name sometimes.

"Hey!" Leni called, skirting around the trailer, just as Lark and Auden were about to enter it. They would be the only two people in the entire Earth Dimension who would be able to see them.

Lark and Auden both paused on the steps, turning toward her.

"Yeah?" Lark lowered her brows.

Leni scratched the back of her neck, trying to find her tongue to speak. "I have this thing I'd like to show you." She couldn't think of what to say—it was like her brain was gone in that moment.

"Sorry," Lark mumbled, "I have to get ready for work, and we don't want to buy anything."

With that, Lark told Auden to hurry in the trailer and said something about solicitors needing to learn to quit bugging people.

Leni stood there with her lips pressed together in a tight

line, ready to hurl herself at the door, beat it down, and tell Lark she could solicit wherever the hell she wanted to.

Two hands of wisdom tugged her backward. "Calm down. She said she was going to work, so let's go to Bubble's and we can try again. And *not* look like a solicitor this time."

"Could you have done better?" She placed her hands on her hips.

"Maybe if they didn't know what I looked like already." Ridley cocked his head. "But, we'll see. I do have a better plan on how to get us back to the store, though."

Leni arched a brow as Ridley snagged the duplicate of Lark's bike. "Hop on, Butterfly." Once the curse had broken, the duplicates of everything had reconnected, including Lark's bike.

Leni sat on the handlebars and leaned into Ridley as he pedaled back to the store, saving her energy. She hadn't realized how much she'd needed this because even her bones were exhausted.

While Ridley pedaled, she watched the clouds move, pretending they were different musicians performing songs. Ridley hit the brakes and she snapped to attention, finding they were back in the parking lot of Bubble's.

Hopping off the handlebars, Leni hid farther down the strip mall behind a tan pillar covered in gum—all the shades of the rainbow were attached.

"How are you feeling?" Leni turned to Ridley. "With the shadows, I mean."

"I'll be fine." She knew he meant what he'd said, but his eyes didn't look *fine*—they were without their usual shine, duller.

Both sat in silence for what seemed like forever when the

sound of a bike crossing the gravelly parking lot came from behind her. Leni spun around and spotted Lark wearing her canvas jacket, along with headphones over her ears.

"Showtime," Leni said. "Let me try this one more time."

Ridley sighed, like he knew she was going to do something stupid. She shot him a glare and slipped out from behind the pillar.

Lark glanced up with fresh red lipstick coating her lips, her eyes narrowing when she recognized Leni. Adjusting her backpack, Lark pressed the kickstand down in front of Bubble's. "You were at my home earlier."

"I need to talk to you." Leni held up her hands. "Not about soliciting!"

While unlocking the door to the store, Lark said, "What is it?"

"I know about the curse," Leni rushed the words out. "And this is going to sound strange, but I need you to go to our dimension."

Without hesitation, Lark pulled out a pocketknife from inside her jacket and whirled around to face her. "I'm not going anywhere. I don't know who you are, but Auden and I broke the damn curse and we're done. Come near me again, and you'll have to talk to my blade." Opening the door, the cowbell rattling, Lark darted inside.

Another sigh came from Ridley as he poked his head around the pillar.

"Why didn't you try and join me?" she grumbled.

"Because I was waiting for you to finish whatever it is you're trying to do." He pressed forward, rolling his eyes. "I'm going to go and talk to her … alone."

"Fine, fine."

Leni didn't think Ridley would be able to charm Lark with his awkwardness this time. Back at the trailer, Auden hadn't said a word—maybe it was possible he would actually be easier to convince than Lark. She wasn't going to waste time waiting for Ridley—he'd have to just be an unhappy camper when he found her gone. Hurrying for the bike, she took off to try and sway Auden.

CHAPTER 11

Music From "How Soon Is Now?" – The Smiths

Ridley opened the door and stepped inside Bubble's, glancing one more time over his shoulder at Leni and her windblown hair. He looked toward the front counter where he expected Lark to be sitting, but she wasn't. Only her backpack and headphones rested there.

As the door closed behind him, he searched down each aisle of oddities for her small frame. Maybe she was in the back because he couldn't find her anywhere. She could've been calling Auden for backup after Leni's poor attempt at an interaction with her.

Ridley slipped his hand into his pocket, brushing his fingers against the butterfly as his gaze roamed over packets of seeds. Why would anyone want to grow tiny bananas when they could just eat a whole one? He picked up the packet and inspected the back—it looked like there would be a lot of work involved in keeping up with the plant.

What was he doing worrying about plants right now? He took another glance at the counter, but Lark still wasn't there. Was she hiding? As he turned the rack of seeds, a loud squeaky sound filled the air, making him cringe.

From behind him, something clicked, and he slowly turned around to find Lark holding her knife, pointed at his heart. There was another time outside the laundromat when she'd held that same knife up at him.

"I thought you said you wouldn't be back," she said between clenched teeth, flicking her eyes up and down him. Behind the anger she was trying to put out, there was worry, and possibly confusion. "Also, what are you wearing?"

Ridley's blinking gaze drifted down to his clothing. He was wearing the same stuff from the day before, a faded *Ghostbusters* T-shirt with a white button-up short-sleeve over it, jeans, Converse, but his usual pork pie hat was gone. He missed that hat already.

"Can you not speak again?" Her brown eyes narrowed with suspicion, and the pocketknife held steady.

"No, I can talk…" Even though he wanted to pull out his Post-it notes and pen from his side pouch right then.

"Where's the black clothing? Where's the mirror? I'm not doing that curse shit again." She took a step back and lowered her gaze to his pocket, where his hand was settled. "What do you have in there?"

Sighing, he fished out the mirror butterfly.

"I suppose it returned to its owner."

His head started to throb around his temples, and his nerves kicked up. "I need to write," he rasped, clenching the side of his skull. It would make it easier, jotting it down. Maybe she'd understand that better than his awkward words. It had worked before, right?

Slowly backing up, but not turning around, Lark scuffed her feet to the counter, never once dropping her eyes from him. He followed her, the pulsing against his skull reducing. Maybe the shadows were staying away for a bit.

Quietly, she grabbed a yellow pad and pen from behind

the counter and slid them across to him. He shook his head and pulled out his own from his pouch.

Wanting to lessen the tension filling the room, he attempted to be humorous when he wrote, *Where's the Ouija?* on the yellow Post-it, and smiled.

Lark shot him a death glare. Apparently, he wasn't funny, and it wasn't the time for him to try to be.

He decided to go with it. She'd either listen to him or she wouldn't. *I need you to hear me out. Can you do that?*

"Maybe?" Lark pursed her lips, clicking her red-painted nails on the counter. For the first time since he'd seen her, he noticed she looked tired. Had she still not been sleeping well since they'd left? There were no dark circles under her eyes, but it was in the way she carried herself. She hadn't appeared that way back at the trailer earlier—he brushed off the observation.

Taking a deep breath, he gathered his thoughts because he didn't want to have to write down everything that needed to be spoken aloud—no matter how much more comfortable it made him. He tucked his notes and pen into his pouch. "Remember when I told you that our worlds are connected and every so often my dimension needs souls to keep the balance or everything would be destroyed?"

"How could I forget that tidbit?" Lark rolled her eyes. "It sounded like something straight out of a film, only it wasn't."

Ridley placed his arms on the counter and leaned forward. "What if I told you there was a way to end the curse from happening to anyone else? To stop it for good."

"I'd say, I'm not sure if that's my problem." Lark brushed her finger along the strap of her backpack. "Auden and I already stopped *our* curse. We didn't suffer for nothing. Neither did Darrin or Paloma."

Those words struck him in the chest, but he had to keep going and get her to sweep that stubbornness right outside the door. Ridley's thoughts shifted to the books he'd read inside Sonya's closet, stories he continued to read even when he'd met Leni. Heroes. Almost all the time the heroes won, but were he and Leni even heroes? From his perspective, taking souls to save dimensions actually might have made them heroes, but for Lark and Auden, they'd be the villains. It was a strange thing, really. A thin line between the two, possibly one and the same.

"What if I told you that you could be a hero in this story, and you are one of the only few who could help to end every-thing? You wouldn't even have to do much." She'd just have to cross over to his dimension and wait until the masquerade started. That was it. But the party could get dangerous…

"I'd say, go talk to the other few who can help." Lark turned away from him, her expression resigned. She opened the cash drawer to start counting the money, like she was pretending none of this was happening. "I've gotta work. Some of us, or most of us, in the 'Earth Dimension' need money if we ever want to do anything with our lives."

Ridley and Leni were both forced to work in his dimen-sion, as well as others, but he didn't want to start an argument. "All right, so when I said a few, I meant two, and we need them both." He rubbed his chin. "You and Auden."

"Listen, um, Ridley…" She paused. "It feels so weird saying this after that name also belonged to Auden's doppel, *pre-filler*, or whatever wanted to lock us in the mirror. Or no, they didn't really. It was the flute player—Leni."

"No, I get it." Ridley didn't want to mention that Leni was the girl she'd spoken to outside—not yet—but he was sure she'd figure it out soon enough.

"Do you?" Lark pressed a handful of bills back into the drawer.

"I didn't know you as a person, not exactly," Ridley started. "I didn't truly know anyone from here. As you're aware, I'm from another dimension entirely, where we think about things differently, though not always. When I chose you, as I told you before, it was because I liked you through your objects and had been taking duplicates from your room the last few years. We have a lot in common, and your music actually helped me after I was found." And Leni, but he left that part out.

"Hold on." Lark's eyes widened and her hands slapped the counter. "What the fuck do you mean you were taking things out of my room? And this was pre-curse? Not just seeing me through the mirror, but actually sneaking in and out of my room? Where I sleep? Where I get naked and change clothes?"

"Oh no, no, *no!*" Ridley hurried on, blinking rapidly and trying to find the right words. Of course, they wouldn't come since he'd never been good with conversation. But he'd never watched Lark in that way—the thought hadn't even crossed his mind. It had been too filled by another girl… "Okay, so it seems I have a lot more to explain, but we don't have the time for any of that right this second."

Lark's face filled with fury as she slammed the cash register shut. "If you want me to listen, then you'll make the time."

His hands gripped the counter, trying to stop them from trembling. "First, I never saw you like that and—"

"But others can peep on people in mirrors from there?" Her voice went high-pitched.

"Yeah, they can…"

Ridley didn't know if Mira's population watched Earth's people *like that*, but he supposed some did. Others might even fall in love with humans on the other side, but there was nothing they could do about it since the person would never be able to see or talk to them. In Lark's case, it was different. He'd guessed as much when Leni had used part of herself and him to create the pre-fillers, when he'd noticed both Lark and Auden could see him. Really see him. Now, even after the curse was done, that suspicion was confirmed.

"In our dimension," Ridley continued, "we take things from rooms, stores, or other places whenever we feel like it, but our bodies don't allow us to stay there for more than a couple of minutes. It's an in-and-out kinda thing. You don't see us when we're there, and we only take the duplicates so you don't notice that either." Except for the one time he'd taken the cassette players for him and Leni, but that hadn't been from Lark's home.

"This is like a nightmare!" Lark shouted, glancing up at the ceiling and back at him. "I swear to God this is a real-life horror movie, worse even. If Imani knew this, she would flip!" She rambled on for a while longer before he could find an opportunity to continue.

"I didn't explain to you last time that we have four rulers where I'm from. Twin kings and twin queens who are the true ones in charge." Lark didn't interrupt him as he went on, but he could tell she wanted to. "They're the ones who take the souls after the curse is completed, to make sure the dimensions don't go off balance and cease to exist. But we recently found out that the real reason behind it is so they can remain immortal." Ridley told her the rest of the story that Quinna had revealed, while she studied him with what appeared to be confusion.

"So they lied, just to be immortal." Lark's eyebrows drew together like she was lost in thought.

This was it. This was the right time for him to bring up Leni and tell her to come inside. "You remember the girl outside, the one you saw earlier at your home?"

"Yeah?" Lark drew the word out slowly.

"That's Leni. The real Leni."

"The flute player with the black cloak?" Lark's eyes widened once again. "That girl who tried to talk to me is *Leni*?" Her expression was hardening—not a good sign.

Ridley winced and swung his hands up. "Yes, but hold on."

The cowbell rang as the door opened, and they both looked in the direction of the new guest. Ridley expected it to be Leni, tired of waiting, but it wasn't. It was a man, maybe in his forties, carrying a clock in the shape of a mushroom. He stopped at the counter and placed his item in front of Lark. "I was seeing how much I could get for this?"

Lark's eyes kept shifting to the side to look at Ridley as she spoke, "Jimbo will be here in about thirty minutes if you want to get an estimate."

"I'll browse around for a bit." He shrugged.

Lark frowned, her gaze sliding over Ridley, and back to the man. "Do you see anyone else in the store?"

The man surveyed the area and turned back to Lark with a

weird look. "Only you." He left his clock behind and walked toward the wall with the bottles of remedies.

Lark's head slowly turned to Ridley—she picked up her pen and wrote a message on the yellow notepad. *Why can't he see you?*

He took the duplicate of her pen and scrawled his message. *It's because Leni used part of us as the pre-fillers so when hers blended with you, you have some sort of sight, I guess. Same goes for Auden. You two are special... That's why we need your help.*

"I'm sorry, I can't," Lark whispered, her voice changing. "I can see the duplicate of the pen..." She seemed to take a deep swallow as she turned and grabbed the feather duster, walked around the counter, then brushed past him toward the weapon area on the other wall.

Ridley chased after Lark and snatched her elbow. "Please, can you at least think about it?"

"I can think about it, but I can't risk Auden's life. He's been through so much, and this already sounds too risky. Kings and Queens? Immortals? Taking souls? Like I said, I'm not a hero," she said in a low voice, peering at the man on the other side of the store, but he wasn't looking in their direction.

He studied her shirt and let go of her arm. "'How Soon Is Now?'"

"What?"

"The Smiths—you're wearing their shirt. That's the song they'd be playing to you in this moment if they were here. Just think it over, and I'll come back tomorrow." Turning away from Lark, to give her space to think, he headed toward the exit to find Leni.

Bringing in Leni today wouldn't help whatever progress

he may have made, if any, but tomorrow they'd go in together so she could explain her side of things. Lark just needed time. But Ridley and Leni were already low on it, so she would need to decide fast.

The humid air hit Ridley's face when he stepped outside. He snuck behind the pillar but found it empty, Leni and the bike both gone. He should've known she would try something like this.

Without a second thought, he took off running to the place he knew he would find her.

CHAPTER 12

With each inch Leni pedaled, her limbs grew limper, but she didn't turn back. She passed a small tan church with a high archway and golden cross on the roof. A large white sign posted out front read, *Jesus Saves All*. Did that include her? Or only people with souls? Because right then, she really needed the saving.

Blowing out a deep breath, she turned down the familiar street with brick houses and mostly pine trees until she found the place she was searching for. Auden's.

His lawn was perfectly tidy with two bright pink flamingo yard decorations. She sighed in relief when her gaze settled on his black van parked in the driveway—he was home. There could've been an easy chance he'd gone somewhere else after leaving Lark's.

Tap on the window or ring the doorbell? she asked herself. *Ring the doorbell or tap on the window?*

A memory came to her—her standing in his backyard in front of his window, dressed in her black cloak, Auden unable to see her face—him frightened.

"Tap on the window it is," she whispered. Ridley would've said getting his attention at the window would scare him, but it was the easiest way.

Pushing down the kickstand, Leni walked around the garden of his one-story house planted with luscious green bushes and yellow and orange flowers. The gate creaked as she opened it to a sparse backyard. Even though she'd been there before, it didn't seem real since she hadn't fully been in control of herself. Yet she remembered everything.

After she passed several windows, Leni came to Auden's room in the back with the curtains pulled open, like they'd been the last time. She peered inside the glass and spotted him right away. He was lying on his bed, staring up at the ceiling. The Ramones poured out from the speakers and Auden was doing drum motions with his fists. Two brand-new band posters spanned the wall.

Tightening her hand into a ball, Leni tapped her knuckles against the glass. Auden jerked to a sitting position, his eyes fully open as they focused toward the window. On her.

Trying to smile so she came off friendly instead of sinister, Leni waved at him like they were old pals. But she inwardly cringed.

The fright vanished, but his brow furrowed as he walked to the window and lifted it up. From his left ear, a silver earring dangled with a stud beside it.

"Yeah?" He paused, studying her face. "You're the girl from Lark's. I don't know what you're soliciting, but I don't recommend trying to sell things at people's windows. Some will pull out a gun before thinking."

This is good. Possibly getting somewhere.

"No, I talked to Lark again at Bubble's and she sent me this way," she lied, or partially so. "Can you meet me out front? I need to talk to you."

His expression turned skeptical. "You can't talk right here?"

"No." She needed him out front so he couldn't slam the window down on her. "It's a life or death situation sort of thing."

"If that's the case, then this would just take up time by me having to stroll out front, but all right," he said with sarcasm. With those final words, he closed the window.

Leni hurried back out the gate and around to the front of the house, where she waited beside his van.

Auden stepped outside barefoot, his gaze sweeping right past her, creases appearing on his forehead. "Why do you have Lark's bike?" His voice sounded suspicious.

Of course it would.

But then she stumbled back, because he shouldn't have noticed that. "You can *see* it?" Leni asked, incredulous.

"Yeah?" Still glowering, he inched forward. "Did you steal it?"

"What? No! I borrowed it." How could he see it? It must have something to do with the connection. That could be the only reason. Leni needed to hurry and reel him back in. She could tell by his scowl, directed at the bike, that she was losing him.

"First," she continued, "I want to say I'm sorry."

Cocking his head, Auden's hazel eyes slid back to her. "For?"

"Everything," Leni whispered. She found herself wanting to cry and she didn't even know why. It wasn't the time for that.

"This is getting too weird." Auden backed up. "I'm going inside and calling Lark."

"Wait!" She lunged forward and clasped his wrist. "Please!"

Taking his arm from her grip, he turned around with a frown. "What is it? Because I know for a fact Lark would never lend her bike to anyone."

"It's not really Lark's bike." Leni sighed. Auden's expression changed from confused to alarmed—he quite possibly believed she was insane. "It's a duplicate. I know about the curse, and I need your help."

Auden's entire body stiffened, making him appear more statue than human. Several seconds passed before his trembling lips finally moved. "What do you know?"

Leni covered her mouth for a moment then dropped her hand back to her side. "I need you and Lark to come with me to the Mirror Dimension. I know a way we can possibly end everything, with no more curses ever occurring."

Auden's lips parted and he slowly backed up. "Fuck that! If you think I'm going to have you take Lark to some other dimension, then you've lost your mind."

She could tell he loved Lark so damn much because he was more worried about her than himself.

"Please," she begged, clasping her hands together.

"Look, that Mirror Keeper told us we were done. But two weeks later, here we are again." Suspiciousness crept back in his face. "Who are you, anyway?"

"I'm Leni." As soon as she said her name, she knew she should've said something else, *anything* else. She should have lied, lied, lied her ass off. But she didn't want to lie—she wanted to be honest. But sometimes honesty was the wrong answer.

"The *flute player*?" His voice rose several octaves. "The *fucking* flute player?"

"I can explain." She moved forward, holding her hands up, pleading with him not to go back inside.

"No, you can't. You're the reason why Darrin's dead," Auden said, anger lacing his words. "Stay away from Lark, and stay away from me."

Leni watched as he took off inside his house, the door slamming shut. She wanted to fall to her knees because she was so, so tired. Maybe he needed time to think it over. However, in that moment, she didn't think he'd ever change his mind. Ridley had been right—Lark's reaction couldn't have been worse than this.

Taking the bike by its handlebars, Leni walked in the direction of Bubble's. She didn't notice anything except for the ground, the cracks running up and down the cement—fragmented, just as her life was. Exhaustion hit her like a tidal wave, and she couldn't control herself from slumping to the ground, the bike collapsing onto its side. She stared up at the sky and the clouds that she wished would play music, when two strong hands scooped her up from the ground and cradled her.

"Why did you do that?" a deep voice asked above her. Ridley.

"Because I thought I could convince him. And I couldn't." Tears welled in her eyes as she studied Ridley's reddened cheeks and damp hair. "Did you run all the way here?"

"For you, Butterfly, I'd run anywhere. You know that," Ridley said. "Lark might still be open to convincing. We'll give them space for the rest of the day." Leni opened her mouth to object. "You don't want to push them into saying no.

I know you're impulsive, but if you want them to say yes, we'll have to stop bombarding them for today. Give them time to absorb it."

He was right. Dammit. Leni hated it, but she would listen.

"Fine," she huffed. "Auden can see the duplicate of things. He was able to see Lark's bike."

"Same for Lark." Ridley shrugged. "They're both on the work schedule tomorrow at Bubble's, so we can try when they come in."

"What do we do until then?" She was tired but not enough to sleep the day away.

"First"—he unzipped her side pouch and pulled out her bottle—"I think you need meds. Next, I'm going to take you to a couple places if you're up to it. You need a break, and so do I."

Her interest piqued as she took two pills and swallowed them dry. "All right, but only if you pedal."

"That was my plan." He smiled and lifted her.

After stopping at a Taco Bell and eating while seated on rad twisty chairs, Ridley paused in front of a red metal building with a flat back roof.

"What is this?" Leni asked, slipping off the handlebars onto loose gravel. Holding a hand at her forehead to block the glare from the sun, she gazed up at the colorful sign. *Arcade Fun House*.

"Pretty much what the sign says." He smiled and tugged her toward a glass door.

As she stepped inside the dimly lit area, there was mostly light coming from the bright screens of arcade games.

"You want us to play games?" Her tone came out incredulous.

"Yep." Ridley brushed past her to the front desk where a woman in her twenties with teased, blonde hair stood. She filed her nails while reading a *Soap Opera Digest* magazine. Ridley popped open the cash register and collected a handful of quarters.

Leni scanned over the area to her left, skimming her fingers across the row of pinball machines. In the middle of the carpeted room rested a few pool tables, and past that were tons of arcade games. Paperboy, Pac-Man, Galaga, Kung-Fu Master, Marble Madness, and more.

"How did you know about this place?" Leni asked when Ridley walked back beside her and took her hand, pouring half the quarters he'd collected into her palm.

"I used to come in here all the time and take candy bars and chips."

They had arcade games in Mira, but Leni had never taken the time to really play. She'd been too busy making mirrors, then in her spare time she would blow glass, watch movies, or listen to albums. But the musical sounds of the games persuaded her to try.

"Go have fun." He tilted his head at the pinball machines and took off in the direction of the video games.

She took a quarter and placed it into the red slot of the pinball machine. Pulling the plunger back, she released and let the ball fly upward. The ball went straight down the center, becoming lost for good. Rolling her eyes at herself, she did it again and this time pressed the buttons at the sides.

After several rounds of not getting any better, but still having fun, she headed toward the Pac-Man machine. Leni played the little bastard three times, each time dying and unable to get past round one.

"I swear it's rigged!" she shouted to the colored ghosts on the screen.

"It takes skill," Ridley said from behind her. She hadn't even heard him stroll up because she'd been too focused on the game.

"To avoid ghosts? It's all chance!" Leni exclaimed.

"Nah. Watch." He placed a quarter into the machine and folded his warm hand around hers, before wrapping their joint fingers around the joystick.

While their hands moved left and right, she watched the screen as Pac-Man avoided all the ghosts, not getting touched a single time.

"See?" He grinned when they made it to round two, his hair falling forward.

"Yeah, yeah, you're the Pac-Man master." She grinned back.

"Ready for our next stop?"

"There's more?" Light still shone through the glass doors, and she was curious to see what else he had planned.

"Yeah, unless you're too drained, then we can head back to Bubble's and rest." His face was full of concern, but her body didn't feel overly achy, only a little weak.

"No, I want to see what's next."

They left the arcade and Ridley pedaled down a few busy streets to a dark building that read *Numbers* in bright white lettering.

"It's a club but only the front is open until tonight, so

we'll have the main room to ourselves for a bit," Ridley said, helping Leni down from the handlebars.

The metal door to the entrance was unlocked, and a man with a mustache was flipping through some sort of logbook on a metal counter. The surrounding walls were all an electric blue, with brightly-colored cassettes plastered on them, and the floor a sparkly black.

Leni followed Ridley into the next room where a string of lights was turned on over a bar covered with rows of glass alcohol bottles. Ridley flicked on a switch and a mirror ball above them illuminated the room with silver flickers. The entire area was the same sparkly black and blue with a spacious dance floor. Against one wall, five long steps led up to a stage. A few metal tables and chairs were propped there, empty for now. Cigarettes and sweat lingered in the air, but also something sweet.

"Oh, you just made the room fancy." Leni laughed as Ridley walked over to the sound system in the corner. He sifted through a few tapes and popped one into the player. The speakers in the back of the room, along the ceiling, filled with static before a recognizable fast beat pulsed through. "Just Can't Get Enough."

After stepping down from behind the stereo system, Ridley didn't come back to where she was. Instead, he went toward the middle of the room. With a smile, he started to sway and move his body to Depeche Mode by himself. Leni covered her mouth and concealed her giggle.

Ridley unzipped his pouch and wrote something on his notepad. Holding up the sheet of yellow paper, he cocked his head. *Come on.*

Even though she knew he could say the words, she still

loved reading his notes because they were a part of him and always would be.

Snapping her fingers and whistling to the beat, she headed to the middle of the dance floor. Leni shifted her shoulders in sync with the singer's voice—she was such a terrible dancer, but Ridley wasn't—he'd always been good.

"Should we go *Footloose* or *Flashdance*?" he asked over the loud music.

Fun or emotional… "Both?" Because either way, both movie-ending dances were freeing.

And so, they danced until their bodies were drenched and spent. They probably shouldn't have danced so hard, but it had helped her not to worry, not to think.

Before they left the dance club, Ridley produced a bottle of alcohol from behind the counter of the bar.

"You don't even drink!" Leni arched a brow.

"You're correct but, maybe for this one night, I will."

Leni rarely ever drank either, but she needed it. Grabbing the bottle from his hand, she followed him out of the building as two women walked inside wearing name tags. Their hair was tightly curled and their dresses skin-tight.

The sun was already lowering, turning the blue sky an orangish pink as Ridley pedaled them back to Bubble's. When he pulled to a stop in front of the store, that was when everything came rushing back to her. She couldn't avoid the overwhelming thoughts. Rebel. Romy. Millie. Lark. Auden. Her dying. Ridley and the shadows.

Her shoulders remained tight as she went inside the store and sat on the floor in the middle of the candle aisle. She opened the bottle of alcohol and took a sip, the strong taste drifting down her throat. Ridley didn't say a word as he plopped down across from her. They passed the bottle back and forth, drinking and drinking.

His hand brushed at his pocket, and she wondered if he still carried the butterfly in there. "Why do you keep reaching in your pocket?" she asked, taking another swig.

"Just out of habit." He shrugged, grabbing the bottle from her.

"Show me."

Slipping his long fingers into his pocket, he tugged out the mirror butterfly she'd made for him.

"Do you still have mine?" Leni hadn't wanted to give it back to him, but that had been one of the only ways she could think of to make him believe she was truly letting him go.

Ridley shook his head, his lips turning downward. "I'm sorry."

She should've expected it would be gone, but something else nagged at her. "Why do you have that one, then?"

"Because I could never damage anything you created," he murmured, peering down at the butterfly. She couldn't stop her heart from swelling or the stupid tears from coming again.

"You haven't had any shadows today," Leni said, changing the subject.

"No. I didn't have any while you were sick except for at the beginning. Maybe my luck will kick in and they'll stay away for a few days." He slipped the butterfly into his pocket and rubbed the back of his neck. "What does she look like?"

Leni tried not to think about Rebel most of the time, because it hurt when she did. For the past couple of months, she'd been shutting those thoughts away, trying to focus on the one thing she knew—her daughter was safe. But when she did think about Rebel, the short memory of her tiny face filled her with completeness, if that were possible. "Like you, mostly you. I don't think she has anything from me, except maybe my olive complexion. Which is a good thing."

"Why do you say that?" He frowned as he examined her.

"Millie once told me I had beady eyes."

A loud rumble of laughter escaped Ridley's mouth. "You don't have beady eyes!"

She tilted her head to the side and fluttered her lashes. "Well, what do I have, then?"

Taking out the Post-it notes and his pen from his pouch, he wrote, *Pretty eyes.*

"I think you mean yourself." She grasped his arm and tugged him forward, scanning his brown eye, then his gray one. "Yeah, definitely pretty."

When she glanced down at his nose, then mouth, she realized he was close, so close that his breath mingled with hers, tickling her lips.

His forehead pressed against hers. "All I've wanted to do all day is kiss you." She could tell he was already partly drunk by the way his pupils were dilated.

"But you won't." She wished he would, the alcohol taking control of her words.

"I didn't say that, Butterfly." Then his lips came to hers in a soft caress, and she could taste the alcohol there, his warm hands cradling her face. He trailed kisses to her ear, light as dragonfly wings. "Please don't ever break my heart again."

If she could've promised him the world right then, she would have, but she couldn't control death from coming for her soon. But she would give him anything—everything— else. Wrapping her arms around him, she held him tight and mumbled in his shoulder, "I'll try."

CHAPTER 13

When Ridley opened his eyes, the world surrounding him was dark, everything the color of midnight. He tried to open his mouth to speak and couldn't.

His heart beat, thumping, thumping to a slow and torturous melody calling to him. But he couldn't draw out the name of it. He followed that light, fluid sound farther into the dark. The blackness enveloping him dissipated, and Ridley discovered himself in a place full of mirrors. They were everywhere. Above him, below him, to the left, to the right, diagonal—long rectangles with wooden frames. In the glass of them all was a reflection of a person—of what must be him, but his face wasn't clear. Ridley's brown hair fell in curls around his blurry chin, and he wore a dark cloak and gloves.

As he stepped closer to one of the mirrors, his face only became more and more blurry until there was nothing, only emptiness beneath his cloak's hood. He reached inside the pocket of his cloak and pulled out the silver flute. Gradually, he brought the instrument to his mouth and blew into it. A sharp squeal rushed out of the flute.

Ridley flicked his eyes open—this time he was awake. But he couldn't see, the darkness had followed him here, the shadows blanketing him entirely. His hands couldn't move to find Leni. Where was she? Where was he?

A clicking sounded, like the clucks of tongues, echoed near his ears. A touch—light, then lighter at first—stroked his scalp before turning sharp, relentless. Shadowy fingernails dug into his skull, scraping and scraping. His scream had no sound. He tried searching for his voice, finally shouting loud and clear. The shadows shifted back, cackling as they shot forward, then vanished.

"Ridley?" Leni sounded panicked, her hand squeezing his arm.

He turned his head to face her, finding her hair disheveled and her eyes with dark circles beneath them. "I'm all right." But was he? Bubble's. They were at Bubble's.

"You weren't breathing!"

"That happened to you before the masquerade, too, remember?" A few days before she'd been chosen, he'd discovered Leni on her bed, still, too still, and thought she was dead. The look she had on her face now was the same one he'd had then. Relieved, frightened, anxious.

"I know, but this time I'm seeing you in the same light, and that's much scarier because I can't see what's happening to you." She brushed a damp lock of hair from his forehead.

The sunlight outside was starting to filter in through the windows, and it would be several hours before Lark and Auden showed up for their shift. He couldn't fall back asleep now, not if he wanted to.

"I'm going to get something for us to eat if you want to stay here," he said, popping his back.

"That's fine, I'm just going to rest here."

Ridley swore he could still hear the whispers and clicking of shadows near his ears. Or maybe it was from inside him…

Ridley and Leni waited on the stools behind the counter for Lark and Auden to arrive. They'd been sitting there for the past thirty minutes because Leni had grown impatient. She'd padded back and forth in the store as though that would make the hands on the clock speed up. He wished it would've worked.

The schedule showed Lark and Auden were both set to be there at ten in the morning, and it was ten minutes until then.

"Do you think we can convince them?" Leni asked. "I really thought I could persuade Auden yesterday, but he wasn't willing to listen."

As a result of the curse, Auden's best friend had died and shouldn't have. Ridley regretted it, but the pre-fillers were unpredictable like that. "Can you blame him?"

Leni hunched over and cradled her face in her hands, appearing tired while staring down at a pencil covered in eyeballs. "No."

"Did you take your medicine?" He should've reminded her about it as soon as she'd woken up.

"I forgot. Too much on my mind." Unzipping her purse, she tugged out the bottle of medicine and swallowed two pills down with her water.

"I know you're worried about *everything*. But you need to take care of yourself, especially if we're going to beat this whole thing at the masquerade. You didn't make it this far to fail, right?" Ridley was worried about Leni getting a fever again like she had in the beginning, but that could've just been an effect of her wounds, mixed with the weakness from her slowly dying. Possibly…

"Yes, Doctor, I promise to pay attention to the time more closely now." She smiled, noticing his serious face, and placed a hand on his shoulder. He couldn't help but think about the night before, him being bolder because of the alcohol, their soft kiss, her saying she would try not to break his heart…

"We need something to keep us focused," she continued. "If you could pick a song right now to describe what's to come at the masquerade, what would it be?"

With a sigh, he picked up a pen on the counter and wrote on a notepad. *"Hit Me With Your Best Shot."*

"Let's hope shots won't be fired." She squeezed the bridge of her nose and continued to read over his words.

A click sounded at the front door and the cowbell rang. Ridley and Leni both jerked as Lark entered. It was five minutes before her shift was supposed to start. The door remained open as Auden followed. Lark wore her jacket with dark jeans and boots, and Auden had on a vest over a Cure T-shirt. As they both walked forward, the duo looked up at the same time and stopped when their gazes landed on Ridley and Leni.

"When you said 'tomorrow,' I didn't realize you meant as soon as we got here," Lark said, shaking her head, her headphones hanging around her neck. "Auden already told me what happened between him and Leni yesterday, and I shared everything that happened here."

Auden whispered something in Lark's ear as they approached the desk, and Ridley could see the flaring of his nostrils. Ridley was finding it hard to think because of the impending confrontation, his thoughts coming to a standstill.

Leni remained quiet, which must've been hard, but he'd told her earlier to let him try talking first … or writing.

Lifting the pen, Ridley wrote what he was trying to say, then he held up the notepad. *I meant early. We need to talk.*

"I don't understand why you're holding up notes again." Lark's brows knitted together. "You just talked to me yesterday."

"He uses the notes because he needs them sometimes," Leni spoke up defensively.

Ridley appreciated her standing up for him, but he didn't need it. He didn't mind that people in Mira found his note-writing odd—it was a part of him. It didn't seem like people would be much different here about it either.

"Oh yeah?" Auden studied Ridley with a neutral expression before focusing his attention on Leni. "What about when he was here and couldn't talk?"

"That was because of the curse." Leni straightened on the stool. "I couldn't talk either."

Auden and Lark exchanged a glance, incredulity and a fair amount of mixed emotions vibrating off them. Lark spoke first, her voice laced with fury toward Leni. "Were you or weren't you controlling Ridley?"

"I was, but I was also being controlled in a sense. Not in the beginning, though." Leni's voice was soft, not making excuses.

Ridley was about to speak up, but Auden's next words came first. "Darrin's dead. Lark's sister was hurt." His voice didn't sound angry when he said this, like when he'd first encountered Ridley during the curse—he sounded defeated.

"I know, and it shouldn't have happened," Leni whispered. "Just, at least listen to what Ridley has to say. Then you can decide if you want to come with us. No one is taking you anywhere by force—it doesn't work like that, not with this."

Lark looked again at Auden, waiting for him to decide.

"Just get on with it," Auden said, "because I'm sure you'll just appear somewhere else if we choose not to, anyway."

Ridley nodded and pushed the notepad aside so he could focus on speaking everything aloud. Time was too short for him to be writing things down. "In our dimension, we're created from ten-year-old liquid mirror glass, so we start working at that age after we're made. But for me, I was kept hidden away in a closet, because my caretaker had wanted a girl. Until two years ago, when I turned sixteen. A woman named Millie found me and brought me to live with her and Leni.

"There, Leni and I became friends ... and more. At times, Leni would have shadows come to her, though no one else around could see them. She'd confided in me about them and the fact that having the shadows meant there was the possibility of her one day becoming the Piper. By keeping quiet, we thought no one could find out. But during a masquerade party at the citadel a few months ago, Leni was chosen to be the Piper, so the royals had always known she could be picked. There are others gifted with the shadows when they're created, so it didn't necessarily have to be her."

"Doesn't sound like much of a gift," Lark muttered.

"I'd have to agree," Ridley said, especially after having experienced it for himself. "After being chosen, Leni uncovered something which, in turn, caused her to push me away. But when she found out her task required fillers once the curse was complete, Leni used it to try and get back what she'd given away."

Leni stayed quiet, watching Ridley closely.

"That was an incredibly vague story." Auden wrinkled his forehead and shook his head. "What did Leni uncover?"

The story made sense to Ridley, but to someone who knew almost nothing about his dimension, he might need to explain things better. "Okay, I can tell this is confusing. Let me try again. On Mira, our dimension, we have four rulers—two twin kings and two twin queens. They were once whole and not split into two. Recently, we found out that it's possible they'd made a deal with another dimension, which we didn't know existed, and became immortal. To keep their immortality, they take souls from here when the need arises, I guess." Ridley didn't know the specifics on that either.

"Sounds disturbing…" Lark trailed off and met Ridley's gaze. "So that's how you're created?"

That was where he was about to get to. Leni hadn't wanted them to tell Lark and Auden, but he'd said it would be the one way of convincing them.

"Yes," Ridley said. "But sometimes, we aren't. It's harder for us, but if a baby is born, it's considered an abomination of sorts by the royals, so the infant is to be killed."

"Hold the fuck on." Auden's eyebrows went all the way up his forehead. "*What?*"

Leni seemed unable to hold back as she got up from the stool and hurried to the other side of the counter. "If you decide to come back with us, you can't tell anyone this."

Ridley got up, too, and went to stand next to Leni.

"Why?" Lark asked. "Not that we would, but doesn't everyone over there know this rule anyway?"

Biting her lip, Leni glanced at Ridley. "We have a baby."

Auden quirked a brow, grabbing at his lower lip. "A *baby?*"

"Wait." Lark held up her hands, her face horrified. "But you just said all babies are *killed.*"

"My caretaker, Millie, took our baby—Rebel—and hid her," Leni said. "I don't know where. But somewhere safe."

"Tell them the rest," Ridley urged, swallowing deeply. This was something he should've told Lark yesterday, but it was better for all of them to hear it together.

Leni nodded, and Ridley noticed her hands were shaking, as was her voice. "Before Millie left, she gave me a few locks of Rebel's hair to remember her by." She paused, her chest heaving. "But I didn't know I would use them one day soon. When I found out about the fillers, another girl named Quinna helped me mix Rebel's hair, mine, and Ridley's together within the liquid mirror glass where the pre-fillers would come from. Once the curse ended, if the pre-filler became pregnant, Rebel would've permanently been in the Earth Dimension, as would Ridley and me. I wasn't ever doing this for myself, I was doing it for *them*, for Rebel and for Ridley. For them to be able to be together and not have to worry about being killed. If you don't turn in the baby to the royals, you die, too."

Auden and Lark blinked and blinked, reminding Ridley of himself.

Lark snapped her jaw shut. "Is that all?"

"Almost," Ridley answered. "When we got to Mira after the curse, Leni was whipped and stripped of her position. Now she'll die when the next Piper is chosen if we don't stop this."

"A new Piper?" Lark's gaze angled to Leni's. "You're not the Piper anymore?"

As if in answer, a crushing started in Ridley's skull as dark smoke poured from his mouth. A rack of coughs escaped him, his body stumbling and falling into a crouched position. Shadows swirled around him, filling the entire room with smoke.

"What the hell is that?" Auden's voice came out shaky.

"What are you talking about?" Lark asked.

"The black shadowy stuff everywhere!" Auden shouted. "Ow!" But Ridley couldn't see him anymore, couldn't see anyone in the whirlwind of black.

Ridley's head pounded harder and harder, while someone's hands held onto his upper arms. Slinky shadows crept closer, swiping their tongues along the edges of his ears. He swatted them away while their whispering rambles stirred, right before the midnight black eclipsed all his senses.

 CHAPTER 14

Music From "The Wall" – Pink Floyd

Leni held onto Ridley tightly, concerned and afraid with what was happening. She knew what was going on with Ridley as she lowered him to the floor. But not Auden. Lark continued to shout Auden's name and telling him to wake up.

While kneeling beside Auden, Lark's eyes filled with tears as she focused on Leni. "What have you done? Do something!" Lark screamed at Leni.

"I don't know what's happening!" Leni fired back. "But I didn't do anything! Did he see the shadows before, during the curse?"

All Leni knew was that Ridley was seeing the shadows, and they were trying to speak to him. But somehow, Auden had seen them, too, yet he wasn't the Mirror Keeper and he wasn't someone else born with the sight.

How? she wondered while looking at Auden's passed out form and trying to shake Ridley awake.

"Shadows?" Lark's nostrils flared as she shook her head. "Neither one of us ever saw anything like that."

An achy groan sounded, catching Leni's attention, and she watched as Auden's eyes slowly opened. His hand drifted to the side of his head.

"Oh, thank God." Lark sighed, grabbing Auden's face and

planting a kiss with her red lips to his mouth. "I thought you were dead."

"I'm here, just waking from a nightmare," Auden grumbled. "That I suppose wasn't one at all."

Ridley coughed, his eyes blinking. He rolled to his side, clasping his skull with his palms.

Leni pressed a hand to Ridley's back and glanced at Auden. "What did you see? You saw the shadows?" Since Leni was released from being the Piper, she'd seen nothing, heard nothing, not even the smallest flutter of movement. There'd only been silence on her end.

Auden stood, his fingers nervously twitching as he straightened his shirt and vest. "There was this dark smoke and then these black shadow things. Monsters? Revelations or some shit? I don't fucking know. But they came spewing out of Ridley."

"I didn't see anything." Lark squinted her eyes as if she might be able to conjure the shadows up right then and there. If Lark had seen them, she would never want to do that.

As Ridley sat up and Leni helped him stand, her right hand clamped around her mouth as she realized something. And it couldn't be good. "I'm not a hundred percent on this, and I know you two are still connected, but I think there's more to this than we thought."

"What does that mean?" Lark asked, holding onto Auden.

"I don't know," Leni whispered. Maybe it didn't really mean anything. But maybe it did...

Ridley was quiet and not looking at Auden, instead darting glances between Lark and Leni. "What if it's the same for you and Lark?"

Leni shared a wary glance with Lark, neither speaking for

a long moment. The truth was apparent in their equally drawn expressions, the dark circles beneath their eyes, the pallor of their skin.

"Have you been feeling tired?" Leni whispered.

"I mean, yeah, but I didn't get any sleep last night. But over the past two weeks, no, I haven't," Lark said. Then she held up a hand. "Are you insinuating that it could be the same for me and Leni, by us being connected? Like would I die if she dies?"

Auden moved in front of Lark, his fists tightening at his sides. "I thought you said this whole curse shit was over and we'd be left alone."

He was right—it should've all been over, yet somehow it might've just become worse. "This is all my fault." Leni ran a hand down her face, not able to look anyone in the eye.

"This needs to be fixed." Auden tapped his index finger against the counter.

The sound pulsed in Leni's ears, but there was nothing she could do about it. More weight was on her shoulders now than before, with not only trying to save herself and help Ridley. There was only one way they could be unlinked from each other and that was through Quinna, but she still didn't know what the hell was going on with Auden and the shadows.

"Imani," Lark said, barreling around the counter and jolting for the phone hanging on the wall. "I'm going to call her."

What could her friend even do? Leni kept the thought to herself as Lark punched in the numbers.

"Have you seen any other shadows over the last few weeks?" Ridley questioned Auden. "Has Lark been feeling tired or running a fever at all?"

Auden dug his finger into his lower lip and shook his head, then stopped. "Something weird did happen last night, though. I had this weird dream with mirrors and darkness. It's hard to describe and unclear."

Ridley's shoulders stiffened, and Leni knew he must've had that same damn dream as Auden the previous night. The one that had woken her up.

"Maybe we shouldn't have come here again," he said, pressing his back against the counter. "It seems slipping back in this dimension triggered something."

"I think…" Leni started. "I think if we're able to put an end to the curse with the royals that we'll be separated for good."

"Are we sure about that?" Auden cocked his head, scowling. "Because Ridley over here said that last time, yet here we all are."

"I mean, it's just a theory." Leni bit the inside of her cheek. "And theories can be proven right or wrong."

Lark walked back around the counter to complete the circle they'd formed. "Imani wasn't home, but I can't just pick up and leave. I have to work and start back up at school soon."

"It wouldn't be that long," Leni said. "A week, tops." The party was in a few days, so she said a week to be on the safe side.

The cowbell rang as the front door opened, making Leni jump. She expected to see a customer walk inside, but instead came a man with warm brown skin, two dark braids hanging over his shoulders, and a balding spot on top his head. He wore sandals, jeans, and a solid white T-shirt while carrying two cardboard boxes stacked atop one another. Jimbo.

"Slow day today?" he asked, skirting around Lark and Auden. He set the boxes on the counter and reached to open a drawer.

"Jimbo!" Lark blurted, causing him to stop. "You arrived at the right time. Who do you see here?"

Pushing the glasses up the bridge of his nose, he straightened and surveyed the room. "You and Auden. Is this some sort of riddle? I'm confused."

"No, but you may be able to help us."

Lark relayed the story of everything that had happened since Leni and Ridley arrived, then about the things they'd told them about their dimension. Lark must've already let him know about the curse before, because he wasn't questioning any of that.

But what Leni didn't understand was if she was connected to Lark, then why couldn't anyone else see her? She supposed she would have to be connected to the other person, and she wasn't.

"Who can see this?" Leni picked up a duplicate of a skull beside her to test something out. Lark and Auden could see both, but Jimbo only saw the original still resting on the counter.

She picked up the original. "Where did it go?" Jimbo asked, adjusting his glasses, but it had vanished from his sight.

"Still there." Auden frowned.

Jimbo removed his glasses from his face and stared at the empty counter in awe. The whole situation was strange, and Leni couldn't help thinking she'd really screwed something up. And whatever it was, she wasn't sure if they could truly fix the situation or not, unless Quinna was right.

"So, can you cover for us for a week?" Lark asked, going back to one of the parts they'd explained to Jimbo.

"I don't mind you taking off from work, but I don't know about all this. Maybe you should let this other dimension worry about itself while we worry about ours." Jimbo said, lines crossing his forehead.

"What if Lark dies because of this?" Auden tugged at his lower lip.

"This is one of those life-defining moments. Something we have to do, even though we don't want to." Lark clasped Auden's hand.

Relief filled Leni, so much so that she wanted to wrap Lark in a hug. She didn't move though, only continued to listen.

Jimbo sighed. "At least let me try a short ritual before you cross over. I don't know how to disconnect you all from each other, but maybe this could protect you somehow…"

"We'll take it." Lark looked from Jimbo to Leni and Ridley. "We're going to go home, pack, and tell our parents we'll be going out of town for an auction for work."

Leni nodded and left Lark and Auden to discuss more with Jimbo about the situation. Exhaustion washed over her. She swigged down the rest of her water and took a seat at the barstool. Ridley sank down beside her as Lark and Auden went out the door.

Jimbo stayed behind and they watched as he flipped the sign over to close the store for a little while.

"I can't believe they said yes." Leni wasn't sure if she was talking to herself, Ridley, or both. But she knew she wouldn't have stopped trying to persuade them, even if they'd said no.

"I'm worried about them." Ridley twirled a pen in

between his fingers, staring at Jimbo lighting a circle of candles. "I'm not sure what he's doing or if it will work. Maybe if we were ghosts..."

There weren't any ghosts in Mira, and this could be due to the fact they didn't have a reflection, that there couldn't be spirits lingering around because of it. And that was the one good thing about not having a reflection—having someone unwanted hanging around in her bedroom would freak her out. But wasn't that what they sort of did when going in and out of rooms in the Earth Dimension? There was so much she never thought about or second-guessed until spending time here.

"I can't see you, but I know you're there." Jimbo released the flame on his lighter and looked in their direction, pointing right to where they were sitting.

Ridley stopped twirling his pen and wrote a message to Leni on the notepad. *He's good.*

If he starts hearing us, then I'll truly be impressed. She wrote back and smiled. *What song would you think about now?*

"*Another Brick In The Wall.*" *Except I would replace teachers with royals in it.*

Leni laughed. She needed that bit of lightness in that moment. But she couldn't help also brushing her fingers against her back, where the scars from the royals lay hidden.

Grabbing some sort of wooden stick, covered in blue and white feathers from the wall, Jimbo started chanting words in another language. He lifted his legs in some sort of dance, then burned a bundle of herbs. The scent hit Leni's nose, grassy and lemony.

It felt like forever before Lark and Auden returned. Jimbo unlocked the door when Lark pushed her key into the lock.

"What did your parents say?" Jimbo asked, re-locking the door after they walked in.

Lark and Auden both carried overstuffed backpacks. What could they even have in there?

"My parents were both fine with it." Auden adjusted his backpack.

"Beth said it was a great opportunity." Lark rolled her eyes. "But Imani still wasn't home, so can you let her know what's going on? I still feel bad about what happened to her during the curse."

Leni's chest clenched up and she stared at the floor, knowing what Lark's pre-filler had said to Imani. That was another thing she wished she could've taken back.

"Just keep these in your pocket. I blessed them." Jimbo handed Lark and Auden each a dark stone. Lark held out her palm to Leni, and she took the duplicate while Ridley did the same with Auden's.

"Thanks, Jimbo," Lark said. "For not once thinking I was crazy."

"I know what it feels like for people not to believe you." Jimbo blew out the flame on a candle, gray smoke drifting upward. "That's why I hear people out first."

Lark smiled, but it dropped as she turned to Leni and Ridley. "What now?"

Leni motioned them to follow her to the rectangular mirror near the front of the store, where she and Ridley had originally come in from.

"Grab my hand," she said to Lark, "and I'm going to pull you through. Ridley will do the same with Auden."

"This won't take us to the Realm of Mirrors first like the other mirror did?" Lark studied the glass and withdrew her knife from her pocket.

"Nope, directly to our dimension." She paused, her heart pounding so hard she swore everyone in the room could see it. "Are you ready?"

Lark and Auden both nodded. Clasping Auden's hand, Ridley tugged him forward and the glass rippled as they stepped through the glass. Leni couldn't see anything on the other side, only Lark's reflection and the absence of hers.

"Well, I'll be damned," Jimbo gasped.

"What did you see?" Lark glanced over her shoulder at him.

"Only Auden stepping through the mirror and disappearing." He sucked in a breath. "Be careful, Lark. I need my best employee to come back and work next week." Leni could hear his tone wasn't as light as he wanted the last sentence to sound.

"I'll be here." Something in Lark's expression told Leni she didn't really know if she would be. Lark's grip tightened on Leni's hand. "I'm ready."

Leni walked them both toward the mirror, the glass rippling around her, sending an electric current down her flesh as she moved past it. With everything in her, Leni promised herself that she wouldn't let anything happen to Lark or Auden while they were here, not after all they'd been through —because of her.

Bonus Track: Back to Mira

 CHAPTER 15

The electric buzzing along Ridley's skin ceased as soon as he finished pulling Auden through the glass. He was now back in the same room he'd originally left with Leni. Ridley watched the long rectangular mirror until Leni and Lark finally slipped through the glass and crashed to the floor. Auden plucked Lark up just as Ridley helped Leni to her feet. For a few moments, he'd been worried they wouldn't have been able to cross the dimension.

Lark and Auden looked around the room with their mouths hanging open. Ridley tried to see it through their eyes—the pools of liquid silver along the floor, the waves of thin smoke in the air, the long rectangular mirrors hanging one by one along the walls. How unreal did this seem to them in the grand scheme of things?

The door cracked open with a soft squeak and a head full of short red hair poked inside, then Quinna fully stepped in. Tufts of her hair stood in different directions, and she wore rainbow-striped pajamas and checkered socks.

"I thought I heard noises in here. Last night I stayed up late, and was still catching up on sleep." Quinna scanned Lark and Auden. "So, you two actually decided to come and try to save the dimensions."

"Um," Lark hesitated, holding her knife higher. "Who are you?"

"I'm Quinna, the one who has been helping Leni and Ridley." She lifted her chin. "In case you haven't been told, the curse is only a façade. A way to help the royals continue their stride with immortality."

"You're the one who tried to help with…" Lark held her arms up as if she was cradling a baby.

"We don't talk about that here!" Quinna snapped.

"Quinna," Leni piped in, grabbing Quinna's arm and tugging her forward. "We have a problem. I think Lark is connected to my pending death and Auden to Ridley's shadows."

Wrinkling her nose in confusion, Quinna shuffled toward a pool of liquid silver. "I suppose it's possible." She pressed her fingertip into the liquid glass and swiped the silver down the center of Ridley's forehead. He blinked as a cooling sensation tingled against his skin. Quinna then turned to Auden, and he dodged out of the way. "It's fine," she said. "It'll wipe right off."

Auden appeared skeptical, maybe a bit frightened, but remained still as she mirrored the motions she'd done with Ridley.

"It feels cold," Auden said, then looked toward Ridley. "His is changing to white."

"Mmm." Quinna pursed her lips and dipped her fingers into the liquid again before applying a thin streak to Leni's forehead, followed by Lark's.

"Not good," Quinna continued as she studied the glowing white streak on Lark's skin.

"What is it?" Ridley asked, swiping the streak away from

his forehead with his shirt sleeve. The coolness slowly dissipated until it was as though it had never been there.

Quinna stepped forward and yanked a strand of hair from Auden's head.

"What did you do that for?" He frowned as he tried to stop her from taking one of Lark's, but Quinna was too fast.

"Ow," Lark said, holding onto the side of her head.

"I'm not sure yet. I was hoping it would possibly unlink you a bit, but I don't think it will." She dropped the hair into another pool of liquid silver. "Leni was right to think that if she dies, then so will Lark. But if you reunite the royals when we perform the ceremony at the masquerade, then all should be well."

"You're talking like it's no big deal that Lark could die," Auden seethed. "What the fuck are we going to do to stop this?"

Quinna remained silent, her lack of words as much a warning as anything else. Auden's face filled with fear, even as Lark gulped, trying to stave off panic. Ridley could see it, though, attuned to their mannerisms after having watched them for the weeks in the Earth Dimension.

"What about Auden?" Ridley asked, trying to redirect the conversation. "What happens to him and the shadows since I'm not dying?"

"He'll continue to see and hear them for as long as you're the Piper." Quinna paused, empathy crossing her face. "And since he's not from here, he'll slowly go mad."

"Like my father…" Auden murmured.

"No," Lark said, placing her hand against Auden's cheek and turning him to look at her. "We're not going to think about that right now. We're going to stay focused on what needs to be done, like we did before."

Auden's eyes caught hers, and he slowly nodded. If Ridley had told him this, Auden probably would've told him to screw off. But this was bad. Ridley knew Auden's number one fear was to inherit the same illness his dad had, and his worst nightmare could become true.

"You all can't stay here," Quinna said. "It would look too suspicious. During the masquerade party is when we'll spill the blood and combine yours together. For now, though, our next step is to retrieve an item from the Realm of Mirrors. In the meantime, you have to find somewhere safe to lie low."

"Hold up!" Auden held up a hand as his throat bobbed. Lark stood next to him, her jaw hanging open in horror. "What do you mean just spill some blood? And whose?"

"Yeah," Lark agreed, her features turning angry. "Like a sacrifice? I'm not playing some weird-ass game and having us die over here."

"Stay calm," Quinna murmured, like she was trying to tame a wild animal. "It will only be a little slice on your palms. Not your throats. Without a little sacrifice, we can't fix the royals. And as you four are instrumental to this whole thing, the blood has to come from *you*."

"What will it do to us?" Lark frowned, suspicious and wary.

"By you joining hands with Leni, and Auden with Ridley, it will start unlinking the connection between you two—your human blood, their mirror blood. It will also link the royals back together. That's what you want, isn't it?"

Lark shared a look with Ridley. He nodded. None of this seemed any stranger than the other things he'd done. A quick glance to Leni showed her deadpan expression, and that reassured him further. He would do anything. Anything to break this. To save her.

"It'll be okay," Ridley whispered to Lark and Auden. He wasn't sure if it would be, but he had hope.

After another beat, Lark blew out a breath. Auden grasped her hand in his and squeezed before asking, "Us doing this at the masquerade will help? You're for *sure*?"

"Yes," Quinna said simply. "It will be the beginning phase."

Ridley sighed in relief when Lark and Auden didn't have further objections. His thoughts moved to something else Quinna had said about the next step in the process, which involved removing an object out of the Realm of Mirrors. The mirrors inside there were firmly attached to the walls until a soul died, as were the plaques with names that couldn't be ripped off. "Nothing in the Realm of Mirrors can be taken."

"Are you sure about that?" Quinna tilted her head to the side.

"I've been in there, too, and he's right," Leni replied, rapidly wiggling her fingers while she thought. "Except for…" Her spine straightened. "The box!"

Ridley shook his head. "It's not from there. I put it there."

"But weren't all things placed in there?" Leni said. "The mirrors were all created outside of there, and so were the plaques."

"Leni's right." Quinna smiled. "Whatever you put in there is a gift to the Realm of Mirrors, therefore you would be taking the box back from it."

Ridley's shoulders relaxed. At least that step wouldn't be

difficult. He'd easily slip into the glass, retrieve Leni's box, and bring it back to his old place. "I can do that today."

"That will be part of the second phase," Quinna said. "After linking hands, the box will be used against the mirror. "Once you receive that, we'll have to figure out a way to retrieve the flute next, which will be used in the final phase. The instrument will then need to be demolished."

"How are we supposed to get the flute?" Leni exclaimed. "That's going to be guarded at all times until the masquerade."

"Would've been nice if you'd mentioned this before," Ridley grumbled. Leni was right. There was no safe way they could get to the instrument.

"I didn't want to worry you about the flute until you had the Earthlings here." Quinna shrugged, meeting both their gazes. "Telling you ahead of time would've added too much pressure and too many things for you to focus on. Now that we're all here, we can figure out a plan to secure the flute soon."

Quinna seemed to think this was all easy, but that was probably because she was doing none of the work. Leni traded a glance with him, and he could read on her face that she was thinking the same thing. Even now, they could still read what the other was thinking.

"All right." Quinna hurried to the door and drew it open, waving them into the next room with the chaise and two chairs. "We've spent enough time here, so we'll meet again tomorrow night."

"Thank you," Leni said, clasping Quinna's hand. "For risking this for us."

"I'm selfish," Quinna said. "It's not just for you but for

me, too, because I'm tired of seeing our world operated this way." Ridley noticed the glistening in her eyes and wondered if her thoughts lingered on the baby she'd mentioned before.

Leni shook her head. "That's not selfish. Take a compliment."

"That would require me to be selfish." Quinna laughed and opened the front door to let them outside.

Once Ridley walked down the few steps, the warmth from the sun washed over him. There was still plenty of daylight. Lark and Auden stood silent as they checked out the scenery around them.

Ridley clasped the handlebars to his bike and checked over his shoulder at Leni. "Are you feeling okay to walk, since there's only one bike?"

"I'm still okay." She turned to Lark, flicking her gaze over her. "And you?"

"I feel peachy keen," Lark said with sarcasm. "It's like an old episode of *The Brady Bunch*. But in case you don't get that, it means I'm okay."

"I know what *The Brady Bunch* is," Leni said defensively.

Ridley and Auden both gave each other a look as he pushed the bike down the cobblestone road. Lark and Leni continued to bicker back and forth about pop culture.

"Won't we get noticed here somehow?" Auden questioned, his hands deep in his pockets.

"If you saw me on the streets in your dimension, would you look twice?" Ridley asked. The only difference was in their blood.

"Depends on if you were wearing your all-black getup or this." Auden ran his finger across his lower lip. It seemed to be his nervous habit. "But I suppose I didn't question you before because I never believed in anything beyond what I thought was real. So, no, if I saw you, I wouldn't wonder if you were from anywhere else."

"Unless your blood spills somewhere before the masquerade, it's safe to say you'll go unnoticed by anyone here."

However, Ridley didn't want them near the citadel because the royals *would* notice. He'd have to find them masks to conceal their identities at the party. Otherwise, he didn't know what the royals would do if they were discovered. But one thing he did know was that they wouldn't let them leave Mira alive.

"Mmm, so I'll stay away from sharp knives." Auden rolled his eyes and angled his gaze upward. "The sky and trees are the same here. Not much different."

Ridley hadn't really seen his own world until he was sixteen and newly released from that closet. When Millie uncovered him and brought him to Leni, he was basically introduced to Mira and the Earth Dimension at the same time. He'd never once questioned their similarities because that was just how things were. But if he'd never seen the Earth Dimension and was going there for the first time, he might've been on the same wavelength as Auden.

"What did you expect?"

"I don't know. Mirrors outside *everywhere,* like inside that chick's house back there." Auden hiked a thumb over his shoulder.

"Some of the places are like Quinna's, but most aren't." Ridley thought about the citadel with its mirrors covering all the walls, or the shop where he and Leni had worked together.

"Fair enough." Auden's fingers twitched as he unzipped

his backpack, pulled out his headphones, and placed them over his head. From the speakers, Ridley could hear and *feel* the heavy thumping beats to "Psycho Killer." Auden used the music to calm his nerves, the way Ridley did with writing his words.

Leni and Lark were still discussing music when the old house with its dark roof and lime-green paneling, next to the mirror shop, slid into view.

"Will you be all right here with them for a little bit?" Ridley asked Leni while Auden and Lark stood talking on the porch.

"Yeah, I'll fill them in on more history." Leni scratched the side of her head, seeming hesitant. "Maybe get them to not hate me as much."

"You're easy to like, Butterfly. When you tell the truth." Ridley tapped the end of her nose twice like he used to. The habit still came naturally.

"That's why I have oh-so-many friends." She chuckled softly, but he could see the sadness and tiredness lingering in her eyes.

"You have me." He blinked twice, his way of showing her that she could believe him.

"I'm glad. Now just be careful and hurry back."

Ridley blinked again and straddled the bike, before pedaling away. He couldn't help glancing back over his shoulder to watch Leni take Lark and Auden into the house where they would be safe … for now.

All was normal as he pedaled toward the citadel. People passed him on their bikes, everyone always looking as though they were in their own world and couldn't spare a moment to wave hello. But that was because everyone's thoughts were usually filled with their daily tasks to be taken care of. Since he'd returned after the curse, this had been the first time Ridley wasn't working at the citadel or at the mirror shop.

Turning down the curved road, Ridley headed down the path filled with planted glass flowers beside it and stopped in front of his house. He popped down his kickstand, inhaling the fruit from the trees while he scurried to unlock the door with a soft click.

As he stepped inside and rounded the corner, his body turned completely rigid. Ridley's chest heaved, his breathing too loud.

The mirror was *gone*.

How was this possible? It had been right here when he'd left. No one could lift it easily but him… Yet it could still be moved. His lungs couldn't pump air as he opened the door and smacked into another body.

Elliot.

"I was coming out of the citadel when I saw you striding up to your house." Elliot held his thumb up and then down.

Hand shaking, Ridley gave him a thumbs up. "But it's gone," he whispered.

"What's gone?" Elliot grasped Ridley's shoulders, holding him steady. "What is?"

"The mirror."

Elliot released Ridley's shoulders, appearing relieved. "Well, good riddance. My guess is you've transitioned away from being the Mirror Keeper. I thought it had something to do with Leni. Next time just say what the problem is right away."

"No, you don't understand," he stuttered. "When we got

back to Quinna's, I was supposed to collect an item out of the mirror to use at the masquerade."

Pursing his lips, Elliot glanced toward the citadel and shook his head. "There are too many guards. We're going to have to wait for the right time."

Ridley was an idiot. He'd held the box in his hands just days before. If only he'd taken the box out and returned it to Leni like he should've done, then this could've all been avoided.

Now, he didn't know if he would ever be able to get it back.

 CHAPTER 16

Lark and Auden stood awkwardly in the middle of the living room, looking from the television to the floral couch to the glass objects hanging on the walls that Leni and Ridley had created back in the mirror shop.

Leni had much preferred the bantering back and forth with Lark on the way here, instead of this uncomfortable silence spreading throughout the whole room, stretching to its breaking point.

"So, are you guys hungry?" Leni asked to rip away the tension, nodding in the direction of the counter and rectangular opening.

"Sure," Lark said, shooting Auden an uneasy glance. "What do you have, *exactly?*"

Auden scratched the back of his neck. "You guys have the same food we do?"

They both were acting like she was going to bring them a bloody sacrifice from the pantry. "We eat tongues of the dead and raw animal feet," she said in a serious tone, fighting a smile.

Auden's Adam's apple shifted, and Lark clenched her jaw.

"Yes, we have the same food!" Leni rolled her eyes.

"Well played. Seems like something I would've done to my twin." Lark walked to the counter and peered through the opening as Leni turned the corner and entered the small kitchen.

Opening the cabinet, Leni pored over the items. Cereal boxes. Chips. Breakfast bars. She snatched a bag of Cheetos for herself.

"I'll take the Cheetos and Auden said he'll eat some of the Cheerios." Lark leaned over the counter.

Leni was selfish when it came to food and she wanted the Cheetos for herself, but she wasn't going to hoard them since Lark was risking her life by coming here. But still. *It's just a bag of Cheetos, Leni!*

"Here." Leni placed the chips in front of Lark and grimly plucked up the bag of Fritos for herself. She wished she'd stashed more varieties here, but she hadn't been there in a while because of the curse. Sometimes at night when she couldn't sleep at her house outside the citadel, she'd ride her bike home and stay here, wishing she could've somehow reversed time.

"I'm going to set up Millie's old room for you," Leni said. "You guys can hang out here for now or go into my room. Wherever." Pivoting on her heels, she hurried to Millie's space because she didn't know how to talk to people, apparently.

Leni closed the door behind her and pressed her back against it, chest inflating then deflating. She tried not to wonder about Lark and Auden thinking about how she'd tried to take over their bodies for her and Ridley … and Rebel. During the curse, when she and Ridley weren't preying after

Lark and Auden, it was as if she was in a dream state when she would blink out from the Earth Dimension and back to hers. She would sleep until the shadows had her perform her next task.

The scent of grapefruit and lilies hit her nose—Millie's calming smell—and a strong, unbearable emotion overtook her. Overwhelmed? Was that what she was? The bedcovers still lay sprawled in a heap because Millie was a blanket murderer in her sleep with her movements. Since Millie left, Leni had never changed out the sheets. She took a seat on the edge of the bed, picked up the corner of the striped blanket, pressed it to her nostrils, and breathed in deeply.

Leni missed Millie so much. She didn't let herself really think about her caretaker being gone until this moment. When she came to the house, after Millie had left, she'd never come in this room. The door would remain shut, and she would pretend Millie was in there sleeping, instead of long gone with Rebel.

"Please be safe," she murmured.

Wiping the wetness from her cheeks that had fallen from her eyes, Leni took off the old bedsheets and grabbed a new set from the closet. She cleaned the dust from the side tables and the headboard before applying the new sheets.

When she was finished, she realized she had to face the two people she was trying to avoid. She wished Ridley would hurry up and get back, because they didn't hate him as much as they did her.

Taking an anxious swallow, Leni opened the door and found the light on inside her room, spilling out into the hallway.

As she crept to the doorframe, she watched Lark and Auden flipping through all the records she and Ridley still had here. Most of her cassettes were all destroyed by the royals, but not her records.

"It's weird how we can pick up everything here, but I guess they don't have the duplicate thing like in our dimension." Lark must've heard Leni's movements because she glanced over her shoulder. "These are all yours?"

"Yes. And Ridley's." She stepped into the room. "You're right—we don't have duplicates the way you guys do."

Everything in here was the same as it had been before they'd left—the pictures on the walls, the record player on the bedside table between the mattresses. That was why she liked coming here so much, even though she hadn't really been gone that long—the nostalgia.

Auden observed the walls, the bright artwork, the band posters. "You have a lot of Bowie."

Leni stared up at a large poster of David Bowie dressed in a long-sleeve striped one-piece and red, knee-high platform boots. "I mean, how can I not? He's the best. I even named… Never mind."

Lark shot her a surprised look. "You named her after one of the songs? That's where the name Rebel came from?"

"Yes," she answered, not breaking eye contact. That day Leni hadn't given the baby a middle name because she'd silently hoped that one day Ridley would be able to choose it.

"I'm surprised it wasn't 'Space Oddity,'" Auden said, taking a seat next to Lark. He didn't sound angry—it was more of an observation and attempt to connect the dots of what he and Lark had gone through.

Leni wondered if she should try to explain a few more things, even if it didn't help. Maybe they would understand *her* better. "When you become the Piper, you either choose the song or the shadows draw it out from you. It's hard to explain, but 'Space Oddity' was our song—mine and Ridley's. I was so passionate about that specific melody—it's why it was the song on the flute."

"I mean, it's a good song," Lark said, digging into the bag of Cheetos, while picking up another record. "Not that I can listen to it anytime soon, but maybe one day."

"What I do want to know," Auden said, "is we killed those doppels—"

"No." Leni shook her head, knowing he was still filled with guilt. "They weren't ever real, even though you think they were. Yes, they moved and breathed, but we weren't in them yet. Neither was Rebel. You did what you had to do." She would have done the same if she were them.

A strange feeling washed over Leni as she sat there. Never had there been many people in her room. Only Ridley, Elliot, Millie, Romy, and Romy's girlfriend. As she thought about it, Lark was the first girl she'd brought here. She'd never even had a girl who was a friend—not that she and Lark were friends. But she found herself liking them there.

"Before Ridley came here," Leni continued, needing to clear something else up, "I had a brother… Remember how I mentioned you could be killed for not turning in an infant? My brother and his girlfriend attempted to run with their baby, and it didn't end well. For any of them." She couldn't help but remember Romy's crooked smile, his long black hair, and his humor. Despite all the time since his death, the sorrow of losing her brother never truly went away. And she didn't think it ever would.

"They killed all three of them?" Lark's hands had stilled mid-movement, a vinyl frozen in her grip.

With a heavy sigh, Leni slowly nodded. "And I don't want you to think Ridley and I were stupid—we did use protection. It's also supposed to be harder for us anyway since we're created, not born."

"If I lived here, I think I'd be celibate," Lark mumbled and Auden quirked a brow at her. "I'm so sorry about your brother."

"Me, too." Leni studied her hands, gathering courage to ask her next question. "If you were in our place, my place, what would you have done? Can you understand the tiniest fraction of why I did what I did?"

Surprisingly, it wasn't Lark who answered, but Auden, his tone heavy with emotion. "Yeah, I get it. I don't like it, but I get it."

Leni didn't completely relax, but she felt a bit lighter, a little freer.

"The mirror shop we saw next door… Is that the same one you and Ridley worked at?" Lark asked, changing the subject.

"Yeah, do you want to see it or something? I can show it to you."

"Sure. If we're in this other dimension for a few days, might as well check things out."

Leni waved them to follow her back into the living room. On the way out, she grabbed the key from the rack on the wall and led them across the grass to the pebbled walkway, which curved to the entrance. Unlocking the yellow door, she opened it and flipped on the light. Bright white spread throughout the room.

Everything looked the same. On the nights when she'd stay at the house, she would secretly slip in here and work on her glassblowing, a way for her not to think, to temporarily forget the world for a few moments.

"This is it," Leni finally said. Memories of her and Ridley started to filter through, and she hurried to brush them back.

To fill up the silence of the place, she headed to the record player and turned on the vinyl that was still resting there. Freddie Mercury's calming voice singing "Radio Gaga" took over the quiet and replaced the air with something they could all relate to.

Lark and Auden strolled toward the unlit boiler in the middle of the room.

"This is rad," Lark said, pressing her finger to the hardened mirror glass. "Like a witch's cauldron or some shit."

Auden leaned over and looked at the silver. "We need to get it lighted." He knelt and glanced beneath the pot.

Leni smiled and froze when her gaze connected to one of the mirrors on the other side of the room. She should've seen and thought about this as soon as they'd slipped through the glass into Mira at Quinna's. But she guessed she'd been used to it. On every single surrounding mirror, not only could rooms in the Earth Dimension be viewed, but Auden and Lark's reflections appeared at the same time. It was odd and noticeable. Leni's hand automatically covered her mouth.

"What is it?" Lark's brows drew together as she took a step toward her.

Uncovering her mouth, Leni walked to an oval mirror

directly across from the boiler and pointed at it. "Your reflections are there."

"Yeah, so?" Lark wasn't getting it. "What I'm more concerned about is, are these places in our dimension? I broke the mirror from my room, so I'm assuming mine is no longer accessible."

Leni ignored Lark's last comment. "You're not understanding. Do you notice how I don't have an image?"

"How could we not?" Auden said, inspecting the mirror closely, and running a finger across the glass.

"You two have to come with me to the masquerade party," Leni said. "At the citadel… That means there will be mirrors *everywhere*. Even with a mask on, your reflections will still show up. It won't be hard to notice that no one has a reflection in the whole party except for the two of you! Some of the mirror objects they have there will make it easier for them to spot you because they aren't linked to other rooms, so you'll be the only thing reflecting on them!" She wanted to hyperventilate right then and there.

"Even with wearing clothes from here, it wouldn't cloak us?" Lark tapped her fingers against her chin.

If that were possible, it would make things so much easier. "No. Even when I take clothing from your dimension, you still can't see them once they're here." If only that could've worked for Lark and Auden, too. Leni thought that her main concern would be needing to retrieve the flute at the citadel, not worrying about their reflections being seen at the masquerade.

Leni's heart accelerated, kicking and kicking with a heavy fight against her ribcage. Tiredness hit her, causing her body to grow weak again. She needed to take more medicine.

"I don't feel so good," Lark rasped, swaying as her eyelids flickered.

Auden grabbed Lark by her shoulders before she could topple and fall.

It was as if the link in their connection was becoming stronger. *This isn't good. Not good at all*, Leni thought as she crashed to the floor.

CHAPTER 17

The sky was already darkening as Ridley and Elliot pulled their bikes to a stop in front of Ridley's old house. Next door, inside the mirror shop, orange light filtered through the glass, so Ridley crossed the grass to the curved entrance. Ridley had told Elliot all about what had happened in the Earth Dimension, then how Quinna had informed them they needed an object from the mirror as well as the flute.

"I was thinking," Elliot started, latching onto Ridley's upper arm, "that I can probably somehow swipe the flute at the masquerade. If I can persuade one of the guards, that is."

Ridley pinched the spot between his eyes. "I'm sure the guards are immune to flirtation. Besides, I'm not sure risking yourself is a good idea."

"I already have, so what's a little more?"

There were now six people involved in this whole thing when one was bad enough. If they were all caught, none of their lives would end well. Ridley's own didn't matter because he would sacrifice his for Leni's in a heartbeat.

Ridley tried turning the knob to the shop, but it was locked. He tapped his fingers lightly against the wood. "It's me."

No one answered. He was about to knock again but then

Leni pulled open the door. Her dark hair was damp and matted against her forehead and neck, the spark in her green eyes dulled.

"What's wrong?" Ridley asked, hurrying inside, finding Lark sitting in a chair at the table with her head against her arms. Auden was beside her, his features strained with worry.

"Lark and I are both experiencing fatigue. I also might have fallen," Leni mumbled. "The new usual. But we're both starting to feel better after taking the meds, so we'll see."

"*Better*?" Elliot exclaimed and moved toward where Lark was seated. "If that's the case, I don't want to know what you two looked like before."

Ridley helped Leni to the table as Elliot introduced himself to Lark. "Aren't you adorable?"

Auden scowled, his jaw clenched. "She's my girlfriend."

"And aren't you just as adorable!" Elliot's attention focused on Auden before glancing at Leni and Ridley. "You really should find a way to bring more Earthlings here."

While Elliot started to ramble on to Lark and Auden, Ridley took a seat beside Leni on the table. He nudged her arm with his to lighten the somber mood she seemed to be in. "What is it, Butterfly?"

"You see the mirrors?" She pointed at the nearest one, bolted to the wall in a diamond position. "What do you notice there?"

For a moment, he thought maybe she was delirious as he inspected the glass. A living room with an elderly man sitting on a couch watching TV and… His gaze shifted to Lark and Auden.

"Their reflections. You're thinking about the masquerade, aren't you?" Ridley also noticed that Elliot's body was blocking some of Auden's reflection in the mirror. Yes, the citadel was covered in mirrors, but there would be a crowd of people there, if not most of the city. Lark and Auden could blend in, but they would just have to try and stay in the middle of everything, as far away from the objects as possible. "It'll be fine. Somehow, we don't have a reflection, but our bodies can still be a barrier to them."

"They'll have more guards out..." And that wouldn't make what they had to do now any easier. She peered down at his empty hands. "Where's the box?"

His fingers twitched to take out his pen and paper to write it all down, but he gathered the words, painful as they were to say. "I have some bad news, Leni." Wrapping an arm around her, he let her head rest against him.

She gave a heavy sigh and mumbled into his shirt, "Oh boy, I don't like the sound of this. But I can already assume you didn't get the box."

"The mirror wasn't at the house anymore. It's inside the citadel walls." He didn't know if the guards had to come and get it or if the mirror had just appeared back in its old place, where it would now stay until a new Mirror Keeper was chosen.

"What?" Leni lifted her head and met his eyes. "This means you're not the Mirror Keeper at all anymore. You'll be required to choose a new one if..."

If they failed and he became the Piper. "I don't know what to do, because now there will be more guards monitoring the mirror during the masquerade." It was like he was developing planner's block instead of writer's block as he tried to think of the next step.

"Easy," Leni said, perking up. "Tomorrow morning, you

can go to the guards and say you forgot to take your box out of the mirror. I'm sure they'll either let you go in and get it, or they'll retrieve it for you."

That could very well work. "Butterfly, you're a genius. What would I do without you?"

Her cheeks pinkened. But before she could say anything, Elliot slid beside them. "I'm going to head out and go work on frames. To not look suspicious, and all that."

"Tomorrow night, we'll all be meeting at Quinna's," Leni said.

Elliot nodded and waved to everyone as he left.

"So, no luck," Lark said, her face no longer pale.

"Not today." Ridley shrugged. "But tomorrow."

Auden was fiddling around with one of the metal rods Ridley and Leni used for glassblowing. It reminded him there was something he wanted to do before going to the house. To break up the tension, Ridley turned on the boiler and grabbed one of the metal rods in the corner.

Leni picked up a rod and stepped beside him. "What are you doing?"

"Just going to focus on something until the morning."

As he started to curl the glass in the boiler around his rod, Leni showed Lark and Auden how to do the same while explaining to them the way they used to make the mirrors.

"We have to tell Jimbo to add glassblowing to the store," Lark said, gazing up at the dangling glass objects from the ceiling. "People would go crazy if they could come in and suggest something to be made."

Ridley focused on molding the wings, the tiny hairs, and the antennae. He stayed silent and in his own head, the words remained sparse. Leni had already taken Lark and Auden back to the house when he finally finished.

He left the shop and walked into the night—the sky was brimming with too many stars to count. If when he was created, his glass was really mixed with the stars, Ridley wondered which ones were a part of him and which ones belonged to Leni. Did they all just pluck pieces from the stars when they came to be? And, eventually, would the star be no more when all its parts were taken?

The thought was both beautiful and disturbing—that something could sacrifice itself so wholly for another.

Ridley entered the house, finding the living room bathed in darkness, but light poured out from his open bedroom. It had been such a long while since he'd stepped foot inside the house. A rush of emotions washed over him as he took in the familiar scent.

Holding the glass object at his side, he headed toward the lit bedroom. Leni lay curled on her side, headphones over her ears, and her eyes shut. He recognized the delicate sounds of "If You Leave" drifting out from her speakers.

A buzzing came near his left ear and he closed his eyes. *Not now.* The low noise went up another octave, then another and another, until it seeped in and out of every single one of his pores. The shadow must've felt the need to come out and play as Ridley folded forward, the black smoke spilling out from his mouth. It was as if thousands of legs were crawling over his exposed skin and clothing. He tightened his eyes, trying to push the darkness away.

"Choose a song," it cooed, almost seductively. A vision curled forward that, even with his eyes closed, he couldn't unsee. A song that hadn't fully played its ravenous melody.

Ridley wanted to choose the song, wanted to play it, wanted to listen to what the shadows needed him to do. His back arched as he was pulled into the direction of the notes, toward *them*. And he found himself liking it, struggling a little less.

"Hey!" a voice shouted, shaking his shoulders. "Come on!"

The shadows faded to gray and burst into ash, then a light charcoal snow fell around him. He felt each of the tiny flakes that hit his skin and faded.

"Ridley?" Leni pressed her hands to his cheeks, her eyes wide. "Are they gone now?"

"I'm so sorry," he said when he finally found air, tears sliding down his cheeks.

"Why are you saying sorry?" she whispered, wiping the wetness away. "There's nothing to be sorry for."

"Because I didn't know what you were truly dealing with before. And for all these years, you had to see these shadows." He'd only been facing them for a short time, while she'd been so young when they started. He wondered if Auden had felt it, or was he too deep in sleep? Ridley hoped it was the latter.

"It's fine." She sat beside him on the carpet. "They'd been there since I was created, so sometimes it was like an extra arm."

"*Fine*? That's not fine." Ridley could tell by the look in Leni's eyes that she was recalling things, and she was most definitely not fine. Even with them gone, she would always remember them.

"What's this?" she asked, picking up the glass object that must've fallen from his hand. "Was this what you were working on?"

"Yeah, it's an orchid bee. One of the most beautiful insects in the Earth Dimension. I made it for you … to replace the other one." He could still hear the way the glass grasshopper sounded when it had melted back into liquid glass.

"This one is even more special." Leni grinned, rotating the bee in her hand, and brushing her fingers along the silvery wings. "Come on." Clasping his hand, she pulled him in the direction of her bed.

Ridley removed his shoes and waist pouch before taking a seat on her mattress. Leaning back on a soft pillow, he opened his arm for her. She settled into the crook of one arm and lifted the blanket over them.

He tried and tried but couldn't sleep, not because the light was still on, but because he just couldn't. And despite wanting to ignore it, he was very aware Leni wasn't asleep either.

Gently pulling his arm out from under her, he hopped off the bed and collected a spiral notebook and pen from his mattress. Leni looked at him oddly, but he couldn't contain himself.

He wrote words as he kept glancing at her until, finally, there was a sentence that made sense. Cheeks growing hot, he flipped it over. *Can I kiss you?*

The edges of Leni's lips tilted up. "Are you reminding me of how I first asked you?"

Ridley didn't know how much time they truly had left, and he hated to admit to himself that he was terrified of her dying. Even if she'd really broken his heart, it wouldn't have changed how he felt.

Without answering her, he dropped the notebook on the floor and came back toward her. He leaned forward, clasped her cheeks in between his hands, and pressed his mouth fiercely against hers, igniting the flame.

He needed to kiss her, really kiss her. The word he drew up in that moment was desperation. And that was what he put into the motion as his lips moved against hers, caressing, pouring out what he could into that kiss. Wrapping her legs around his waist, Leni drew him forward so he was settled in between her legs as close as he could get.

The way she was kissing him in return was as if she was spelling out the words—missed, sorry, afraid, and faith. Rolling with her to his back, Ridley ran his hands beneath her shirt, up the warm skin of her spine, careful of the healed wounds.

"Does it still hurt?" he asked, lifting his fingertips.

"No. Don't stop touching me."

She lifted her shirt and slipped it over her head. His came next, and her pants followed, until all the clothing had come off, quicker than it ever had.

Leni's lower body shifted back and forth against his as her lips traveled to his neck, tickling, teasing, then right to that spot below his ear, driving him mad with want. Her head lifted and her gaze caught his, worried. "Not yet," she whispered, and he knew she wasn't completely ready after everything to go all the way.

Neither was he. "Not tonight," he agreed.

But that didn't mean they couldn't explore every inch of each other's bodies in different ways. Her lips kissed down his chest, lower and lower until they were right where he needed them to be. He groaned from her movements, his hands fisting the sheets. After he felt as though music had exploded around him, he flipped Leni to her back and returned the favor, until they were both spent.

Leni softly pressed her lips to his one more time, cooling the flames, before curling into the crook of his arm.

Even with no music playing, it seemed to still be around them, in their kisses, their touches, their caresses, their love for each other. Among other things, music had bonded them, and that string would never fray.

The light seeping in through the window woke Ridley. Leni was still lying fast asleep in his arms, snoring softly. He slowly peeled himself away to put on some of his old clothes from the dresser. Smiling to himself, he threw on a pair of jeans and a *Gremlins* T-shirt.

Ridley knelt beside the bed and pressed his chin to the mattress as he ran a finger against the pinkened scars of her back.

Her eyes opened, taking a moment to focus. "You're leaving already?" Her voice came out groggy.

"I'll be back as soon as I can."

She traveled a hand through his hair and smiled. "Keep your words to a minimum and try not to stab the royals."

"The second one is going to be hard." He placed a delicate kiss to her forehead. "Don't forget to take your meds."

Leni closed her eyes as Ridley left their space and headed to the bathroom. When he came out into the living area, he found Lark alone. She was sitting on the couch and eating out of a cereal box.

"I'm heading to the citadel now," Ridley said. "But you can listen to records, watch TV, or whatever."

Lark placed the box down on the coffee table and stood from the couch. Her gaze softened a fraction as it fixed on him. "I understand now why you chose me."

"I had already told you why." And he remembered the reason not going over well with her or Auden.

"I know, but I actually got to *see* your collection and your rad taste in music. I mean, it's still messed up, though." She paused and bit her lip. "But if you'd gone to our high school, I think we would've been friends."

"And Leni?"

"Yeah. And Auden." She chuckled. "Auden might've taken longer to join us, though. Just be careful, all right?"

Ridley pulled out his pad and pen from his pouch and wrote the words, *Thank you.*

After parking his bike at his house behind the citadel, Ridley crossed the bridge toward the two guards, blocking the entrance he needed. He gave the secret code and straightened so it appeared like he wasn't bothered by anything. "I need to see the mirror. There was an object I left inside it before it was returned here."

"You'll have to discuss that with the royals," the one on the left said and swung the door open for Ridley to enter.

The sitting room was empty except for the next two guards in their yellow jumpsuits and helmets. He followed the vibrant rug toward them as he scanned each of the mirrors. One showed a family at a kitchen table eating breakfast.

Another reflected a girl applying green eyeshadow. He avoided studying the rest of them after Lark had freaked out about people from Mira watching others.

Ridley came to a stop at the end of the rug and gave the secret hand signal. "The guards at the front let me in to see the royals about retrieving my item from the mirror."

Neither guard said a word as they both opened the doors. It was as if they'd been expecting him.

All four royals glanced up from their glass thrones as he entered. Brand was studying a newspaper, while Anson and Calliope sipped on mugs of something.

Portia adjusted her orange blazer sleeve and set down her magazine. "You've chosen to grace us with your presence."

"You took the mirror back," Ridley said. "I left one of my items—a jeweled box—in there, and I'd like to get it back if that's all right."

"I'm assuming you already know why the mirror is no longer in your possession?" Portia swept a lock of auburn hair behind her ear.

"Yes." He knew if he lied, they would know since they most likely guessed Leni had already discussed her last visit here with him.

"Ah, well, we'll just pretend like it's a secret until the masquerade." Brand smirked. "As for your item, you should've already taken it out."

"It will only take a moment for me to grab my box." Did his last word sound desperate? He felt like it might've, unless that was all in his head.

"So you want to go to the box?" Portia's tone rang of boredom.

"That's right."

"Guards!" Brand shouted while grinning wickedly. "Take him to the mirror."

As soon as the words fell from Brand's lips, he knew something was wrong. Ridley shouldn't have done this today—he should've waited for the masquerade. He spun for the door, but two hands slammed down on his wrists.

"I don't know where you've been wandering off to," Portia purred. "But we would rather you remain here until the masquerade. Besides, we think it's better you stay away from Leni since you already know what's going to happen to her anyway."

The guards removed Ridley's waist pouch and dragged him backward, while he twisted and shouted, trying to break free from their hold. Their grip didn't slacken as they took him out of the room and down a long hall, turning down several corridors to a spiral staircase leading to one of the towers. They took him up it until he was outside a familiar door.

A guard who was overseeing the area opened the metal entrance, and the hands holding Ridley threw him into the tiny room. His eyes met the cursed mirror resting in the center.

Behind him, the door slammed shut and locked, leaving him trapped in the too-small space with only the mirror for company.

CHAPTER 18

Music From "Forever Young" – Alphaville

Leni tapped her fingers anxiously on the couch while Lark and Auden sat on the floor, zoned in to *Children of the Corn*. Every time Leni watched, it made her want to stay away from cornfields for the rest of her life. She wasn't into horror movies like Lark and Auden seemed to be, and even then, she couldn't focus because Ridley still hadn't returned.

For what had to be the hundredth time, Leni shifted her gaze to look at the cuckoo clock on the wall. As soon as her eyes met the hour hand, the bird popped out, startling her. *Damn bird.*

Since Ridley had left, hours had now passed. The trip shouldn't have taken this long for him to go into the citadel and retrieve the box—something didn't sit well with her about the situation.

She couldn't help letting her thoughts drift to the previous night with Ridley. Him with her. Her with him. Them together. Warm skin against warm skin. Lips against lips, and those lips in other places. Leni had wanted to be with him in the way they had been before, but she'd been too scared after being surprised with a baby. Yet after the masquerade, would there even be a tomorrow for her?

"Did you see that?" Lark laughed and shoved Leni's leg.

"I must've missed it." Leni tried to focus back on the TV but had been zoned out for most of the movie because of her mind going in different directions.

Auden turned around and frowned. "What is it? You're acting different than you have been."

How did she normally act? They had barely been around her. Leni supposed less fidgety, for sure. Blowing out a breath, Leni glanced at the clock again. "It's just ... we have to meet Quinna in a little while and Ridley should've already been back." She rubbed her clammy hands against her jeans. "I think I'm going to head to the citadel and see if he's still there." But she didn't want to leave them here alone...

As if Lark could read the concern on her face, she said, "We'll be fine. We have Malachi and Isaac to hold our attention. Then Ash can entertain us from *The Evil Dead* next. Or maybe *Sleepaway Camp*—which, if you haven't seen it, the film has one of the best endings in cinematic history."

Leni hadn't seen that movie, and she shuddered to herself about those creepy corn kids.

"Besides," Lark continued, "if someone from this 'citadel' busted in here, would you really be able to stop them from doing anything?" She didn't seem unnerved about that possibility.

However, Leni was. Lark was a strange bird, but one who Leni wouldn't mind looking up to right then, because Lark was right.

If guards did come into the house from the citadel with their weapons, what could she do? She was just a girl. Even when she had the flute, the only person she could control with the instrument was Ridley. It wasn't as though she could call in all the mice from the Earth Dimension to go and attack the royals at the citadel. But oh, how that would be handy if she could. Running her hands down her face, she was going to do like Lark did and carry a damn pocketknife on her.

"I'll try and make it fast." Leni stood from the couch and strapped her pouch at her waist. "If anyone knocks on the door, don't answer it, unless you hear me or Ridley calling for you."

"We'll have the knives ready," Lark said.

Auden and Leni both rolled their eyes. Speaking of knives, Leni opened the drawer in the kitchen and placed one of Millie's pocketknives into her pouch.

When Leni straightened, a dizzy spell washed over her and she had to catch herself at the counter. Even with the medicine, she was feeling tired faster. Lark's eyes were still rimmed with dark circles and if Leni could see her own reflection in a mirror, she knew hers would appear the same purplish shade.

"Let me leave you some meds, just in case," Leni said when she noticed Lark swaying a bit on the floor.

"Thanks," Lark answered as Auden scooped her up and set her on the couch, making her laugh.

Leni fought back a smile as she placed a few pills on the coffee table and headed out the front door.

Fumbling with the chain of her bike, she finally got it off. It had been a while since she'd ridden these wheels, at least a few months. She'd kept a different bike at the citadel since this one had too many memories.

A light mist sprinkled down on her as she pedaled along the cobblestone road to the citadel. She didn't mind the rain that cooled her heated skin. Nausea and exhaustion ate at her as she continued past bright green and pink rectangular buildings, but she forced herself to remain steady.

One more day to get through and then tomorrow night would be the masquerade. Whatever would happen, would happen. And if things went her way and she lived, Leni couldn't help wondering about Rebel. Could she go and search for her? She didn't dare let herself hope. Because even if the kings and queens were reunited, that didn't mean the rules would change. They would still be the same rulers. Or maybe they wouldn't, since two personalities would be merging together.

Several other people on bikes or on foot passed her in the slowing mist, most wearing neon-colored protective rain gear in case the angry clouds truly decided to unleash their fury.

Maybe Ridley wasn't even at the citadel any longer. He could've stopped somewhere else or even gone to see Elliot to let him know he had the jeweled box. But there was that pricking in her brain telling her something was wrong.

Rounding the bumpy curve of the pebbled path, Leni's body jostled to the side and she gripped the handlebars tighter. Trees with branches shaped like monstrous claws slipped into her view, then Ridley's blue house directly behind them. The bike wouldn't go as fast as she wanted it to. Finally, Leni slowed as she skirted around his home to the front door, where she spotted his bike on the porch.

Heart pounding, Leni hopped off her ride, not bothering to press down the kickstand. The bike toppled to the ground as she sprinted for the entrance to his house and threw open the already-unlocked door. Wiping mist from her forehead and cheeks, she hurried inside, shouting his name.

"Ridley!" she yelled again, venturing into the clean

kitchen, his organized bedroom, then the bathroom—nothing. He wasn't there. She inhaled marshmallows and cinnamon, but of course she did—he lived here.

His bike was still there, so that meant he had to be in the citadel. But how many hours should it have taken him to get the box? Leni flew out of the house and looked in the direction of the brightly-colored citadel. If he could speak mind to mind to her in that moment, Ridley would've told her not to be impulsive and to just go home. But Leni was impulsive, and she didn't care.

She should've gone with him that morning, especially after learning things about those jackasses in the citadel from Quinna. Her stupid thoughts couldn't help but remember the whip slamming down against her flesh again and again, how each strike made her secretly want to die yet not give up at the same time.

That little demon of a voice in the back of her head told her not to disrupt what Ridley could be trying to do, but what if something did happen to him… What if the royals *knew* they were up to something? *Shit.*

Tired of her back and forth thoughts, Leni pinched her inner wrist to stop. Her nerves were on edge and she couldn't go to the citadel door appearing flustered like this. Digging her nails into her palms to keep herself focused on something else, she headed to the front of the building and crossed the bridge with a confident face but a fearful heart.

As usual, two guards remained at the door under the black horse helmets. Leni wished she could see the guards' expressions to read what they might be thinking. Lifting her chin, she craned her neck up at them when she got closer to the door. She moved her fingers and hand in the secret code. "I need to speak to the royals." Despite her fast-beating heart and her tired limbs, her voice came out steady.

"They won't see you," the guard on the right boomed under his helmet. "After your last meeting, the royals said they have nothing left to say to you."

She had to get in there, if only for a few minutes.

"It won't take long, I promise." Even as she wanted to get down on her knees and plead with them, Leni didn't let her mask slip.

"News traveled fast about the lashing." There seemed to have been a little sympathy in his words. "I suggest turning around in case you don't want a repeat of what happened. The royals do what they believe is necessary."

Leni couldn't just turn around, not without some sort of answer. "Can you at least tell me if Ridley came here?" Her insides were screaming, demanding, needing to know.

"He's been contained," the other shorter guard said. "And he isn't allowed to leave."

Leni's heart got stuck in her throat. "*What?*"

The shorter guard tugged at the cuff of his sleeve. "Nothing can be done. I'm sorry."

There wasn't anything Leni would be able to say for them to let her in. With a nod, she took off on a sprint down the glass bridge, making it sway more. Tears filled her eyes, and she didn't care if they saw her running away.

She needed to get to Quinna's home sooner than this evening. But first, she needed to get to Elliot, then go back to her place to gather Lark and Auden. There had to be a Plan B. But she wasn't sure what Plan A had been to begin with. So maybe what she needed was just an organized plan.

Straddling her bike, she took off down the pebbled path as

a wave of exhaustion hit her. The mist had stopped at some point, and the sun peaked out from the pale clouds, hitting her with its rays, making her want to get off the bike and take a nap from the tiredness. But she fought through it. She would continue fighting until her dying breath if she had to.

After pedaling as hard as she could, she arrived at Elliot's place, which wasn't far from her home. Outside, wind chimes created from old Coca-Cola bottles and orange and yellow pieces of glass clinked together.

Throwing open the door, she listened to the sound of a hammer striking metal reverberate off the frame-filled walls. Alphaville was playing somewhere in the back of the room. In the corner, Leni spotted Elliot working over a dusty table, wearing a black apron, goggles, and leather gloves.

"Elliot!" she screamed, stumbling forward.

His shoulders jerked, then he whirled around, lips set in a tight line. "Next time, don't yell like that. I almost disfigured my hand." But he couldn't stay mad for long—a small smile formed across his lips.

"It's Ridley. He went back to get the box from the mirror this morning." Leni inched forward, catching herself on the wall, causing a few frames to rattle on their hooks. "The royals have him and I'm not sure what to do, but we need a plan."

Tearing off his gloves, he strode to her and helped her sit in a chair. His face was concerned as he fussed over her for a few precious moments. Leni didn't like all this pampering that was happening, but she was too drained to refuse the help.

"Did Ridley retrieve the box before he was captured?" Elliot asked, handing her a can of soda resting on the table.

"I'm not sure if he was able to go in and take it out or not, but my guess is no. All I know is he went into the citadel and didn't come out."

Elliot cradled his head in his hands, moving his mouth like he was talking to himself. Finally, his gaze latched onto hers. "Let me go to the citadel since I need to drop off some completed mirrors anyway. Maybe I can gather some information, then I can meet you guys tonight at Quinna's."

"That's a good plan." Leni stood from the chair, wobbling. "I'm going to take Lark and Auden over there now."

Elliot grasped her arm at the elbow, preventing her from falling. "Do you need me to bring you to them?"

Leni shook her head and unzipped her waist pouch, pulling out two more pills, praying they would hold her over for at least the rest of the day and the next.

Gathering what strength she had left, Leni left to retrieve Lark and Auden. She prayed Ridley was safe for the time being, but her focus drifted to the fresh scars on her back that twitched at the memory.

With everything in her, she hoped that wouldn't be his fate.

CHAPTER 19

Music from "Major Tom" – Peter Schilling

Ridley inspected the confined area, then the mirror without its drape. The room felt like it was closing in on him, threatening to swallow him whole. His heart pounded with desperation to get out. He automatically reached for his pouch, for his notepad, but the guards had confiscated them. His hand fell to the glass butterfly in his pocket—that was at least still there.

The royals had thrown him in here to wait until the masquerade, but at least they had sequestered him in the same room as the mirror. He could go in and retrieve the box and figure out the rest later. Crawling forward, the mirror rippled around him, the hairs on his forearms lifting as he pressed through the glass.

For a moment, he thought the box might not be there at all anymore. Panic threatened to seize him, choke him more, but his vision cleared. And there it sat, just as he'd left it, on top of the table.

Ridley shifted forward to scoop up the box when the veins on the sides of his head hummed and pulsed harder. *Not again. Not again.*

The purple walls surrounding him slowly darkened to obsidian. Then the light buzzing grew louder and louder until it sounded as if a bee was hovering right beside his ear, preparing to sting. He swatted at it, colliding with nothing. The noise echoed at his other ear, and he slapped the side of his head.

His eyes darkened as the shadows seeped out from behind his irises, causing his vision to give way. Blindly, he walked forward, frantic, trying to clear the world so he could grab the box and go.

"Ridley," a shadow whispered.

"Come to us," another purred.

The black lightened, as if another color was mixing with the darkness, until he could see again. Down the hall, the shadows beckoned him forward, their whispers only increasing instead of fading.

Throat bobbing, Ridley picked up the box. Something was telling him to follow, while another voice at the back of his head demanded he leave.

But this time as they lured him forward, the shadows were different. They weren't taunting him. He entered the hallway from the triangular room, glancing at each face in the mirrors. One after another turned to Ridley, their eyes settling on him, whispering his name, repeating it again and again. In Lark and Auden's mirrors, they moved their lips, saying his name, too.

The woodsy scent of the room altered to a new smell like burning paper. His heart pounded as black flames licked up from the bottom of the mirrors to the top, crackling and flickering, until all of the mirrors were entirely darkened. Except for the cursed one from where he'd entered.

A coldness filled the room—frost gathered on the mirrors. Ridley shivered, goosebumps collecting on his skin. Plumes of dark smoke exited his mouth when he exhaled. From the end of the hall, near the cursed mirror, shadows barreled back toward him, dancing to the buzzing music they were creating.

He stumbled backward, prepared to run, but they were faster, swimming around and around him, preventing him from passing.

"Go and watch," one buzzed in his ear.

His feet moved of their own accord toward the cursed mirror where a silvery movement danced. Ridley stepped closer until he was directly across from the mirror. His thoughts spun wildly as he planted his hand to the glass, attempting to hurry and pass back through. But the mirror didn't ripple. He banged on the glass, but the mirror didn't crack or shift.

Something took hold of him, and he could no longer move his hand away from the glass. The force pulled him somewhere new, until he could no longer see anything within the Realm of Mirrors. It was as if he was standing within a memory. No one in the room could see him. In front of him stood a man with dark hair and a woman with auburn curly locks—Brand and Portia, their twins not by their sides. Portia took a step forward, wearing a long silky dress, tears streaking her cheeks.

Ridley was in some sort of bedroom with a large canopy bed. Beside the bed rested a wooden cradle. Portia leaned forward and drew something out from inside. A doll? A white bonnet covered its head and the body was draped in the same colored nightgown. Ridley inched closer until he could see it wasn't a doll at all, but a baby. As Portia brought the child up to her chest, it didn't stir.

"We can try again," Brand said, rubbing his tired face.

"They all die!" Portia cried. "She's the first one to come to term and she still died. If I can't have a baby here, then why should anyone else?"

The scene changed to where Ridley and the two royals were all standing in the throne room.

Portia shoved at Brand's chest. "I need her back, Brand."

"She can't come back," he said, but in his voice, Ridley heard the desperation. He wanted it, too.

"The shadows. We can make a deal with their dimension, and they can give her back to us."

"We can try, but will they listen?" Brand grabbed Portia's hand and intertwined their fingers.

What was going on?

Around Ridley, the scene changed once more.

Portia and Brand stood back in their room. From the cradle, Portia lifted the same baby cloaked in white, but only now she was nothing but a pale skeleton. Nausea stirred in Ridley's stomach.

Across from the two royals stood a mirror, the same cursed one Ridley had carried around. The glass was obsidian in color, and it rippled. A shadow arm pierced through, pulling itself from the mirror. Ridley stiffened. But the shadowy guest wasn't coming for him—it moved toward Brand and Portia, circling above them.

"We want you to bring our daughter back to us whole," Portia said and handed the baby to the shadow.

"Your dimension will require souls from another," the shadow rasped. "For that, you will have to link your world to theirs. It will take time to acquire the souls, but in that duration, you will have your counterparts by your side to absorb them."

"We don't have time," Brand sputtered. "We age and could die by the time this is completed."

"That's why the counterparts will be by your side. You will remain immortal until then. Be warned—while you're connected to the Earth Dimension, it will affect your people." The shadow took an obsidian flute from somewhere within its darkness and handed it to Brand. As it touched the king's palm, the shade of the instrument changed to silver.

From the glass, the darkness cleared and reflected an image of Brand and Portia. The one who looked like Brand stretched a hand through the glass and crawled out. Anson. Then the image of Portia repeated what Anson had done. Calliope.

As Ridley moved forward, the scene changed again.

A shadow hovered in front of Brand and Portia with the twin royals at their sides. "You have enough souls. The deal can be made now. Destroy the mirror and break the flute."

"We've changed our minds," Brand said.

Portia nodded in agreement. "We rather like having the immortality."

Words fell from the shadow, and Ridley strained to hear them but couldn't. His hand was pushed back from the cursed mirror, and the Realm of Mirrors pulled back into focus.

"Shit," Ridley murmured, staring down at his hand and the room. "All this nonsense about worlds being destroyed definitely wasn't true."

It was all to get their baby back, and then they changed their minds. How could someone do that? They'd told the shadows they preferred the immortality.

Ridley had to get out of there, and he needed to get to Leni. The blackness of the room dripped back down, releasing the walls once again to purple and clearing the rest of the mirrors. Gripping the box, Ridley pressed his hand to the glass, and this time it rippled against his skin. He darted through the mirror and slipped to the other side.

As soon as he returned to his prison of a closet, he jolted forward, ramming his shoulder against the door. It didn't budge. The metal was too heavy. He did it again and again until his arm ached. On the other side of the door, a guard threatened to leave him without food if he did it again. He didn't care. There wasn't any way he was getting out of there today.

Ridley gazed down at the box, hoping he could give it to Leni at the masquerade, or before it.

Being in the confined room, trapped and unable to leave, felt too much like Sonya's closet. He wanted, *needed*, to escape. *Now*. He yearned for his pen and paper. Too desperately. There was nothing for him to read to distract himself from his memories, from what he'd just witnessed. All Ridley could do was look at the box.

Quickly, he crossed his legs and sat on the floor. He opened the box until he could see the velvet inside. *Purple*, he repeated over in his head. *Purple.*

But purple wasn't what came. Because his temples were throbbing again, and the darkness slithered out from him once more. The thing about the color black was that it could overpower any other. Shadows crawled across the floor, horns protruding from their heads. The shadows had never really been a part of him or Leni. They'd been there because of a deal the royals had made. They were linked to some Shadow Dimension and to the price the royals had silently agreed to pay.

In Ridley's hand, a shadowy flute appeared, and his eyelashes fluttered at the thought of having the real one in between his lips. Leni had chosen "Space Oddity" as her song, and as the room seemed to chant for him to choose his own, he knew which one he wanted to pick when he had the instrument in his hand. Because, like Leni, "Space Oddity" was the song of his heart, too.

And with that melody, he would call forward the souls that his Mirror Keeper would want. He tried to brush it off, shake his head, not remembering Leni having it this bad. The pain came at his temples, throbbing, throbbing, until the room became a complete shadow, until he became one as well, then he slipped into darkness, falling to the side, his eyes remaining shut.

Ridley had been at Leni and Millie's for around a week. His thoughts were all there, but his words were still stuck inside his head. They wouldn't come out right. The world was such a big place, much larger than the closet he'd spent six years in.

Sitting on the edge of his bed, he took out a Shakespeare book and copied the words down in his notebook like he always did.

"You know you don't have to force the words out," Leni said.

He glanced up at her face and blinked. The word he had for her was beautiful. She didn't look like the girls in the books he'd read. There was something different about her soft features, and he liked them.

"Talking to me through blinking is fine. I'm starting to understand you in the way you speak by your movements."

Taking out a note, he wrote down words. I want to speak.

"Then it looks like we have a lot of practice to do." She started a record and let "Major Tom" fold the music around them.

A shuffling outside caused Ridley's body to jerk, and his eyes flew open. He rubbed the side of his head, wondering how long he'd been passed out.

"Can I take a look at the frame in there?" A familiar voice. Elliot... "I have a client who described something she wanted, and I remembered the mirror had a similar design. It'll only take a moment."

"Sorry, no one can go in for the next few days," the guard said.

"Why? It will literally take only a few seconds."

"There's someone being held until the masquerade."

"Oh. All right, I'll just tell my client she'll have to wait until after the party." The scuffing of Elliot's footsteps sounded as he left.

Leni must've told him what was going on, and Ridley knew she was going to try to plan something. And all he could do was sit in this room, waiting and thinking about the possibility that Leni could die the next night.

 CHAPTER 20

Leni shot through the front door of her old home, expecting to find Lark and Auden still in the living room watching horror movies. But they weren't there. All she could think about was the chat they'd had about someone bursting into the house while she was gone. However, the door had still been locked.

Her heart kicked up as she walked the hallway to her room, then slowed when the musical sounds of Cheap Trick carried out to her. Rounding the door frame, she spotted Auden and Lark lying on the floor with their eyes shut, listening to the music.

She didn't want to disturb the moment, but she had to.

"Change of plans." Her voice came out panicked, even though she hadn't meant for it to sound that way.

Both their eyes flew open and they scrambled to sit up.

"Where's Ridley?" Lark asked, lifting her chin and gazing past Leni's shoulder, as if expecting to find him there.

Leni's chest heaved as she thought about what could be happening to him. "He's being held at the citadel until the masquerade."

"Oh shit." Auden stood and pulled Lark up beside him. "So what does this mean?"

That was something she wished she could figure out, but

at least she had a next step. "This means we're going to Quinna's place now. There has to be a way to get him out before the masquerade." But she wasn't sure how.

Lark stopped the player, the music fading out to silence. "All right. It's a minor setback—that's all."

A minor setback would've been Ridley coming home without the jeweled box, but maybe Lark was right.

"We're going to walk." Leni waved them to follow her. "It would be better not to have bikes parked outside Quinna's."

Once they headed out of the house, they trekked down the cobblestone path toward Quinna's. Leni wondered if Elliot was going to find out anything new.

The bones and muscles inside Leni still ached, and she tapped Lark on the shoulder. "Are you feeling okay?"

Shrugging, Lark tilted her head and squinted at a few of the tall teal houses with dark green roofs. "Just achy, sort of like I have a cold or something."

"That sounds about right." Leni studied a few of the signs about the upcoming masquerade. "Tomorrow, I want you to stick close to Auden at all times, just in case we faint or something." She turned to Auden. "And if Lark does, get her, and yourself, the hell out of there. Forget about anything else."

"Done." Auden picked at his lower lip. "I'm not going to blame you."

"What?" Leni knew he could be talking about a million different things, but she had a feeling she understood what he meant. She just wasn't sure if she could discuss it without releasing a flood of emotions.

"With Darrin. Knowing about everything, these dimensions, it could make monsters out of anyone. But I can see you aren't one."

"I'm sorry." Tears pricked her eyes and that seemed okay enough for Auden because he nodded, clearly not wanting to talk about his friend any longer.

Auden and Lark both put their headphones over their ears as they traveled the rest of the way to the outskirts of the town, where Quinna's red house was partially hidden in the cluster of trees.

Leni went up the uneven porch steps and knocked on the door, tapping her foot as she waited. A few seconds later, it swung open. Quinna peered out, wearing an apron and her short hair mussed.

"You're all early," Quinna hissed, running a hand through her hair and only making the tufts messier.

"It's important," Leni pleaded. "It's about Ridley."

Quinna clenched her teeth as though debating what to do, but then she finally motioned them inside and pointed them to the creation room. "Just go in there and keep your voices down to a whisper."

Leni passed the furniture in the sitting room and opened the door, the metallic odor stronger than last time. She stepped inside the room—light steam hovered above the pools of silver liquid in front of the full-size mirrors.

"What are you doing?" Leni asked as Quinna took down a large ladle from a tool rack in the corner. Lark and Auden were inspecting the liquid pools in the flooring.

"Working," Quinna said hurriedly. "A client is picking up a child soon, and this one is stubborn, not wanting to come out just yet."

"You're creating one?" Lark's interest piqued as she craned her neck and took a step closer to Quinna. "Can we see?"

"I guess?" Quinna batted Lark to move back a little and looked at Leni. "So, what is this about Ridley?"

"He's been taken by the royals and won't be released until the masquerade tomorrow night." Leni couldn't help her thoughts from returning to all things grim with what the royals could be doing.

"How the hell did he get himself in that position?" The ladle fell from Quinna's hand, thumping on the floor. She hurried to pluck it back up, a frown on her face.

"You did tell him to go and retrieve something from the mirror." Leni couldn't help but blame Quinna in a way, yet it wasn't as if she'd forced them to do anything. She had only told them what they could do to stop the whole curse situation. But still.

"That was the easiest task out of all three things to collect." Quinna spun the liquid silver with her ladle in a clockwise circle.

"Not when he isn't the Mirror Keeper anymore and the royals took his mirror back! And then they decided to take him too!" Leni's lungs weren't keeping up with her, and she was finding it hard to breathe again.

With a low growl, Quinna pressed a gloved hand across her cheek and lowered her head. "Okay… Let me think about this."

"Elliot went to the citadel to see if he could find out something—*anything*. So hopefully when he gets here, we'll at least know where Ridley's being kept."

"Let's discuss this more after I finish here." Quinna's voice came out in a struggle as she churned the liquid harder. "I have to create this child or things are going to look sketchy."

Nodding, Leni plopped down on the floor beside Lark and Auden. She'd never seen a person be created. When she was made, she recalled being in the room, but she didn't remember anything before that, or even being drawn out of the liquid.

Quinna continued to spin the glass, the liquid seeming to grow thicker as each second passed. The steam above the pool became lighter.

"Whoa," Auden said as a shimmery silver light flickered atop the liquid, flashing bright like a shooting star.

A hand shot upward. Silver from the liquid coated the child's skin, but underneath rested a dark tan. Setting down the ladle, Quinna grasped the hand and pulled the new guest forward.

The child wore a plain white gown, also coated in the liquid. Beneath the silver covering the girl's long hair, it appeared blonde. Quinna snatched a towel from the rack and wiped as much silver as she could from the girl's face, arms, and legs. Through it all, the girl's eyes remained shut while her chest rose and fell, breathing in the world around her. Then her lids opened to a light blue, taking her surroundings in, but her lips remained silent and shut.

"I'm going to bring her into the front room and wait for the client. Just make sure to keep your voices down." Quinna glanced at the three of them, who were now speechless.

Leni had seen some wild things in the dimensions. She'd even created mirrors, but nothing like this—not life.

As Quinna guided the girl into the front room, Leni continued to stare. That was how she'd once been, how everyone was at first. The words were in their heads, but it would take practice for them to come forward. Ridley's was longer, and he still had to battle with it because of what Sonya had done to him by keeping him in that closet. Yet Leni liked who he was and wouldn't change anything about him.

"I don't understand," Auden whispered, getting up and kneeling at the pool. "Are there just bodies floating down in there waiting to be born?"

"That seems creepy." Lark joined him and studied the liquid, about to press a finger in.

Leni tugged Lark's hand back. "I'm not sure if you can touch it. Best not to." But as Leni gazed at the flickering lights of silver, she was curious, too. "There aren't bodies down in there. The best way to explain it is how in your world, and I suppose also here, is that the male has sperm floating around inside him… When the silver light flashes, the first one to make it toward the light in the center, which acts as an egg, gets created. But the process is faster because we only use glass that is ten years old, so that's why we're created so big."

Auden's mouth curled up, baffled by the concept. "So odd."

"So cool." Lark grinned.

A knock at the front door sounded and Leni's body stilled. She placed a finger over her lips, and they all remained quiet. Two female voices started talking—Quinna, and the other presumably the client.

The client's voice appeared elated as she chatted to Quinna for what felt like forever. Leni wanted to just say, *Grab your child and go, lady!* She couldn't quell the anxiety rushing through her veins.

Finally, the voices faded away and the front door shut, the sound echoing throughout the house.

Lark nudged Auden with her elbow. "It's like the stork

scenario when the bird brings a baby, only this isn't an infant, but a larger kid."

"That seems accurate, and bonus is, you get to skip diapers," Auden said.

Leni couldn't help thinking about Rebel. How she was a newborn, not a tall child. Rebel needed bottles, diaper changes, naps, and holding. All those things, which Leni hadn't done, became Millie's responsibility instead. She shoved the thoughts and disappointment back down.

For the remainder of the time, Lark and Auden passed a small notebook back and forth while Quinna cleaned up the room. Lark must've noticed Leni's somber mood because she then passed the notebook to her. On the paper were lyrics from "Go Your Own Way." Leni smiled and was about to write something back when a knock came at the front door.

The three of them sat with shoulders tensed until Elliot's voice boomed through the house and Quinna told him to be quiet. Leni stood as soon as the door opened to the creation room. Quinna stepped into the space, followed by Elliot and his tight-lipped expression.

"Did you find out anything?" Leni edged toward him.

"I did." Elliot moved to the center of the room, past Lark and Auden. "Ridley's being kept in the room in the tower with the cursed mirror."

"What!" Leni shouted. She lowered her voice for the next words, but the vehemence was still there. "They have him in that tiny closet?"

"Yeah." Elliot nodded. "He'll be okay in there until the masquerade. I mean, the royals could've been doing worse to him."

"No." Leni sighed. "You don't understand. Ridley came

from a closet after Millie found him. Remember? He'd been inside there for six years. That's his number one fear—being trapped in a small area."

"There really isn't much we can do until the masquerade, especially with a guard at the door."

Slipping by someone guarding the area wouldn't be possible, but there had to be a way.

"Listen," Quinna interrupted and grabbed a dark green box from a drawer under the tools. "I want to show you something." Opening the box, she pulled out a long, silver object. A flute. *The* flute.

Leni sucked in a sharp breath, and she knew she was practically beaming that they had it. "You took it?"

"No, I created it." Quinna smiled. All the hope vanished from Leni. "Tomorrow at the masquerade, we're going to swap this out with the real one."

"That still leaves the box," Auden pointed out. "You'd still be missing it."

Lark clicked her red nails against the floor. "This seems like everything will be too rushed."

They were right.

As Leni stared at the flute, she thought about how there wouldn't be enough time to do what they needed to. But then an idea came to her, a rather stupid one, but it could make things easier and have them prepared for the next evening.

Leni smiled. "I have a better solution."

"This is pretty dumb," Auden whispered, squatting behind Leni and Lark at the window, wiping invisible dust from his Sex Pistols shirt.

It was early morning and the sun was barely entering the sky. The guards' shop had just opened maybe thirty minutes earlier.

"Shh, we're going to be fast," Leni whispered back. "What do you see now?"

Auden stood, peering into the window. "Elliot's still talking to the guy."

Come on, Elliot.

Timmy was someone Elliot had most recently had a fling with, but they weren't serious. So Leni wasn't sure if the idea would work or not. If it didn't, she'd just have to go in there with Lark and hold him at knifepoint.

"Wait, he's now being lured to the back by Elliot." Auden smirked. "I guess he was able to do it."

But how long would they have?

"All right, it's been more than five seconds." Lark headed to the door and knelt beside it. "Just two uniforms, right? Small and medium?"

"Correct. I'll grab the helmets." Leni hurried next to her. "Now!"

Auden discreetly opened the door and held it as Leni and Lark tiptoed inside. Leni headed toward the dark helmets, while Lark veered right. The inside of the guards' shop smelled heavily of grease and iron.

Black helmets shaped like horses lined the entire wall in neat rows. Leni collected two on the far side off cedar shelves, careful not to clink them. Then she quietly spread the remaining helmets out, so the missing ones weren't as noticeable.

With both helmets in her hands, Leni rushed outside, past Auden holding the door, to the side of the building. She set the light metal onto the pebbled ground and looked for Lark.

Where is she?

Leni peered through the window and Lark had one uniform in her hand but was still searching through sizes for the other. She should've just told her to grab whatever and leave.

Nerves on edge, Leni ran back inside while Auden bulged his eyes at Lark, seeming to tell her to hurry the hell up.

Leni started fumbling through the bright yellow jumpsuits when voices sounded from the back room. *Small.* She'd found it. The voices were growing closer. *Shit.* Hurriedly, Leni tossed the uniform to Lark and watched her run out the door. Auden stood, holding it still, and Leni waved at him to release the door because she wouldn't make it out.

The door shut just as Elliot and Timmy entered the front room. Trying to appear casual, she leaned her elbow against the counter.

"I knew it!" Leni said, slapping the front desk with her hand, rattling the jar of pens.

"What are you doing here?" Timmy asked, his lips swollen and face flushed. "You're not the Piper anymore, so you shouldn't even be in here."

"Elliot wasn't home, so I came here looking for him." She tried to keep her gaze from glancing out the door or window.

Elliot clenched his teeth, silently begging her not to say anything stupid.

"I'm going to have to report you to the royals." Timmy

rubbed the back of his neck. "*But* I'll do it after the masquerade tonight. Wouldn't want to disrupt their day."

For all Timmy knew, Leni might not be alive tomorrow.

"That's fair." She nodded. "But I really do need Elliot to help me move some things at the house."

"Thanks, Timmy," Elliot said, grabbing Leni and pulling her to the door.

Timmy looked as though he wanted to argue, but he must've been too smitten by Elliot's kiss. She knew if Elliot hadn't been there that Timmy would've reported her right away.

Once they were outside, Elliot turned to her. "Please tell me you got the stuff."

"Yes, we did." She smiled at him. "And I owe you for that in there. We couldn't have done this without you."

Rolling his eyes, Elliot followed Leni to the side of the building where Lark and Auden were waiting with the supplies already inside the backpacks.

"All right," Leni whispered. "I'm going to drop you two off at the house, then Elliot and I have a mission to complete."

CHAPTER 21

Music from "Always Something There To Remind Me" – Naked Eyes

Ridley didn't know how much time had passed when he awoke, but it had to be early morning. He hugged his knees at his chest and kept his head pressed against them. Slowly, he said letters over and over in his head, then spelled out words, anything for him to forget he was still in this closet. Going back into the mirror and hiding didn't sound any better, not after the images he'd seen from the shadows.

He remembered the first time he'd seen the shadows rising up from Leni, when she'd played that first note on the flute. When he'd bumped into Lark, then Auden, to start Phase One of the curse. All of that had been because of her melody—or the shadows—leading him to do things he didn't want to do, even though he'd chosen Lark and Auden.

He couldn't think about that. About what he'd done, what he'd been forced to do. In an effort to break from his thoughts, he repeated songs in his head as a distraction. He was tapping his fingers against his thighs to the upbeat intro to "Always Something There To Remind Me," when the door creaked open.

Before him stood a lanky guard with the same dark horse helmet as everyone else. There was no difference between them, and underneath the helmet, were they even people at all? He wondered how they were at home. Did they laugh? Did they cry? Did they love? Was this just something they had to do, the way he and Leni had to create mirrors or perform tasks for the curse?

"The royals need to see you," the guard demanded.

"I thought I was supposed to be in here until the masquerade," Ridley muttered.

"If I were you, I wouldn't question anymore. Just do as requested unless you want to find a whip against your flesh like your little friend."

Ridley's cheeks heated with fury, but he kept quiet as he stood from the floor.

The guard grasped Ridley's arm and yanked him to the spiral staircase. He walked down the steps, keeping his head lowered. At the bottom of the staircase, the corridor stood empty. All the doors were shut, and neon masquerade masks with feathers now hung across the walls, prepared for the evening.

As they rounded the corner, the two guards at the entrance to the throne room pulled open the doors to the large area. Up on the stage sat the royals in their high-backed chairs, just like the day before. Did they ever go anywhere? Or did they just remain seated there until it was bedtime?

Maybe they don't sleep at all. Too high and mighty with their immortality that they'd ruin lives to keep it. Ridley wanted to question them about the Shadow Dimension, about the child, about everything, but that would only make matters worse for him, which would trickle down to Leni and the others. He had to make his move with them tonight, not now.

"I apologize," Brand said, setting down a glass of what

appeared to be tea, "that we had to do it this way, but you seem to be drifting in and out."

Blinking, Ridley nodded and held his tongue. An easy feat for him normally, only this time, words were fighting to spill out from his mouth.

"Since you already know what's going to happen tonight," Portia purred, "we'd like to know who you would choose to be your Mirror Keeper."

"Why are you asking this now?" Ridley frowned. "Leni didn't have to choose right away last time."

Brand gestured at the air. "We decided it's best to begin the curse directly after the masquerade. The dimensions are already starting to fracture since the last curse didn't succeed. As you're aware, there has never been a time where a curse wasn't completed."

Probably because you cheat, Ridley thought. If hints were never given, then how would the cursed ones ever win? He was sure that some never even went into the mirror to figure things out.

"Who will you choose?" Portia asked, cocking her head at the same time Calliope did.

"I'm not choosing." Why should he put someone in the same predicament he'd been in? The only way he'd be choosing was if the shadows forced him.

"No?" Brand seethed. "That's fine, but tonight at the masquerade, the flute will make you, if you refuse. I'd suggest you stop being difficult."

"If I'm so difficult, then why don't you pass the position on to someone else?" They'd easily gotten rid of Leni, even though it had been his fault the curse hadn't succeeded.

Portia curved her fingers around the ends of the chair's

armrests. "Once the flute is in your hands, we'll make sure you're one of the best we've ever had. Now, do you want to choose?"

Ridley shook his head—he didn't even have to think about it.

"Then you won't be coming out of the room again until tonight." Brand waved the guard over to collect Ridley. It wouldn't have mattered if he'd chosen, because they would've still sent him away afterward.

Ridley needed to at least try to keep up an appearance. He should've done that as soon as he walked in. "The truth is... I need time to think about who I want to help me. Someone who is willing to follow."

Portia's lips curved into a dangerous smile. "That's more like it."

Like before, the guard clasped his hand around Ridley's arm in a tight grip, his fingers digging into his muscles. The guard shoved him out of the throne room toward the staircase leading back up to the tower. Ridley's heart sped up at the thought of having to return to that closet of a room. He was already getting tired of this, sick of having to listen to every-one. Even back at the mirror shop, it was always about following orders, creating X number of mirrors, and never a single thank you from the royals. And this stupid guard was gripping him so harshly when he hadn't even fought back.

As they stood before the door to the mirror's room, Ridley knew he had to do something. He still needed to get the jeweled box to Leni. All his life, he'd never been violent with anyone, and he didn't want to be, but sometimes ... there was no other choice, especially when it was about standing up for what was right.

Ridley tried to tap into *Terminator* mode as the guard unlocked and opened the door. Barreling forward, Ridley ripped off the guard's helmet, meeting his stunned gaze. Ridley clenched the collar of the guard's uniform and swung a tightened fist into the man's jaw. The guard stumbled backward and struck his head on the knob. His body collapsed on the floor, eyes closed.

Ridley stood, chest heaving, stunned. Too many emotions floated through his head at that moment. And he couldn't decipher what he was feeling or think of the words. Kneeling, he pressed a shaking hand to the guard's pulse—it beat a healthy pattern against his fingertips. *Alive.* One word came to mind—*relieved.*

Using quick movements, Ridley dragged the guard into the tiny room and placed him in front of the mirror. He was maybe in his early thirties with a shaved head and a long scar on his chin. Ridley then stripped off the guard's yellow jumpsuit and scrambled to put it on over his clothes. After picking up the jeweled box from the floor, Ridley placed the helmet over his head—it was surprisingly light and reeked of sweat.

He slipped out from the room and bolted the door, silently apologizing to the guard. The uniform felt tight against his muscles as his arms swayed, but it would do well enough.

Rotating his shoulders back, Ridley walked down the spiral staircase and into the corridor. He just had to make it past the two guards at the door to the throne room and then the two outside. Neither of the guards inside questioned him as he strode past, but as he headed out the front entrance, one of them stopped him.

Ridley gave the hand signal and moved forward when one

of the guards placed a hand on his chest, peering down at the jeweled box. "What's that you got there?"

He'd already prepared a lie, his voice coming out confident. "A gift I brought to work, so I can give it to my girlfriend on the way home." Flipping the box over, he showed the guard the bottom. "Her name's Butterfly and I got this engraved for her. See?"

"With a name like Butterfly, I hope she gives you some action for that gift." The guard chuckled and stood back in his straight position. Ridley must not have lost his aggressiveness from earlier, because he wanted to punch that guard in the face, too. "Next time, I advise you not to bring anything like that here, or it will get confiscated. You should know the rules."

With a nod, he shuffled across the bridge. His heart hadn't calmed, and sweat dripped down his face from the heat of the helmet. He quickly rounded the bridge and scurried toward his house, dodging anyone he could. The trees blocked most of his view and he stopped behind a thick trunk to remove the helmet. Leaning against the bark, he breathed deeply, drinking in the sweet air.

Ridley took one more gulp of air, then sped toward his front door. He went inside and shoved the helmet beneath his bed, tore off the jumpsuit, and stuffed it under there, too.

He went back outside, pulse spiking to get off the citadel property as soon as possible. Hopping on his bike, he pedaled down the path to Leni. While gripping the box in one hand, he knew what he was going to do. Give Leni the box then come right back to the citadel, because he'd have to retrieve the flute. And the only way to do that would be to get it during the blasted masquerade.

Sweat soaked his curls as he pulled up the cobblestone driveway to his destination. Ridley patted his pant pockets, realizing he didn't have a key on him, so he knocked on the door, waiting for someone to answer.

The door slowly drew open and Lark peeped her head around the edge, before fully swinging it toward her.

"Where's Leni?" Ridley brushed past Lark, spotting Auden right behind her.

"What do you mean where's Leni?" Lark whirled around to face him. "Isn't she with you?"

"No?" Why would she be with him, when he'd been held at the citadel?

"She went to get you out!" Lark shouted.

"I got myself out!" Ridley's voice went up on the last word. *Leni*...

"Oh no…" Lark covered her mouth.

"Damn…" Auden folded his arms and pressed his back against the wall.

Ridley exchanged glances between the both of them. "What?"

"She went with Elliot to the citadel to swap out the flute and bust you out." Lark cringed as though she didn't want to be the bearer of bad news.

Butterfly, what have you done?

CHAPTER 22

Music from "You Shook Me All Night Long" – AC/DC

"I can't go to that masquerade, Ridley. I just can't." Leni said, *straightening her dress.*

"It'll be fine." Ridley set down the AC/DC record. "You won't get chosen. No one else knows."

Yet Leni had been chosen. And she wished with everything in her she hadn't been. There'd been no stopping it.

Leni and Elliot had brought Lark and Auden home after stealing the guard uniforms from the shop. They then headed to the citadel, where they now both stood hidden within the trees, behind wide trunks. She'd already taken the jumpsuit out of her backpack and put it on, but the helmet still rested in her fingertips.

"I don't know if this is going to work," Elliot said as he slid on the black helmet over his tight curls.

"It *will* work, but you don't have to risk it." She had originally planned on going by herself, but the night before Elliot had said absolutely not. And she'd refused to risk Lark and Auden coming here before the masquerade.

"Why?" Elliot's voice came out muffled through his helmet. "So Ridley can yell at me because I let you go in by yourself? Besides, you haven't been feeling well."

"I'm feeling fine," Leni lied. Her muscles were aching

more than usual, even with the meds, but she could hold it together—at least, she hoped she could.

She swiped her hair behind her ears, the shorter locks coming forward. Before placing the helmet over her head, she scooped them back again. "You already mentioned last night that someone needs to guard the door when I go in for the flute."

"I know," he groaned, still messing with his helmet to make it straight. "I'm just worried more about you than myself."

"Likewise, but about you." She drew up the zipper on the front of the uniform over her clothing. It was a little loose in the shoulder area, but the rest was fine. Even the helmet wasn't bobbing around.

They walked out from behind the shaded trees into the glaring rays of the day. Leni was already starting to perspire under the thick uniform and helmet. She didn't know how the guards who stood outside could wear these things all day long. Same went for Lark and that heavy jacket she always wore.

Leni led the way and took the path leading toward the glass bridge, the light of the sun reflecting off the blue side of the citadel. A heavy breeze stirred, making the bridge sway as they crossed it toward the guards.

She wondered if Elliot's heart was beating as hard as hers and if he kept swallowing as much as her in order to not freak out. By the looks of it, Elliot's movements seemed fine, but he always appeared assured. Except for the day when Rebel had been born. That was the only time she'd seen him horrified.

The guard on the left held up a hand, stopping them. Leni

wanted to rub her clammy hands against her uniform, but she kept them loose at her sides.

Leni and Elliot both flashed the standard hand signal, and the guard pulled open the door, allowing them inside. As much as she wanted to go to the tower where Ridley was being held, they first needed to switch out the flute.

They entered the mirror sitting room and headed down an empty corridor on the right. Colorful fans of bright pinks and yellows hung on the wall. A kitchen attendant wearing a blue jumpsuit and a horse helmet pushed a cart of food past them. Leni caught a whiff of buttery biscuits and strawberries, causing her to lick her lips. She'd have to worry about food later.

At the end of the hall rested the spiral staircase, and Leni picked up her pace. The handrail was a glistening red and she held onto it as she ascended the steps.

The walls at the top were covered in neon-green bricks. A petite guard stood at the metal door, leading to the flute.

"The royals sent us up here for shift change," Elliot said, his tone leaving no room for questioning.

"Good, I'm starving," the female voice answered. She turned and opened the door and collected a tall and muscular guard from inside the flute room.

After the two guards were out of sight, Elliot stood his ground while Leni slipped inside the room. She knew she only had a few minutes before the actual guards for the new shift would arrive. The area was small, like the room where Ridley was, yet his would only have one guard protecting the outside. In the center of the space rested the flute within a clear glass case.

Reaching forward, she hesitated before lifting the glass

top off the box. For a moment, fear swept over her, and she secretly never wanted to touch the real flute again. But she had to. She could do this.

Leni unclenched her fist and brushed her fingers against the familiar silver ridges of the instrument. She imagined the shadows rising out of her and flying to the flute like a beacon. Nothing stirred. She had to remember she was no longer connected and wouldn't ever be again. Dead or alive.

She quickly plucked the deceptive flute from inside her uniform and swapped it out with the real one. With hurried motions, she slammed down the glass lid, harder than she should have. But it remained uncracked.

A smile spread across her face as she patted the instrument at her chest. Leni folded her arms behind her back and waited for the real guards to arrive. It was only a couple seconds later when the door opened. No words were exchanged as the new guard slipped into place and she came out the door to meet Elliot and the other one.

The swap seemed to go smoothly and easier than she'd expected. Hopefully, the royals and the guards would never know. *One room down and one to go.* She followed Elliot down the spiral staircase, the flute feeling heavier in her uniform than it should've.

They took the corridor to another hallway decorated with colorful masquerade masks. The masks were practically begging Leni with their empty eye sockets to try one on. And she would've if the situation wasn't so dire.

The spiral staircase at the end of the hall neared, and she hurried up so she could get to Ridley sooner. Her fingers fluttered at her sides with anxiety, because she'd have to think of a way to really get him out. She could just tell the guards the royals requested he be transported to another room.

Perspiration beaded along her forehead and upper lip when she reached the top of the staircase. She frowned inside her helmet as her gaze swept the area, spotting the metal door without a guard.

"Are you sure he's here?" Leni hissed, striding for the door. "Why would they leave it unguarded? Unless they took him somewhere else?"

Elliot pressed his hand against the side of his helmet. "It was guarded yesterday."

Leni unbolted the door and cracked it open. She let out a gasp when her eyes connected with a man on the floor wearing boxers and a thin white T-shirt. His chest rose and fell, but it was obvious he'd been knocked out.

What did Ridley do?

"I didn't know he had it in him." Elliot softly chuckled. "Let me see if the box is still in there." Without another word, Leni studied Elliot as he pressed his head inside the cursed mirror, the glass rippling. A second later, he tugged himself out. "It's gone." The guard hadn't stirred once.

"We need to get out of here." Leni stepped backward out of the room. "*Now.*" She bolted the door with a soft click once Elliot came out.

"We're okay," Elliot said calmly. "I have another plan that will make this easier, and this should've been in the original plan, anyway. I'm going to stay here."

"What? No." Why would he want to do that? So he could get caught?

"Look, if Ridley escaped, the new guard who gets here will take notice. The first thing he'll do when he comes in later today is pull open the door and find that gift inside." He pointed several times at the door.

"I don't know," she murmured, but his idea wasn't a bad one.

"It'll be fine, and I'll meet you here tonight."

"You'd better be careful."

Backing up against the wall, Elliot flicked his hand at her to go. And that was what she did. It was a way to ensure his safety.

Leni took steady steps down the stairs and toward the front of the citadel. The flute kept tapping her chest as she walked. Even though she knew she would need to blow into the instrument for it to create music, she was still worried a melody would go off and catch the guards' notice.

As she padded down the hall toward the sitting area, Leni's body grew heavy with exhaustion and the room started to sway. Leni's knees buckled and she caught herself on the wall, preventing her body from slamming onto the floor. But it wasn't a quiet catch—the sound had echoed throughout the corridor.

A guard rounded the corner, most likely one who was watching the door to the throne room. "What are you doing?" his voice boomed as he sauntered toward her.

Leni's eyes widened when she recognized his voice, the shape of his strong body. It was the same guard who'd struck her back over and over with the whip. She tried not to let her body tremble as she hid her nervous expression behind the helmet, or let her anger grow as she yearned to reach for the knife she had tucked away.

"I don't feel so well," she said unsteadily and forced herself to straighten.

"Do you need me to take you to a healer?" He reached for her helmet and she ducked out of his grip.

"Don't touch my property!" she snapped. "I can go there myself if I need to. I'm at the end of my shift and it's just my … monthly cycle. My body always gets weak during this time." If she didn't get out soon, she knew she would collapse at any moment, then the guard really would remove her helmet.

The man's body stiffened, and he took a step back as if her words had sickened him. He wasn't worried about the blood from her back before but hearing about a monthly cycle made him uneasy? *What a dick.*

"Go." He shooed her away.

She tried not to run for the front entrance as her mind and body wanted. Instead, she pushed herself to walk at a normal pace out the front door of the citadel.

Once she hit the fresh air and was out of sight from any more guards, Leni hightailed it toward Ridley's house while digging out the pills she'd stashed in her bra.

And sure enough, his bike was gone

CHAPTER 23

Leni

Music from "Crimson And Clover" – Joan Jett & The Blackhearts

Ridley was free of the cursed mirror room. He'd broken himself out, and somehow the citadel hadn't noticed. Leni rested behind the tree trunk where she'd changed earlier, allowing the pills to kick in. It had been too close with the guard inside almost catching her. But now as her breathing evened, she needed to get to Ridley and find him as soon as possible. Maybe this was easier, how it had happened. Maybe it was easier he'd gotten himself out of that ridiculous room.

Leni had already stashed the helmet and uniform in bushes deeper in the wooded area. She wouldn't bring the evidence with her. When she felt as though she wouldn't drop like a dead fly to the ground, she hopped on her bike and pedaled toward home.

She weaved around the path to the cobblestone street, then picked up the pace, turning too fast around a corner. A woman carried a bucket of apples and Leni nearly collided with her. The woman's curses could be heard for several more seconds as Leni pushed farther past the bakery and fruit shop.

A guy with green hair came out of the meat store, lugging a basket full of paper-wrapped meat. Leni narrowly missed crashing into him, too.

"Sorry!" she called over her shoulder.

The trip going home from the citadel was a short distance, but this time it was like crossing dimensions and getting nowhere.

Along the edges of the street, people were walking with bright sun umbrellas like the Earth Dimension had in Japan, except with different designs painted on the top. The wind kicked up a notch when she turned on the path toward her house.

Mrs. Kirby at the flower shop was planting blue and purple orchids in vases outside. She was a prickly woman who never said hello to anyone. Leni ducked her head because she didn't want to be recognized. She turned up the curved path toward her house and hopped off her bike.

Lowering her brows, Leni scanned the porch and the side of the house, then the mirror shop next door for Ridley's bike.

Is he not here? What if he'd been caught somewhere outside the citadel? Maybe he went somewhere else. Leni's heart pumped with apprehension as she pressed down the kickstand and propelled for the door.

Sweat coating her face, she took out her key, unlocked the door, and pushed it open. "Has Ridley come here?" Leni shouted, entering the living room.

Lark and Auden both lurched forward on the couch, looking like they didn't want to answer. It was clear they both knew something with their tick-tocking eyes, settling anywhere but on her.

Scratching the back of his neck, Auden pointed toward something resting on the counter—her jeweled box. "Ridley brought it here for you."

"Okay…" Leni drawled, taking a few steps toward the

counter. She was afraid that if she were to touch the box, it would mean Ridley had truly dropped it off and left.

Lark stood from the couch and picked up the jeweled box, handing it to Leni. "He was here, but he knew if he stayed, the plan wouldn't go smoothly for tonight. If the guards found him missing, it might affect the masquerade and the citadel allowing people in. When we told him what you were trying to do, that didn't go over so well either."

The man had been knocked out when she'd left, but once he awoke and started beating on the door, his sounds would signal the guard who would be replacing Elliot. "So he went back to the citadel to turn himself in?" Leni rubbed her temple. "Like that would make things better?"

"No." Lark shrugged, wearing an expression of pity. "He was going to sneak back in after he knew for sure you hadn't been caught."

"After knocking a guard out?" Leni seethed. "How could he think that was a good idea? 'Hello, guard, sorry for punching you in the face, but here I am?'"

Auden pursed his lips, fighting a smile, as if he would've done the same thing. Leni narrowed her eyes at him, wanting to knock the smirk off his face. Insufferable. Everyone today was insufferable.

"If it helps you sleep tonight, I think he did make the right choice," Lark said. "But I would've been pissed too."

Leni didn't care who thought he made the right choice because it was the *wrong* choice. And for now, they would all have to deal with that decision. With a nod, Leni finally took the jeweled box from Lark's palms. She rotated it in her hands, reading the words at the bottom, like she had a few days ago when inside the cursed mirror. Words from Ridley to her. *For Butterfly.*

"So…" Lark lightly brushed her toe along the carpet. "Was that really a gift from Ridley to you before it had been in the mirror?"

"Yeah," she whispered, hugging it to her chest. "The best gift."

"It's what saved us," Lark said, biting her lip. "That, and Ridley's hints with the glass butterfly and the Ouija."

Leni had known what he was trying to do during the curse, and the shadows in her had tried to get him to stop. At times, she knew the shadows thought they'd done enough, but Ridley kept finding his way back to Lark and Auden.

"I'm glad," Leni replied, meaning it. A few weeks earlier, she hadn't regretted the curse, but now she'd gotten to know Lark and Auden, little by little. "Ridley's right about me being impulsive, and I'm relieved he was able to see the wrong in everything. It took me longer, but I see it too."

"During the curse," Lark started, "Auden and I each had code words that we still have. Not that they were necessary, but you and Ridley should do the same. Just in case you ever need them."

"What were they?" Leni asked.

"Can't tell you, then they wouldn't be code words." Lark grinned.

Auden tapped the top of the box in Leni's hands. "There are a few things inside Ridley left for you. If you want to read them alone, you can."

Leni gave a brief nod, not wanting all the eyes on her any longer. "I was able to get the flute, so it looks like we have everything." Except for Ridley. Her shoulders slumped of their own accord when she turned to walk down the hall and into her room.

Tiredness washed over her as she sank down onto her bed. With shaky fingers, Leni opened the box, the purple velvet catching her attention first, followed by two white, folded sheets of paper. One small, the other larger.

She took out the large note and opened it first.

Leni,

I wish I could've run into you for a few minutes, but you're impulsive as usual. Apparently, I guess, so am I. I'm going to believe you got what you went for and that I'll see you tonight, unless I run into you on the way back. There's more to discuss that I uncovered, but I don't want to leave it in a note. Talk to Lark and Auden.

I love you,

Ridley

The blood in her veins boiled, and she wanted to scream in his face, but he wasn't there for her to do so. Instead, she refolded the note and shoved it into her drawer. Then she fished out the second note from inside the box.

Unfolding the small letter, she focused on the few words written in Ridley's hard to read handwriting. *"Crimson And Clover."*

The last time she'd heard the song was near the van in the Earth Dimension. Auden had played it on his record player for Lark while Leni had been standing outside. The song hadn't been the Joan Jett version she'd liked, but the original. Still, she loved it, too. The Joan Jett cover was one of the first songs Ridley had played for her that he'd discovered on his own. She'd always liked Joan's tone of voice, but more so when he'd put it on the record player. That was the first time she'd also listened to the song.

"What is this?" Leni asked, hovering over Ridley's bed. She was still tired from the night before with the shadows disturbing her again, but she'd been lucky she hadn't screamed and woken Ridley that time. Millie was mostly a heavy sleeper, so she rarely heard Leni.

With a few blinks and a tilt of the lips, Ridley picked up the record and placed it onto the player, letting "Crimson And Clover" drift out from the speakers.

"I feel like I should know this version, but I don't." As the beats poured out from the player, she found it odd that it was so close to the Tommy James & The Shondells version, yet so different at the same time.

Ridley tapped his fingers against his thigh to the song. She sat on her mattress across from him and started whistling. Together, they created their own music while he watched her and she watched him, both smiling.

Wiping the tears that had started to slide down her cheeks, Leni stashed the small letter in her drawer too, then shut the lid on the jeweled box.

Continuing to hold the box, she took a deep breath and went back into the living room to Lark and Auden. "What did he tell you? He told me you two would let me know something."

"Um, there's another dimension," Auden answered, looking as though he wasn't sure if he believed it himself.

"Like the one Quinna mentioned to me?" Leni frowned, not knowing where this was going.

"Yeah," Lark said. "A Shadow Dimension, which is really

where the shadows are from—the ones you guys have all seen. That's how all this came about. The king and queen made some sort of deal with the shadows to bring their dead baby back to life. For that to happen, your dimension became linked to ours. The royals' twins came out through the cursed mirror that Ridley carried, making the four of them immortal. The souls the royals took from our dimension, that the twins absorbed, were supposed to help bring the baby back, but when the time came, the royals refused to give up immortality. And now here we are."

"A baby?" Leni gasped. "The royals had *a baby* that they desperately wanted back, yet they still want everyone else's to die?"

"Seems that way," Auden said, sounding pissed.

Leni thought about the shadows and how they had to have come from somewhere, but she'd always thought they'd been created with her. Yet Ridley had never been made with them.

She jerked her head up. They needed to get things ready for that evening, and time was drawing closer for her to meet with Quinna, and hopefully Elliot, at the masquerade.

"Pick out the costumes you two want from my closet."

She was going to save Ridley, make sure Lark didn't die, and ensure that Auden wouldn't go insane one day from seeing the shadows. Or, at least, she would try.

With everything in her, she would try.

Chapter 24

Music from "I Know There's Something Going On" – Frida

Ridley hoped Leni wasn't still inside the citadel. He hoped she hadn't been caught. He hoped she'd changed her mind about trying to swap out the flutes. But if she did complete her task, from what Lark and Auden had told him, Leni said the flute Quinna gave her was an exact replica of the original.

Before Ridley left, he wrote two notes to Leni because he believed she would succeed. And he would find out when he arrived back at the citadel. At least the jeweled box was in safe hands, for now.

Pulse throbbing, Ridley took a shortcut and skirted around the back alley of square buildings on pier and beam. It reeked of garbage, and he normally avoided this route, but it would get him there a few minutes faster instead of venturing past the meat and fruit shops. Words, spray-painted in various colors, graffitied the back of the buildings. *Anarchy. Believe. Melancholy. Stop. Why? No more.* He wondered who wrote them and whether they felt the way he did about Mira? Or was this just something personal in their lives? He'd never know those answers.

Pedaling harder, cheeks hot, Ridley took the bike in a downward dip and passed a few civilians carrying stacks of books. Once he arrived at the citadel and made sure Leni was in the clear, he was going to turn himself in.

But Ridley had a plan, and he wasn't going to announce it to the world that he'd escaped. He'd make sure the royals never knew what he did. Or, at least, he would try.

Ridley took the pebbled path and cut through the trees, trying to make sure he stayed out of sight. Lucky for him, no one stood guard in the back of the citadel where his house was. Was the house even still his since he wasn't the Mirror Keeper any longer? He supposed it was, until later that night.

Ridley ran over small twigs and leaves as he sped by the trees. The ground was uneven as he rounded a thick trunk covered in moss and broke through the forestry at the back of his house. He parked his bike in front of his door and hurried inside to his room. As he reached under his bed to collect the helmet and uniform, a part of him had thought they might've vanished, like the mirror had. But no, they were still there.

With quick motions, he tugged on the jumpsuit and zipped until halfway up, it got caught. "No, not now." He pulled at the zipper again and let out a frustrated groan when it wouldn't budge. "This can't be happening." Grinding his teeth, he yanked it one more time and the zipper shot upward. A sigh of relief escaped him as he picked up the helmet and placed it over his head. The smell of sweat from the previous guard invaded his nostrils once more.

Ridley slipped out the door and shuffled toward the front of the citadel. The bright colors of the glass building glistened beneath the sun's rays as he crossed over the bridge, his spine straight while he tried to maintain confidence. One good thing that came out of this was the helmet concealed his hesitant expression. Within his outer layers, Ridley's heart and bones rattled, prepared for the guards to grab him and haul him off to the royals.

Yet, they didn't. He gave them the secret hand signal, and the guard on the left pulled open the door, letting him wander inside.

First, Ridley turned right, taking the hall covered in fans to the flute room. He went up the spiral staircase, his breaths increasing. At the top stood a guard at the door. If they had noticed the flute was gone, there most likely wouldn't be a guard standing there.

"Need something?" the man said in a deep voice.

"No, I think I went up the wrong staircase for the mirror room."

"It happens." He gave Ridley directions on how to get where he needed to.

Ridley nodded and smiled to himself because Leni must've gotten away. As he descended the spiral staircase, he begged for the shadows to stay away until he could get back in that closet. Even though the situation wasn't ideal, even though he was frightened to be back in that tight space.

Taking measured steps, he passed the guards in front of the entrance to the throne room and entered the corridor with the face masks. His heart calmed momentarily because he'd bypassed all the big dangers. The only one left was the guard in the closet, and he'd have to somehow convince him to keep his mouth shut.

Killing him? he thought while venturing up the spiral staircase to the tower. Ridley shook his head. He could never do anything like that. Maybe he should've brought duct tape and something to bind the man's wrists together. But if the royals pulled Ridley out, like they had earlier, then that would disrupt the plan.

Ridley lifted his head at the top of the staircase, his movements halting when his gaze fixed on another guard standing before him. Tall and lean, his hands the color of copper. Why was there a guard already here? Before Ridley had escaped, the guard on duty hadn't been there that long. Maybe about an hour. Or had the royals found out Ridley had gone missing? But then wouldn't the guards outside have checked him if they'd discovered Ridley had escaped wearing a guard's uniform?

Neither Ridley nor the guard spoke. Ridley had sunk back into his own head where he couldn't draw out what to say or what to ask. He tightened his fists—he'd have to knock this guard out, too. The other option was to let the royals think he didn't make it out, let himself get caught… He'd go with option one.

He lunged forward, and the guard grabbed Ridley by the collar and slammed him up against the wall. His head struck the metal of the helmet as it hit brick.

Ridley grunted and punched the guard in the stomach. The guard cursed and grabbed at his abdomen. There was enough space for Ridley to rip off the helmet and prepare for a punch. He froze when he recognized the face. Elliot.

It was a mistake to stop. Elliot shot forward and shoved Ridley to the floor, pain radiating up his spine. Words. Words. Words.

"Stop," Ridley finally shoved a word out. "It's me."

The anger in Elliot's face dissipated and turned to confusion, then recognition. He yanked off Ridley's helmet, his eyes widening. "What the fuck are you doing? Why are you back?" he hissed and got off Ridley.

It did seem stupid for him to come back, but sometimes stupid was the only way to do things. "Because it would make things easier for tonight if I was here. The box is with Lark and Auden, and I know Leni came for the flute. Did she get it?"

"She has it." Elliot nodded and helped Ridley off the floor.

Ridley exhaled slowly. "Did she make it out, then?"

"I don't know, Ridley." Elliot scooped up his helmet and placed it back over his head. "But I'm assuming so. I haven't heard any disruptions in the citadel."

"Why did you stay behind?"

"Because," Elliot said in a whisper-shout, "we came to save you, but your ass was gone! And when shift change happens up here, I didn't want the guard on duty to come looking inside the room and see the present you left behind." He cocked his head. "By the way, nice job."

"So we have everything then." Ridley couldn't believe it.

"Except for you and, I suppose, the mirror."

"For now, but we'll both be there at the masquerade." Ridley pulled out a knife from his pocket. "Lark gave me a tip and told me to bring one of these, so I'll still be able to do the blood part when the time comes."

"That Lark…" Elliot chuckled as though he'd known her his whole life.

Ridley rolled his eyes. "She's taken."

"Just ruffling your feathers. But it does seem you're rather protective of her. Not as a lover... Possibly a friend?"

"She doesn't see me like that, though."

"But you see her like that."

Ridley shrugged, because Elliot was right. He quickly changed the subject and pointed at the door. "How are we going to do this?"

Elliot crossed his arms. "How were *you* planning on it?"

"Letting him out and me going back inside. I was still trying to think of a way to convince him not to go and tattle-tale, though."

"Ridley, Ridley, Ridley, he would've gone straight to report it to the royals." Elliot wrapped a hand around Ridley's shoulder. "Let me handle this, while you play along."

Shifting his hand lower, Elliot gripped Ridley by the upper arm and thrust open the door. The guard Ridley had knocked out released a groan and sat up, rubbing his head, his eyelids flickering.

"Did you let him escape?" Elliot seethed at the guard, shaking Ridley's upper body.

"No!" The guard stood up, now wide awake and rubbing his jaw. "He punched me in the face after ripping off my helmet."

"The royals will have your ass for this, so I suggest keeping your mouth shut." Elliot threw Ridley inside the closet. "Give the guard back his uniform unless you both want lashings."

Impressed by Elliot's acting skills, Ridley unzipped and peeled off the uniform. Elliot handed the guard the helmet after the man yanked his jumpsuit from Ridley's grasp. Beneath his helmet, Ridley knew Elliot was smiling at him as he shut the door.

"You're lucky it was me who found him and didn't report it," Elliot spat. "I won't save your ass if this happens again."

The guard seemed to fumble with his words as Elliot continued to reprimand him.

Ridley sat and hugged his knees to his chest, trying to forget how he was back in the one place he didn't want to be. This time, he reached inside his pocket and fished out a small notepad and pen he'd taken when he'd gone home. With these two things, he would distract himself until the masquerade.

While he wrote words and lyrics, the shadows didn't come out, but at the back of his scalp, under his skull, he could feel their hands crawling inside, waiting for their moment to emerge once more.

The last thing he wrote before resting his head against the carpet were lyrical words from "I Know There's Something Going On."

CHAPTER 25

Leni slipped the feathered bird mask over her face. Everything was obscured, except for her eyes and nostrils. The mask was purple and silver with a long glittering beak. She wore a violet leotard concealing her body, along with silver gloves and a matching cloak to hide the flute and the jeweled box she'd be bringing to the masquerade. The items would need to come out right before Ridley's announcement when the mirror would be lugged out.

Grasping the bird beak of the mask, Leni adjusted it so she could see more clearly. She hated wearing things over her face, or at least the one other time she'd been to a masquerade at the citadel. But it felt confining, like it might never come off. Yet she'd collected several masks over the years because she liked the look of them—when not attached to her face. Taking a deep breath, she left her space and went into the living room where Lark and Auden were dressed and waiting.

Lark was in black from head to toe—leather pants, a frilly button-up shirt, and cloak. The mask was embellished with dark fur and sequins, covering all but her lips and chin. Beside her, Auden stood with folded arms, probably thinking how stupid this was. His ram mask exposed the same amount of flesh as Lark's did. It was entirely black except for the golden ears, and the horns spiraling out to the sides. The wardrobe had left him with little to choose from besides a gaudy jacket made of gold brocade, a black shirt with ugly buttons, pants that looked uncomfortably tight, and gloves with holes at the thumbs.

At Leni's right side rested the weight of the box. The flute was snuggly tucked inside her left pocket, while her knife was hidden inside her boot.

"You two have your knives?" Leni asked.

"I mean, it's part of my daily dress, so yeah." Lark smirked.

"Yep." Auden pulled his out, flipped it open and pushed the knife back into his boot.

They each needed a blade for when the time came to draw a line across their palms. Leni hadn't seen Elliot since the citadel, but she knew what he and Quinna would be wearing tonight. As for Ridley, she hoped he was okay, and her chest ached every time she thought he might not be. But he was strong, stronger than her.

"Nervous?" Leni asked Lark, who looked a bit stiff.

"Sort of? I'm not a fan of going to parties anyway, and this seems extravagant."

Lark was right about that. Leni didn't know how extravagant a party could get until she'd been to the last masquerade.

"Let's get this show on the road, then," Auden said and moved for the door.

Leni and Lark followed him into the night. The dark surrounded them with a full moon illuminating the area brightly, dark shadows flickering wherever its light hit.

"Full moon?" Lark groaned. "Seems about right."

They each grabbed a bike from the back of the house and

headed for the masquerade. Millie had five spares that hadn't been ridden in a while—Leni had pumped the tires with air earlier.

As she pedaled across the city, her limbs grew heavier. Even her heartbeat sang a sluggish song instead of a healthy tune. Leni glanced at Lark and even with a mask concealing most of her face, she could tell by the way her lips turned down that she was struggling, too. Other people dressed in masquerade costumes were headed in the same direction on foot or wheels to see who the new Piper would be.

Leni pulled to a stop at the front of the citadel, where bright lights were glowing from each side of the building. Rows and rows of bikes were all parked near the forest trees, but it appeared that most people had chosen to walk.

"People aren't afraid of having their bikes stolen?" Lark asked, pressing down her kickstand.

"Why?" Leni frowned. "We can easily take one from a mirror if we need to."

"I wish it were that easy for us," Lark grumbled.

Auden wrapped his arm around her shoulders and pulled her close. "Looks like someone may be getting a new bicycle for their birthday."

"Oh, hush, you know I love my rusty set of wheels." She smiled.

They trekked their way to the glass bridge, and as Leni drew closer, the music of "Any Way You Want It" pounded its way through the speakers, brushing against her eardrums.

Guards stood at the door in their usual helmets, checking guests but letting most enter. There were rarely issues in Mira. People were trustworthy, but that was because they were too scared of what the royals could do.

Leni held her breath, hoping she wouldn't be one chosen for a check. The girl in front of her, wearing a jester mask with blue and pink diamonds alternating across it, was pulled to the side. Another guard tugged on Auden and her heart leapt. He was quickly patted down along his legs and upper body before being released to enter. He'd had a good idea about them all placing the knives in their boots.

Once over the threshold, Leni breathed again and scanned the mirrored walls. The lighting was dimmed for the masquerade, and all the mirrors appeared to be shrouded by darkness. She couldn't make out any reflections of Lark or Auden—yet.

"This is really weird," Lark whispered at Leni's ear as they shuffled across the colorful carpet toward the throne room.

A tall guy wearing a tiger mask bumped into Leni, and the box inside her cloak moved forward. She adjusted herself so it wouldn't slide out of its pocket and topple to the floor.

In the throne room, behind a group of people laughing, a sense of déjà-vu poured over Leni, and her slowing heart rocketed. She'd been panicked the last time she was here, worried about being chosen—there'd been no joy like what these people were having. The bout of panic was seeping into her pores right then, only this time it was worse than before.

The room was dim except for the colorful lights where the royals were seated on the stage. A mirror ball dangled in the center of the room like the one from the club where Ridley had taken her to. It cascaded its silvery glow across all the dancing guests in the room. Some wore masks only covering their eyes or had entire helmets over their heads. Most of the women swayed in dresses with puffy sleeves and several layers of material. Others skipped out on the dresses and had chosen pants like her and Lark. The guys were styled in tight pants and swanky blazers with high shoulder pads.

Seated upon their thrones, both Brand and Anson wore button-up, long-sleeve white shirts with shiny red vests. Their masks were shaped like golden wolves, covering half of their faces. Beside them were Portia and Calliope, regal as always. Their dresses were white and poofy with frilly lace covering every inch of the fabric, like they should've been going to a wedding instead. Or possibly visiting Marie Antoinette some-where in the past. Their white masks only wrapped around their eyes, while their hair was styled in an updo with ringlets spilling out from the top.

Leni peered around, searching for Elliot, Quinna, or Ridley—someone—*anyone*. She was surrounded by strangers in masks dancing all around her, closing her in. Her body wanted to collapse to the floor in the tight circle of people.

A tap came on her shoulder, and Leni whirled around, prepared to kick the person if she needed to. Her shoulders relaxed when her gaze met a guy wearing a mask resembling a goat head. The horns were a dark blue while half the face of the mask was gray and the other a shimmering white.

Leni latched onto Elliot's wrist and whispered near his ear. "What happened? Is he all right?" He didn't hear her over the music, so she repeated herself.

Pulling back from her, Elliot glanced toward the royals. All four were sipping on their wine and snacking on some sort of dessert covered in chocolate syrup. Elliot cupped her ear and seemed to speak as loudly as he could without being heard. "He was fine when I left. He came back while I was here, and I had to collect him a costume for the masquerade.

But after he got dressed, there was a shift change, so I don't know anything after that."

That didn't relax her in the slightest. Leni looked toward the stage again, but there still wasn't any sign of the flute, the mirror, or Ridley.

"Have you seen Quinna?" Leni asked, scanning the crowd for a pink flamingo mask.

Elliot shook his head and surveyed the crowd. Lark and Auden were doing the same, while still trying to look part of the scene by shuffling side to side to the music.

One of Elliot's hands clasped her upper arm. "Over there in the far corner."

Leni's gaze followed Elliot's, expecting to find Quinna. Instead, she spotted two guards, dressed in their usual uniform, standing beside someone. A person wearing a Guy Fawkes mask and a black velvet cloak. Ridley. She would notice his curly hair and body build anywhere.

"You like what I picked out for him?" Elliot asked.

"It's fitting." The edges of her lips tilted upward. It did sort of feel like a rebellion of sorts. But she didn't know how they were going to get to him in time.

Leni tapped Lark and Auden's shoulders and nodded in Ridley's direction. Lark cringed when she discovered that Ridley wasn't alone.

A girl wearing a pink and silver flamingo mask sauntered up to them, as if materializing out of nowhere. Quinna's dress was voluptuous in the sleeves, but the rest clung to her body and fell just past mid-knee. "Here we are. I'm assuming everything is taken care of so far, since no one randomly showed up at my house again." Quinna beamed, then her smile faded when she spotted Ridley in the corner. "This doesn't bode well."

The crowd started to shift from behind Leni, and she looked back to see several guards lugging in the cursed mirror toward the royals. They carefully set it down on the floor, in front of the stage, as the glass flute box was brought in on a golden stand. Leni's heart picked up, fighting against her ribs to break free. The time was getting closer, and she didn't know how to get Auden to Ridley.

Music floated in and out of Leni's ears until she could barely make out what it was. Dizziness swept over her. The room was spinning—people were spinning—she was spinning. Brand was handed a microphone from one of the guards and the music lowered.

"It's time to make the Piper announcement." His voice boomed loud and clear throughout the crowded room. "Then it will be a party for the rest of the night."

The crowd cheered, not realizing what this proclamation truly entailed. They didn't know about souls being taken from another dimension and used for the royals' own purpose. The blood in her veins ignited, thinking how she'd been used for this, how Ridley had, how others had, and it could keep continuing on and on if they didn't put a stop to it.

"Do it," Quinna said, her eyes blazing. "Auden, you're just going to have to find a way to Ridley. I didn't think the guards would be hovering over him the whole time."

Leni remembered when she'd been here last, how she and Ridley had been near the back of the room with no guards surrounding her. She took out her blade from her boot at the same time Lark did. With the knife, Leni drew a stinging line down the center of her palm. Lark appeared pale, like she wanted to throw up as the blade bit into her palm. Silvery blood bloomed to the surface on Leni's hand, crimson on Lark's.

Auden observed Ridley, but there was no way he could get to him just yet.

Lark reached forward and clasped her hand with Leni's, joining them together. A warming sensation tickled at her palm as she stayed locked onto Lark.

Come on. Come on. Come on, she said to herself as she let go of Lark and fished out the box from inside her cloak, prepared for the next step.

Ridley was finally being moved, closer and closer to the center in front of the stage. Something gleamed in his hand, and she watched while he casually slid it across his palm as if he wasn't doing anything at all. The guards didn't notice as they placed him between the mirror and flute, then stepped away. There was now a good enough space for Auden to get to him.

"Go." Quinna nudged Auden and Elliot forward.

Flicking open his blade, Auden sliced it across his flesh—bright red blood bubbled up—and pushed across the crowd to get to Ridley. Auden broke through the last barrier of people and charged for the stage. Ridley lifted his hand as soon as he saw Auden. Elliot barreled toward a guard, who was already darting in Auden's direction, and knocked him hard to the floor. Ridley clasped Auden's hand and was pulled back by a guard, while two others hooked onto Auden. Hopefully the connection had been enough. Auden hurried and slipped back into the crowd.

The royals searched, aware of the chaos beginning to stir. Something dark was in Brand's other hand—a gun. The guards weren't allowed to carry weapons—no one was. That didn't mean the royals couldn't break their own rule.

Lark ripped the mask off her face to get a clearer view. "Give me the box," she said and tore it from Leni's hands.

"No, wait!" Leni shouted as Lark sprinted forward, leaving no room for error, shoving people aside.

The gun in Brand's hand lifted and Leni shot forward, but she couldn't bust through the worried people in front of her. Her gaze met Auden who was shouting and trying to break free from the two guards holding him, not removing his frantic stare from his girlfriend. Lark didn't once look up at the royals or notice the gun that was about to be pointed at her.

Quinna kicked the person, wearing a yellow elephant mask, in front of her who wouldn't move. But it wasn't enough. Leni's body was growing weaker by the second, so she knew Lark's was too. *Boom.* The gun went off and Leni wanted to shut her eyes, but she couldn't. It didn't strike Lark —the bullet hit another body who had bolted in front of Lark. Elliot.

The crowd screamed as their nervous and confused looks shifted in terror. Lark didn't stop, though, not as she hurled the box toward the center of the mirror.

An ear-piercing shatter came from the mirror, reverberating around the throne room, the sound feeling like it would never end. The box hadn't passed through—the mirror had broken into too many pieces to count as they all collided with the floor.

The ruckus only increased with people screaming louder, watching with horror, and running out of the throne room instead of helping. Maybe Leni would've done the same if she didn't know what was going on, but she did.

Her eyes caught on Elliot, his body unmoving on the floor. She gripped the sides of her cloak and rushed by his side. As her hand clasped onto his arm, a buzzing erupted somewhere straight ahead. From the shattered mirror, when the last piece of glass struck the floor, dark shadows poured out, their bodies shifting and moving in stiff angles.

Leni wasn't the only one who could see them—everyone could, because the pandemonium only increased.

Auden ripped himself from the guards as their stunned gazes saw what was coming out of the mirror. Several of them took off running with the crowd. The gun went off again, pushing a bullet through the helmet, then head, of a guard—it was the male who'd lashed Leni's back. Auden ducked toward the floor as another blast rang in the air, and the bullet sliced through the chest of another guard. More bullets came until there were none left to be fired.

Leni had to complete the last step, even with her body swaying with delirium. For a time, the flute had been like a demonic home, and she would make sure it didn't have to be for Ridley or anyone else. She stayed near Elliot as she retrieved the flute, the cold metal brushing her fingertips. With one hard thrust, she went to crack it in half. Nothing. It didn't budge. Why wasn't it working?

Brand's gaze met hers, and he must've realized what was happening. The coward appeared too scared to come after her without any bullets left. "Ridley is to be the new Piper," he seethed into the microphone, seemingly determined to enact her death before it was too late.

It *was* too late. Leni's heart slowed and slowed, her body

slumping to the floor on its side beside Elliot. She wouldn't even know if he was dead or alive. And Leni was sorry, so sorry, because somewhere in the room, she knew Lark had also fallen.

"I choose Leni to be my Mirror Keeper!" Ridley screamed across the throne room.

"You can't do that!" someone spat. Possibly Portia.

Leni's eyes fluttered open, her body no longer fading, her death halting. She wasn't better as she gingerly sat up, but she wasn't feeling worse, either. *What's happening?*

"I just did," Ridley said, his voice smug, so different than he'd ever sounded.

Another body, wearing pink and silver, came out from behind a speaker and jolted for the stage. Portia tossed something to Brand—another gun. His hand came up again, this time for Ridley. But Quinna was too fast. She knocked the gun from Brand's hand—it slid off the stage and onto the floor with a clang.

"Give Ridley the flute!" Quinna shouted, just as Brand wrapped his hand around her throat.

Leni launched the flute at Ridley, and he easily caught it with one hand. Maybe this would work, maybe it wouldn't. No matter what, she'd be with Ridley, whether as his Mirror Keeper after he'd broken the flute, or in death. By the way things were going, if they didn't succeed, Brand would kill them both.

Chest heaving, she watched as Ridley held the instrument between his hands, the shadows swarming around him like he was their guardian. With one swift move, and Portia deciding to finally move toward him, he brought the instrument down over his knee, breaking it in half.

The world around them shook, the shadows hissing and buzzing, scattering all across the room. Others poured out of Ridley and joined the rest of the shadows, all swirling in sync with each other. In a single line, they came swarming back, circling and circling until they shot toward the stage, straight into Quinna.

Brand's hands fell from Quinna's throat as his feet skated across the stage in an uncontrolled manner toward Anson, like two magnets being drawn together. The same was occurring with Portia and Calliope. Leni stood with her hands on her knees, lungs aching for more air. In a matter of seconds, the royals were no longer four entities, but two.

What now? she thought as her eyes found Ridley. He wasn't looking at her, but at Quinna.

Quinna's hand fell from her throat and balled into a fist. This wasn't going to be good, whatever it was. While the two royals gripped their chests, Quinna took out a knife and lunged forward. She didn't hesitate as she plunged the blade into the chest of the one queen left. Portia let out a gasping noise as silver blossomed out from her wound. Brand peered at Quinna, terror written across his face, and started to backpedal. No one was left in the room to defend him—all the guards had already fled or been gunned down.

A spring of shadows slipped out of Quinna and surrounded her. With what looked to be fury on her face, Quinna shoved the knife into the king's chest just as she'd done to the queen. Leni didn't know what the hell was going on—she thought they were only supposed to rejoin the royals, not murder them. But after everything that had happened, she wanted to murder them, too.

A low groan came from the floor—Elliot. Ridley was already at his side, speaking words that Leni couldn't hear.

She searched around the empty room for Lark and Auden, but they weren't there—they were gone. There wasn't a single dark shadow hovering in the air, either.

Tightening her jaw, body trembling, Leni took off her mask and walked toward the broken mirror. Along the floor, the shattered remains of glass caught her attention. Or better yet, what was in them. The shards before her weren't blank. A girl was reflected there—*her*.

CHAPTER 26

A hand wrapped around Leni's shoulder, and she glanced back, horrified, at Ridley. Quinna was now on the floor beside Elliot, helping him up. Leni couldn't comprehend what was happening. In the mirror pieces' reflections, *she* was there.

"What is it?" Ridley asked, his face filled with concern.

"Look!" Leni gasped and pointed at the glass. She knelt and, with her unsliced hand, she scooped up a slender shard covered in rigid edges, careful not to cut herself.

Hand trembling, she brought the glass up to her and Ridley. His eyes widened when he focused on what she was seeing. Within the mirror was a reflection of not only her, but Ridley as well. His curls, his mismatched eyes, his constellation of freckles. Her…

She didn't know what to think. It had been years she'd lived without ever seeing herself. But there she was. Green eyes, a narrow gap between her teeth, a light scar on her cheek where she'd fallen after she was first created. Leni didn't find herself beautiful, but she wasn't ugly either. Just a girl…

The low music had stopped as "Our House" came to an end, enveloping the room in complete silence.

"Elliot." Her voice wavered.

Quinna had ripped off part of her sleeve and Elliot was pressing it to his shoulder. As she drew closer to him, she noticed the cloth was almost completely covered in his silver blood.

His breaths were coming out hard, uneven. "I think I need a healer in a little bit, if they didn't run off, too. Just glad the bullet didn't strike something I needed. Like a heart." The words came out playful, but his face fell into a wince. His gaze angled to the shard in her hand, and his body turned rigid when he stared at himself.

As Leni surveyed the room, it wasn't only the cursed mirror reflecting their images—*all* the mirrors were.

"Where are Lark and Auden?" Ridley whispered, taking a step forward.

"I don't know!" Leni's voice came out panicked when she realized they still weren't there. "They were here one second, then gone the next. I'm certain they didn't just leave the party."

Her heart pounded and pounded because they were supposed to keep them safe. But now, she didn't know what the hell had happened to them. Did the shadows do something to them? As she came out of her shock, looking at the dead bodies of the king and queen on the stage, Leni peered at Quinna. Her dress and hands were coated in blood, and Leni didn't know how much of it belonged to the royals. Quinna stared at the three of them with an unreadable expression while holding onto Elliot. The shadows had gone into *her*...

Quinna was the one who'd told them some of the backstory and how to get rid of the curse. Leni wasn't dead. Ridley wasn't the Piper anymore. What Quinna had said was true. But something felt very, very wrong. No one spoke.

It was like a game of who could stay silent the longest, until Leni finally asked, "What the fuck is going on?" She gestured at the royals who both lay slumped in awkward positions. Blood had bloomed from their chests and pooled onto the stage. "Why did the shadows go into you?"

Ridley shifted forward, and Leni yanked him back by his shirt. She didn't know what Quinna was capable of.

"I had to do what needed to be done." Quinna motioned at the air, sounding like the same girl, not someone capable of villainous acts.

Elliot focused on Quinna, his vein thumping at his neck. "It looks like I missed a lot. Please explain to me what's happening."

"When something dies," Quinna said, placing a hand against her splotchy red cheek, leaving traces of silver behind, "you shouldn't try to bring it back."

"What died?" Ridley asked, stepping closer again. This time, Leni went with him, not quite understanding what Quinna was trying to say.

"Me." She placed a hand over her heart. "It may beat, but I was still dead before."

"You look alive to me!" Elliot exclaimed, shaking his head.

Leni settled her gaze on the royals—no emotions of regret stirred at the fact that they were lying there dead. She was more fearful of what would happen to Ridley and the others because of this.

Quinna sat down on the edge of the stage like she was going to tell a story. "In the beginning, there were two royals before they split apart, as you know. What I didn't tell you was they'd created me through the natural process. When I was born, I died within a few days."

"You're the *baby*?" Ridley's voice ricocheted off the walls.

"What baby?" Elliot asked, his brows pinching together.

It was all coming together now. Quinna had mentioned a baby—the shadows had shown Ridley one.

"When I went into the mirror yesterday," Ridley started, "the shadows, who are really from a different dimension, showed me how the two royals had made a deal to bring back their dead baby. That's why they needed all these souls. Not to keep the balance, but to get *you* back." His gaze landed on Quinna.

"That's right." Quinna nodded. "And you saw how they weren't really split apart, though, right? Their other halves came out from the cursed mirror. After that, this dimension became connected to Earth's. But." She stopped talking, her voice sounding as though she might shed tears.

Leni, Ridley, and Elliot all stayed silent, watching and waiting for her to continue. Quinna had been the royal baby... And Leni knew what was coming next because she'd already heard it from Lark and Auden.

"When Brand and Portia's other halves collected enough souls," Quinna continued, "they didn't want to bring me back. They chose to remain immortal instead."

"But then how are you here? And why would they still kill all the other babies?" Leni couldn't help but think about Romy and his baby. How such selfishness from the royals had been the cause of her brother's death.

"Because babies born naturally have a soul attached,"

Quinna said. "They're innocent, new, and can be absorbed too… No one here would know they had one though, since the deal with the Shadow Dimension prevented their reflections from ever showing in mirrors. Until now." Leni's stomach twisted, and she covered her mouth to prevent herself from hurling. "As for the shadows, they finally decided to release me to try and put an end to this. They were all a slave to the curse, too. Whether they are truly good or bad would be for you to decide. However, now you know I didn't help you from the kindness of my heart when you wanted to take over Lark and Auden's lives."

"But you didn't know they would win." Leni wrinkled her nose. That seemed like a risky game. "Even when you were the Mirror Keeper, you broke free."

"It was a gamble that won, and as for being the Mirror Keeper"—Quinna cocked her head—"I fibbed about that so you'd believe me. It wasn't a story I'd wanted to share yet."

"What about the reflections we now have?" Ridley chimed in. "Lark and Auden?"

"You had souls all along—they were just absorbed by the royals as you were created. When the royals were pulled together on the stage, it was because their soul was coming back to them so it could be reflected. There were always reflections on Mira—the worlds were never off balance, only our dimension was off-kilter because of selfishness and greed. As for Lark and Auden, they are safely back at home in their dimension."

Safe. They were safe. A thought struck Leni—Quinna had killed her own parents. And Leni couldn't say she blamed her for it.

"What now?" Leni stared once more at the royals lying dead on the stage.

"Well, I think it's time we go back to a healthy world, don't you think?" Quinna shrugged. "No more slaving away with mirrors, no more crossing dimensions, just us being ourselves. I'll take over my parents' positions, but guide everyone, not try to dominate. I'm sorry I didn't tell you the truth upfront, but as you can see, because of my parents, I have quite a few trust issues."

"But what about the souls for the people in the Earth Dimension?" Ridley asked. "The Realm of Mirrors in between?"

"No need for that anymore." Quinna batted a hand at the air like everything was taken care of. "The souls are inside you, as theirs are, and now the reflections are all just that … reflections." She paused and drew out a folded sheet of paper from a pocket in her dress. "What's more important is that you two have a baby to find and bring home."

CHAPTER 27

Leni scanned over the note and her hand shook as she gave it to Ridley. He pored over the words Quinna had written. Directions.

"You know where she is?" he asked, his gaze connecting with Quinna's.

He didn't know what to think about anything she'd said. None of it. Quinna was the baby he'd seen in the mirrors—the *skeleton*—the one the shadows had shown him. Somehow, the shadows were a part of her, and she was a part of them.

"How?" Leni moved toward her as if she didn't believe the written words, like they might be some kind of trick.

"You gave me her hair, remember?" Quinna smiled and swiped a hand through her own short strands. "How did you think she would've been able to go to the Earth Dimension?"

"But you didn't say anything!" Leni shouted.

Quinna's smile disappeared. "Because that wouldn't have done any good with the royals still alive, especially since you had wanted to keep her safe. You had your caretaker go and hide her and didn't want anyone to know, remember? Besides, now that I've inherited my parents' throne, things will be a-changin' here."

Ridley wanted to believe the good in Quinna. There had

been goodness in his life from people like Leni, Millie, and Elliot, but not from how the dimension was run.

"Elliot," Quinna said, dropping back down from the stage, "you took a bullet for someone you barely knew. How would you like to be a part of my royal guard? You, along with Leni and Ridley, who are the only three who chose to stay and not run."

"Mmm." Elliot exchanged a glance between Leni and Ridley, while holding Quinna's sleeve to his shoulder. "No more slaving away with frames?"

"No more slaving away with frames," Quinna echoed.

"All right, then," he said.

Leni and Ridley remained silent, but Quinna answered for them with a grin. "Good. You two can start when you get back. I'm sure you want to go to Rebel in the morning."

"I'm going to take Elliot to the healer's room," Leni said softly. "Thank you."

Ridley could tell there was a lot spinning in her head, the same way words were whirling around in his.

He and Quinna followed Leni and Elliot to the healer's room, where they found her barricaded behind the door. Quinna chose to stay with Elliot while the healer removed the bullet and told him it was a lucky hit.

Leni and Ridley walked out of the castle and into the night. The citadel had been abandoned and Ridley was sure there would be more chaos before the storm could clear. But at that moment, he just wanted to sleep.

He tugged Leni in the direction of the Mirror Keeper house—he didn't have the energy to pedal back home. It looked like she didn't either, with the way her eyelids fluttered.

"Is your body feeling better?" he asked when they got to the front door.

"Yeah, just tired." She smiled. "That was a risky move, choosing me as the Mirror Keeper. How did you know it would work?"

"I didn't." It had been the first name that had popped into his head, and he'd hoped it would work.

As they entered the living room, he thought about Lark and Auden, wondered what they were thinking. The mirrors were all sealed off now, so there wasn't a way he could tell them goodbye and thank you. It somehow felt like an open-ended book.

He scooped Leni off her feet, and she let out a breath as he carried her to his room. Ridley placed her on the bed, and they both removed their cloaks and boots.

Leni sunk into her pillow and turned to face him. "Lark told me she and Auden had code words during the curse."

"Oh yeah? Did she tell you what they were?"

"It's Lark—of course she didn't." She grinned. "I was thinking, if we were to have code words, what would they be?"

Ridley adjusted his pillow and shifted closer while thinking, until the words came to him. "Music and mirrors."

She wrapped her arm around his waist and inched even closer. "Yeah, those would be perfect."

He tipped her chin up with his finger. As soft as a butterfly or orchid bee's wings, he kissed her lips. She dipped her head down to his collar bone and pressed her mouth there, just as softly. He closed his eyes, holding her tight, and for the first time in his life, his mind truly stayed quiet.

In the morning, Ridley knelt beside Leni, his chin against the mattress. She was still asleep, her face appearing angelic without a worry in the world. He nudged her shoulder to wake her, and her eyes flicked open. With a smile, he held up a note where he'd written, *Ready, Butterfly?*

He was anxious, too anxious. While the words in his head had quieted the night before, they were brewing a thunderstorm now.

Leni peered at the note, reading his message. "I'm so ready."

After she got dressed, and they checked on Elliot, they headed outside into the morning light. Ridley's bike was still in front of the house, while Leni went to scavenge hers from the collection. Some of the people must've run off and left their wheels behind after the chaos had broken out at the masquerade.

Ridley and Leni ventured out of the city to a place where there was mainly forestry. Sky-scraping redwood trees covered the area with trunks the size of houses. On the way, they stopped once to eat chips and fruit that Ridley had packed into his backpack. When they started up again, they passed a glistening waterfall, and he thought maybe one day he'd like to go camping out here. He'd never done something like that. The only places he'd ever traveled were cities through mirrors for a few minutes, or the recent times to the Earth Dimension during the curse. When he'd worked with Leni in the mirror shop, they never had off days where they could just go journey somewhere.

Eventually, as he pedaled around a bend, a small house—

or more of a shack painted a hunter green—slipped into view. It was made out of wooden planks with an uneven roof. Farther out, past the hills, were other similar houses, but he didn't know if they were abandoned or not. The hunter green one was supposed to be where Millie was.

"Do you think they're really here?" Leni asked, pulling to a stop.

"I don't know." Ridley looked toward the brown door, his fingers fidgeting. "I hope so."

Stepping off his bike, he walked to the door beside Leni, up two wooden stairs that creaked and moaned. With a closed fist, Leni reached up and knocked several times.

No one answered.

"Should I break a window and climb in?" Leni craned her neck at the blue, curtain-covered window.

"So you can scare them if they're inside?" Ridley banged hard on the door. "Millie! It's me and Leni! It's okay!"

"Like that won't scare them half to death?" Leni rolled her eyes. "Plus, if anyone is out here in those houses, I'm sure you just woke the whole town."

No one came out of any of them.

The door in front of him cracked open, and Ridley couldn't help but blink. Millie peeked out, a bandana covering her dreadlocks. She appeared the same, but it had only been a few months since she'd been gone, not years. And as he studied the wrinkles at the sides of her eyes and lips, he couldn't help but realize how much he'd truly missed her.

"What are you doing here?" Millie hissed. "Have you lost your minds?"

"We have a lot to explain to you," Leni said. "Have you noticed the mirrors aren't working? The royals had a daughter who murdered them and is now in charge. We can all go home now."

Millie's mouth opened and closed again, baffled. "You're going to have to go into more detail than that." She opened the door and pulled Leni inside. "I haven't had to go into the mirror for a few days. I keep it hidden under the bed."

"I know this is going to sound crazy, but we have reflections now, too…" Leni said. "We have a lot to talk about."

Millie furrowed her brow as Ridley stepped into the house. There wasn't much inside—a bed, a rocking chair, and a small oval basket in the corner. From the basket, a soft grunt sounded, and a tiny fist poked at the air. The breath in his lungs caught.

Neither Ridley nor Leni moved toward the basket. He knew she was as frazzled as he was. There had been babies he'd seen in mirrors, but he'd never touched one, much less held one.

Millie nudged him forward, and he crept closer until he stood hovering over the basket. Inside rested a baby with skin the color of Leni's and brown curls matching his.

"Pick her up," Leni whispered next to his ear.

"But she's sleeping." Ridley wasn't sure if he should disturb her—she appeared so peaceful with her eyes closed.

"I think it'll be fine to wake her this one time," Millie said from behind him.

Rebel let out a big yawn, her eyes opening. Their voices must've disturbed her.

Unable to contain his smile, Ridley reached in for Rebel and a tiny grunt came, followed by a loud wail. He froze, panicked, not knowing what to do.

"Pick her up." Leni laughed.

Gently, he scooped Rebel up and the crying slowly ceased as her gaze latched onto his. Eyes that were the same shade as his—one brown, the other gray.

"I'm glad things worked out this way instead of us ending up in the Earth Dimension," Leni murmured. She glanced back at Millie, who had pulled a large square mirror from beneath the bed and was staring at her reflection with her jaw practically unhinged.

Peering down at Rebel, then back at Leni, he said, "If you hadn't given Quinna our hair, this wouldn't have been possible."

Leni rested her chin on his shoulder, careful to not jolt him and Rebel. She began to whistle a tune to him he knew well. "I Was Made For Lovin' You."

Ridley hummed it along with her while Rebel softly cooed, as if she was trying to join in on the music.

 EPILOGUE

Ridley touched the glass that once had access to go into Lark's room, where he would uncover what he considered treasures. He wondered how she and Auden were doing, but somehow, he knew they were all right. As for Mira, it had been a month of changes, but changes for the good. People were getting to choose what jobs they wanted to do, and Quinna implemented a currency exchange program similar to how people in the Earth Dimension paid for things. The world wasn't perfect—and most likely would never be—but that was okay. It was better, and that was what mattered.

"Are you all right?" Leni pressed her chin on his shoulder.

"Yeah." He released the glass and turned to face her. "Just wish we could've at least said goodbye."

"Sometimes goodbyes are too permanent." Leni lifted her chin and turned his face toward hers. "Maybe this was better. More of a, 'maybe one day we'll meet again.'"

Ridley stared past her, across the mirror glass shop, at Rebel sleeping in a bassinet. They didn't create mirrors here any longer, but he and Leni still made glass objects in their spare time. "I think Rebel wants us to shape something for her."

Leni took Ridley's hand and pulled him across the room until they were standing in front of Rebel. She lightly stroked the baby's cheek. "I think she said she wants a snail."

Ridley looked at Leni's chest covered in different characters from *The Neverending Story*. "Like the racing snail on your shirt?"

She laughed. "We can certainly try."

Ridley pressed his forehead against Leni's, breathing in her scent. "I love you, Butterfly."

"I love you," she whispered back. Her green eyes had never looked so bright as they did in that moment when her gaze caught his. "I think tonight I'm ready, if you are." She quirked a brow, as if daring him.

And he wanted to be dared.

His hand roamed up the back of her shirt, touching the softness of her bare skin and the light scarring. The happy feeling of purple completely washed over him. "I'm ready."

"Good, we have that matter settled." She grinned, her body arching into his before turning to walk toward the boiler.

Ridley glanced at the mirror one last time and whispered, "Keep listening to good music."

Lark stared at the mirror in her room. The one thing she never thought she would replace after trashing the old mirror. She had questions and no answers, and she'd hoped this would've gotten her some. But no. The mirror at work hadn't given her any either. Nothing and no one did.

She didn't know if Elliot was still alive after taking a

bullet for her. She didn't know if Quinna was still pulling weird bodies out from puddles of silver in her house. She didn't know what happened with Leni and Ridley or where their baby was. But Leni must not have died since Lark was still alive, and Ridley must not have become the Piper because Auden had stopped seeing shadows.

Thank God for that.

An entire month had gone by since she and Auden had poofed out of the Mirror Dimension and returned inside Bubble's late at night. Every day Lark had to work, she would tap the mirror at Bubble's to see if there was a possibility of her going back for a few moments. At home, she would do the same thing when she woke up.

Lark tapped her red nails again at the glass, when there was a knock at her bedroom door. She'd heard his engine only moments ago.

Dropping her hand from the mirror, Lark opened the door to find Auden there in a Black Flag T-shirt and jeans. She'd just seen him yesterday, and he still took her breath away today. Hurriedly, she tugged him through the door before Beth or Paloma could come down the hall and ask him more questions than they probably already had. Every time he came over, Beth would hound him with news stories, as if he cared. But maybe he did, because he would sit there and listen.

"What's this for?" Auden asked, rubbing away the line between her brow.

"Oh, I was just trying to see if I could go through the glass. You know, cross dimensions … *again*." She sighed.

"Mmm, and what would you have done if you could?" He smiled, showcasing his bottom row of slightly crooked teeth as he pushed a lock of curly hair behind her ear.

"I would've called you and told you to hurry your ass over here."

His grin grew wider.

A clink-clinking sound came from behind her, causing them both to jump. As she whirled around, a folded sheet of yellow paper flew out from the mirror and fell to the floor. Lark scrambled to pick up the paper and unfolded it, her hands shaking.

I wasn't going to say anything, but since you keep tapping on mirrors, I thought I better let you know that Ridley and Leni are fine. Baby Rebel is with them. Elliot is indeed alive. Day by day, Mira is becoming better. But that's because I'm the ruler now. I was the baby Ridley told you was given to the Shadow Dimension, so yes, I'm alive, and yes, I defeated my parents. And sorry, no one can crawl through mirrors anymore since our dimensions are now unlinked. Except for me. So stop tapping on the glass!

Quinna.

Lark inhaled sharply. "So, that left me with more questions than answers."

She folded the note back up and placed it on her dresser. The main thing she'd needed to know was that Ridley and Leni were fine. And they were. Yet she still missed them in a way.

"Strange..." Auden frowned at the paper. "But now you don't have to worry about knocking on mirrors and trying to cross dimensions."

"I suppose." She moved toward Auden and wrapped her arms around his neck. He pressed his lips to hers and she pulled him closer, deepening their kiss. They both fell to her mattress, and Lucy hopped off the bed. The cat hadn't hissed at the mirror when Quinna threw the note, so that must've been another good sign.

Lark lifted her head while Auden's hand ran up the back of her shirt to the nape of her neck, his fingers drawing music notes across her spine. She couldn't control the shiver that escaped her.

"What song do you want to cue this time?" Lark grinned as warmth washed over her, while sliding her fingers through Auden's soft hair.

"I think this is a David Bowie mood." Auden trailed kisses up her neck to the spot right under her chin, and she fought back a moan.

"Still no 'Space Oddity' yet." She chuckled, toying with the button of his jeans. "Maybe in a few months, though."

"How about 'Rebel Rebel', since there was a reunion and all?" He lifted a brow and with the tip of his finger, he lightly wrote words from the song up her back.

"You read my mind."

Lark's lips crashed against Auden's, drinking all of him in. Her body practically melted into his as their movements sang the lyrics of the song to each other until they were flushed, their breathing unsteady, and she knew their love was one that would last through anything.

Thank you so much for reading Music & Mirrors!

Authors always appreciate reviews, whether long or short.

Subscribe to Candace's Awesome Newsletter for the latest news and giveaways!

ACKNOWLEDGMENTS

I'd first like to thank the readers for sticking with me to see Part B of this duology and wanting to learn more about Ridley and Leni!

Elle, thank you so much for taking me under your wing at Midnight Tide Publishing and for believing in this duology as much as me!

Brandy, you thoroughly went through this manuscript and helped to shape it! Jena, I didn't think I'd love a cover as much as I did Lyrics & Curses, but I love this one even more!

Amber D., you have helped me in more ways than one! Donna, you believed in this series early on and have been a rock! Amber H., you always manage to find the final touches that need to be completed, and I appreciate it so much!

A special shoutout to Jenny Hickman for being freaking amazing, Ann for your kindness, and to Pat, Vic, and Kattie who continue to stick around since the beginning!

One day, I will find that DeLorean time machine, and we'll actually get to visit 1985 and possibly travel to the Mirror Dimension!

ABOUT THE AUTHOR

Candace Robinson spends her days consumed by words and hoping to one day find her own DeLorean time machine. Her life consists of avoiding migraines, admiring Bonsai trees, watching classic movies, and living with her husband and daughter in Texas—where it can be forty degrees one day and eighty the next.

MORE FROM CANDACE

Wicked Souls Duology

Vault of Glass

Bride of Glass

Marked by Magic Duology

The Bone Valley

Merciless Stars

Cruel Curses Trilogy

Clouded By Envy

Veiled By Desire

Shadowed By Despair

Cursed Hearts Duology

Lyrics & Curses

Music & Curses

Letters Duology

Dearest Clementine: Dark and Romantic Monstrous Tales

Monstrous Tales

Dearest Dorin: A Romantic Ghostly Tale

Campfire Fantasy Tales

Lullaby of Flames

A Layer Hidden

The Celebration Game

Mirror, Mirror

Faeries of Oz Series

Lion

Tin

Crow

Ozma

Tik-Tok

Demons of Frosteria

Frost Mate

Frost Claim

Vampires in Wonderland

Rav

Maddie

Chess

Knave

Standalones

Between the Quiet

Hearts Are Like Balloons

Bacon Pie

Avocado Bliss

These Vicious Thorns: Tales of the Lovely Grim

www.ingramcontent.com/pod-product-compliance
Lightning Source LLC
Chambersburg PA
CBHW030807210726
48290CB00002B/461